GIRL

LAST

SEEN

HEATHER ANASTASIU
ANNE GREENWOOD BROWN

ALBERT WHITMAN & COMPANY
CHICAGO, ILLINOIS

To all the musicians in my life—AGB

Library of Congress Cataloging-in-Publication
data is on file with the publisher.

Text copyright © 2016 by Heather Anastasiu and Anne Greenwood Brown
Published in 2016 by Albert Whitman & Company
ISBN 978-0-8075-8140-7 (hardcover)
ISBN 978-0-8075-8141-4 (paperback)

Printed in the United States of America
10 9 8 7 6 5 4 3 2 1 BP 24 23 22 21 20 19 18 17 16 15

Design by Ellen Kokontis
Cover images © Shutterstock.com

For more information about Albert Whitman & Company,
visit our web site at www.albertwhitman.com.

TWISTED

Lyrics by Lauren DeSanto

Music by Lauren DeSanto & Kadence Mulligan

It's you who's got me upside down
and you don't even know it.
Your words they've got me spinning
like a sick and twisted poet.
Please, I'm begging, just come clean
cuz you're a cheat, a scarlet letter.
I'm tangled in this twisted life;
you always think that you know better.

Oh, it's such a twisted life.
Don't know which way is up.
You got me turned around.
I'm drowning in my cup.

I'm at the crossroads of my own perplexities.
You're the beating heart beneath my floorboards, see?
I'm swallowed up in guilt, my darling.
I can hardly breathe
cuz I'm twisted up and turning
in my own Greek tragedy.

Oh, it's such a twisted life.
Don't know which way is up.

You got me turned around.
I'm drowning in my cup.

Oh, it's such a twisted life.
Don't know which way is up.
You got me turned around.
I'm drowning in my cup.

WEB-STREAMING VIDEO, LOCAL KLMN NEWS

Friday, March 30
6:50 p.m.
Footage from the Night of
Kadence Mulligan's Disappearance

A woman with shoulder-length blond hair and a plastered-on smile holds a microphone as she stands to the side of a crowded coffee shop. A makeshift stage can be seen beyond her shoulder. A small area is cordoned off so people can still make their way to the counter and order their drinks, but otherwise the patrons are packed into folding chairs, some sitting on laps. They turn around and wave, smiling at the camera. For several moments, the woman stands frozen, grinning as if waiting for an invisible countdown, and then she begins to speak.

"Kristi Clemens, reporting from Cuppa Cuppa coffeehouse in Pine Grove, Minnesota, for KLMN 5 Eyewitness News. In our weekly Community Now web featurette, we join local teen YouTube sensation Kadence Mulligan to bring you this live-streaming concert."

Clemens continues smiling, and her bleached teeth flash with every word. "As many of you already know, Mulligan and bandmate Lauren

DeSanto first shot to national attention last year when their songs "Sing to Me, Calliope" and "The Twisted Life" received over a million hits on YouTube and the duo was invited to participate on the national television broadcast *America's Talented Kids*.

"And no one is prouder of their talented kids than Pine Grove residents." Clemens turns to the group behind her, then crouches to hold out the microphone to a girl who looks about eleven years old. Her hair is in ponytails with magenta streaks at the ends. "Can you tell me what's brought you out tonight?"

The girl's eyes get big. "Because I'm a Kady-Did! I follow all her music videos and her fashion-tip tweets. She sings, like, oh my God, amazing! I want to be like her when I grow up."

Other tween girls bunch together to get in the camera shot and shout, "Kady-Dids forever!" with an ear-piercing screech. Clemens laughs and pretends to cover her ears. When she stands up, she holds out the microphone to the woman standing with the girl.

"So I imagine that's something you're used to?"

The woman laughs. "Yeah, well, at least Kady's music is something I enjoy too. Plus, she's a great role model for our daughters. That's why we couldn't say no when they asked us to bring them here tonight." Some of the other women in the crowd nod.

"And you?" Clemens holds the mic out to a teenage boy in black pants and a printed tee. "Why are you here?"

"Kady's music has *substance*. You listen to the lyrics, and it's"—he furrows his eyebrows like he's thinking of the right word—"*deep*, y'know."

"And she's hot," says another guy behind him, and the group laughs.

"It's not just Kady though," says another person. Clemens is busy trying to chase the voices with her mic. "Lauren wrote most of their songs before she injured her vocal chords and had to stop singing."

"Aaaaand now she's making coffee at Kady's concert," says another guy, maybe the same one who commented about Kady being hot. "Way to go up in the world." More laughter.

Several of the people in the group look over to the left. Clemens jerks her head in that direction in a less-than-subtle manner.

The camera pans over to the coffee counter where a girl works feverishly, running between an espresso machine and the refrigerator. The guy at the register calls out another order to her from the long line waiting on the opposite side of the counter, and she nods as she pours dark liquid into a small cup. She spills some of it on her hand and winces.

But then she stops her activity as her eyes lock on a point at the front of the shop. She just stops and stares, swallowing several times.

After a couple of hissing noises and the reporter's whispered, "The stage, pan to the stage!" the camera finally swings that direction as well.

A girl with bright magenta hair that's teased and shaped into a low beehive steps onto the small stage. She's wearing a vintage-looking blue-and-white polka-dot dress. She grins and raises her arms to wave at the crowd as she steps up to the microphone. The crowd is already clapping and screaming for her.

"Oh my gosh," she says, laughing and looking overwhelmed. "This is so awesome! I can't believe all you guys came out tonight to hear me sing."

The screams get louder and some wolf whistles join in. There are a few calls of "We love you Kady" from the young girls, and then all at once their young voices screech together, "Kady-Dids forever!"

Kadence grins. "So how about we play some music!" she says, raising one fist and then grabbing her guitar. The crowd roars its approval.

She begins to strum and then leans so close to the mic that her lips seem to brush it as she begins to sing:

It's the last chance for Calliope.
One last song for you and me.
Dance on the island,
Dance on the sea.
It's good-bye, baby,
Good-bye to you and me.

ONE

LAUREN

Cuppa Cuppa
Saturday, March 31
5:50 a.m.

The song ends.

Before the morning DJ can tell me what a *grrrreat* day it's going to be, I kill the radio and silence him. I'm not ready for words. Not this early. Not today. The parking lot outside Cuppa Cuppa is still cast in deep purple, the sun about as excited to start the day as I am. Which is to say, not at all.

I don't make any effort to unbuckle my seat belt. Instead, I reach into my bag and pull out a pen and small notebook. *Purple sifted, sifted light.* It's against doctor's orders, but I can't help humming as I scribble across the page. If I don't get the line down now, I'll forget it later. Then I write, *Everything's gonna be all right*, which will do for a rhyme. For now. I'll come up with something better later.

I toss the notebook onto the passenger seat and face the inevitable. I need to get out of the car. I have to get out of the car. *I have to get out of the car.* My shift starts in ten minutes, but I do not want to go back inside. Last night was crappy, and the memory of it is still going to hang thick in there, mixed with the smell of roasted beans and scalded milk.

I closed up the place after Kady's show, less than seven hours ago, then never fell asleep. I wonder if it's too late to call in sick. From the parking lot.

I pick up my cell phone and think about that, turning my phone over and over in my hands. The fact that I can think about *anything* is give-me-a-gold-star amazing because God knows my head is a twisted mess.

I glance up at the coffee shop again, then roll my eyes. This job is all I've got now. It's enough reason to get out of the car. Besides, a hot mug of rejuvenating decaf green tea might do me some good. Detoxify the night and all that.

I roll up the sleeves on my flannel shirt and push my glasses up my nose (too tired for contacts this morning). Stepping out of the car, I adjust the long strap of my bag across my chest. The tassels that hang from the bottom of the bag snag on the thick, black tights I'm wearing under my favorite cutoff shorts. It's not quite April. Still cold, but I'm so ready to be done with long pants.

The closed sign still hangs on Cuppa Cuppa's front window. I knock on the bright green door, and after a few seconds Charlie, my boss, lets me in.

"Good morning," I whisper.

I'm not whispering because of the early hour or because Charlie is hungover—which he probably is. I've been whispering since Halloween. That's when I got food poisoning so bad I had to go to the hospital, which is where I picked up some lovely throat infection. I haven't been able to talk any louder than a rasping whisper since then.

"What's with the flannel?" Charlie asks. "Where's your uniform shirt?"

So much for trying to detoxify the memories from last night. Bam. Front and center. That didn't take long. "Um, *hello?* You told me to toss all the old ones out. You said the new ones had come in."

Charlie grimaces. "They have, but when I opened the package this morning, I saw that the logos say *Pucca Pucca*. I have to send them all back."

When I raise my eyebrows at him, he adds, "Hey. It wasn't my fault."

Ha. He probably screwed up the order. "Fine by me," I croak out.

"*Jesus,*" Charlie says as the phone starts ringing. "How long are you going to talk like that?"

I shrug in response because I don't like going into the details, like how when things didn't get better with my voice right away, I had to see an ear, nose, and throat doctor. Like how the ENT first put me on total vocal rest for two months and handed me a mini whiteboard and a black marker. So I could *continue to communicate.*

I remember thinking, *This has to be a joke, right?* I mean, it had to be a joke. She was so blasé about the fact my life was ending.

But things only got worse when I told Kadence later that night. Or rather, wrote it on my whiteboard.

∎   ∎   ∎

"But it will get better," she said, looking up from the board to my face. "Right?"

Hopefully, I wrote.

She glanced down at the word, then back up at me. "Hopefully?" Her voice rose, pitch by pitch with each syllable.

They don't know how long it will take. It'll just happen one day.

"That's all the doctor said?" she asked.

I understood Kadence's frustration. I had already bailed on three of our performances by that time, and we hadn't been able to record any new videos for our YouTube channel. She was getting irritated by how long I'd been out of commission. The same anxiety I'd felt when Kadence and I first became friends roiled through my belly.

I'd been on the cusp of Loserdom—with a capital L—when Kadence moved to town in seventh grade. She was popular within five minutes of walking in the front door. Why she picked me to be her best friend I'll never understand. That first year I lived in fear of her dropping me like a lead balloon. When I lost my voice, that fear came roaring back.

That's all, I wrote.

"So what do I do?" She twisted a long bit of magenta hair around her finger.

I sighed and used a tissue to clean off the board. Writing everything out was exhausting. So much went left unsaid. I wrote: *What do you mean?*

"It's been three weeks since we put out any new music. We have fans," Kadence said. "Fans with expectations. Have you looked at the views on our YouTube videos? We've gone from one-point-three million views on "Twisted" to only three hundred thousand on "Calliope," and the view count on all of them is leveling out. No growth. That's like a death knell. And in the comments, people are starting to ask when we'll have a new song."

They'll have to wait, I guess.

"Have you even tried to sing?"

I could only stare at her. Was she even looking at me? Did she not see this freakin' whiteboard? Tears pricked at the back of my eyes. I opened my mouth to say something but then closed it again. What did she expect of me? I couldn't even talk, for God's sake!

"Things are building for us, Lauren," Kady said, apparently not noticing my distress, "but Internet fame is fickle." She threw up her hands. "We either have to build on our momentum or forget it. It's about number of views. The numbers grow, or they go stagnant. We need new material."

This isn't my fault, I wrote, still fighting back tears. Kady never appreciated tears. She always snapped at me that the Major—her dad—hadn't defended this country for thirty-five years just so we could be crybabies. She only cried when it was useful, to get what she wanted. Like an extension on her math homework.

Kadence rolled her eyes. "I'm not saying you did this to me on purpose."

My eyebrows shot up. What did she mean, *to her*? I would've thought she'd be more empathetic. Kadence had once been hospitalized with a horrible allergic reaction to peanuts, and I'd visited her every day.

"We need a plan for going forward," she added quickly, so maybe she was empathetic enough that she could easily read my thoughts. I guess that was something.

Well, I can't sing. I'm not even supposed to play guitar. This was the most surprising part of the doctor's orders. I swallowed hard and looked away from Kadence.

"You can't even play guitar? You can't even play backup for me?" Kadence's voice was rising again. Pretty soon only dogs would be able to hear her.

I shook my head. I didn't want to write down the reason. It would take too long to explain how playing our old songs would trigger the muscle memory in my vocal cords, how they'd flex and rub together, and how it would slow down the healing process. So the doctor said anyway.

It was going to be a tough rule to follow. Maybe I could avoid our old music, but how could I walk away from my guitar? My ukulele? I already had new lyrics running through my head. *Life sucks and then you die.*

Kadence shifted uncomfortably and tucked her hair behind her ear. *What???* I wrote.

"Would you be mad if I put something out on my own?" Or...in other words...your life is over. We'll reassess in two months.

My stomach knotted. She was going solo? I scrubbed out the previous messages and wrote, *You mean without me???????*

"Just this one time," she said.

. . .

"Just this one time, Mark," Charlie says into the phone.

My mind snaps back to reality like a rubber band. I recognize the look on Charlie's face, not to mention the name of the person he's talking to. It's the landlord calling again. Cuppa Cuppa is behind on the rent.

"We've got a new plan for bringing in more business. Kadence Mulligan played a show here last night...Yes, *her*. My number one barista is Kadence's best friend." Charlie glances over and winks at me. Nervously, I pull my dark brown hair forward over my shoulder and start to work it into a braid.

"Lauren set it all up. The place was packed, and the local news even did a piece. Can't beat free advertising," Charlie says. All last night he'd been practically fangirl-ing over Kadence. It wasn't a good look on a twenty-seven-year-old pre-alcoholic. He'd been bouncing around, making sure Kadence had plenty of water and that the news people got a good shot of the Cuppa Cuppa sign on the back wall.

I'm sure I was the only one not digging the show.

Last night, everyone could see that Kadence had star potential. Only I knew how much went into the act. How choreographed the whole thing was. How I was the one who had written the lyrics that she was singing with such a pang of personal angst.

I mean, come on. I was the word girl. It was the fortunate consequence of being a total bookworm for the first twelve years of my life. Kadence might have brought me into the land of the ridiculously cool and beautiful, but I was still a literary nerd at heart.

We'd argued over the second verse of our song "Twisted." She wanted to change the line that went "I'm twisted up and turning in my own Greek tragedy" to "I'm twisted up and turning cuz you're so super sweet."

God help me. She simply didn't understand the symbolic nuance of my version. I tried to be diplomatic, but she thought I was too clever for my own good. For our own good.

Fortunately I won that battle, though last night Kadence had sung the line as she'd originally wanted to write it. She didn't make eye contact with me, but she had to know that I noticed. You can't just rewrite a song. Not once it's published and out there in the world. I mean, imagine if Dickens retroactively changed the beginning of A *Tale of Two Cities* to: "It was the best of times, it was the French Revolution times." Come on. *Really?* But then, it wasn't like I had any control over our music anymore. Maybe I never really had. Maybe I'd been part of the audience all along. Singing harmony to the Kadence Show.

For a long time, I was drawn to the Kadence Show like everybody else. I was so close to her—to that energy that made you feel like your life was amped a few shades brighter than everybody else's. I got so close that I couldn't see what it was doing to me. Like Icarus flying too close to the sun.

There's nothing like a couple of months of enforced silence and losing *every-freaking-thing* you care about to stimulate a little introspection. Question: Who was I without Kadence Mulligan? And how could the friend who was more like a sister drop me so easily?

"Yeah, two weeks. Two weeks is great, Mark," Charlie says over the phone, sounding relieved. "Thanks. Thanks so much." He hangs up and turns to me. "Last night was great."

"Yeah, it was." He doesn't notice that my smile is the fake kind you plaster on just to be polite. The kind that covers secrets.

TWO

JUDE

I slept the sleep of the dead last night. I wake up to the birds chirping. Goddamn birds. I flip onto my back and reach for my iPod. It's an old one, three versions back. Bought it off eBay for twenty bucks. I turn on some System of a Down. "Chop Suey!" blares through my docking speakers. Oh yeah. I nod my head to the hard beat. Screaming lyrics instead of happy birds chirping. Much better.

I sink back into the cheap mattress, a particularly annoying spring digging into my back. Dad's at the other end of the double-wide, no doubt sleeping one off from last night. Nothing will wake him up.

The memory of Mom's voice from last summer echoes in my head. "Why do you want to go back to live with your dad again?"

"Miss my old school."

"I thought you hated that place." She looked away and took a slow drag on her cigarette. Her hand still shook even though she'd been clean for eighteen months.

I turned my back to her and looked out the kitchen window at the little patch of grass that made up her front lawn. It wasn't that it was hard to lie to my mom or that I was bad at it. I just preferred not doing it to her face. "I grew up there, Mom. I want to go back for senior year."

She sighed, a long breath that wheezed through her teeth along with a cloud of smoke. She padded over in her old house slippers and put a hand on my back. "Fine, honey. I'm just going to miss having you here. You've gotten so handsome," she said with a laugh. "All the girls in town will riot now that you're leaving."

Handsome. I scoff at the memory and get out of bed, the springs creaking in protest as I walk to the mirror. This is the same room I spent my childhood in, back when Mom and Dad were still together. The same room of all those angsty, crap-ass junior high years alone and miserable, cursing my stupid face and skin. My dresser is one of those antique kinds, with the mirror attached. I trace my fingers over the spiderweb fractures fanning out from the spot where I'd planted my fist in eighth grade after Lauren DeSanto screwed me over, helped along by her bitch of a new best friend, Kadence Mulligan. All because of my face. No one called me handsome back then.

I had acne. And not "Oh poor kid, he's got some zits" acne. It was the volcanic, painful kind where you have dime-sized lesions that last for a month and leave lifetime scars. Not just on my face either, but on my arms and back too. Christ, even my legs.

And Lauren, who had been my best friend until seventh grade, dropped me like the proverbial hot potato as soon as Kadence Mulligan came to town. Lauren even started calling me *freak.* Monster. Creep. And then later, stalker. That was the one that stuck. At the time, I couldn't believe Lauren could treat me so badly. I thought it had to be because of Kadence. Kadence, so *shiny*—that was the word for her—but mean to the core. Who knew so much darkness could hide behind a pretty face?

9

Oh, wait, I thought, smirking. *I do. I know exactly how much a* handsome *face can hide.*

I look at the image reflected back at me in the fractured mirror. There's a particularly powerful drug for the worst cases of acne. My dad, in a random bout of giving a shit, didn't want me to go on it because he did when he was a teenager and it made him depressed. Wanted to kill himself. Almost did. Besides, we couldn't afford it anyway. But then Mom got a job with health insurance. First thing I asked for was the drug. I promised I'd be extra careful about my moods and let her know if I ever felt off.

I felt off. I never told anyone. The medication started working, and for the first time since seventh grade, I could see my face again. I was being reborn.

That was when I first came up with the plan.

Lauren had never known how right she was when she called me a monster. But I was only what she and Kadence had made me. Whenever my moods went dark, I didn't think about harming myself. No, not myself.

I get my video camera—another eBay purchase—from my dresser drawer where I keep it beneath my T-shirts and socks. I tug on some jeans, a sweatshirt, my boots, and then I'm out the door. I leave System of a Down playing on the off chance it will wake up Dad and piss him off. I'm not usually such a dick. Most of the time, I just don't care enough. But if there's a passive way to stick it to him...well, hell, why not?

I grab my coat and jog down the stairs of our rickety trailer. It's sunny and in the mid-fifties. Warm for Minnesota in late March. I only feel like I can breathe once I'm out in the woods beyond the trailer park. I take the path that only I know and inhale the sharp scent of the towering evergreens. There are the subtler smells of spring too—fresh growth out of last year's rot. It feels clean out here. It's good to clear my head, especially on a day like today when my thoughts are so twisted.

I flip open the viewer on the video camera to watch the footage from last night. I'm suddenly nervous that I forgot to click Record or something else happened to mess up the image, but then my muscles relax as the music comes out of the crappy little speakers.

I hate hearing Kadence's voice. She's so tinny and pop sounding. She's been total crap without Lauren. Everyone knows Lauren is the actual musician in the group. I might hate her too, but I'm not one to deny talent. Kadence, on the other hand, is more for "show" than anything else. Such a goddamn diva, up there playing her guitar, her burgundy hair catching the lights.

She's grinning seductively out at the crowd, making eye contact with every guy there, and probably all the girls too. That's her specialty after all. Making people want her. Publicity whore.

There's a tightness in my stomach and my hands ball into fists, just like they did last night. Just like they did last year when I first saw Lauren and Kadence's YouTube views start to skyrocket and I knew I had to come back.

The camera view suddenly swings from Kadence to Lauren, who's watching Kadence perform from behind the counter. She's smiling, but I can see past it. She's miserable not being up there onstage. My gut twists, but not with rage. I click the camera shut and put it back in my coat pocket. I put my palms against my eyes. Damn it, I hate Lauren. *Hate* her. I'm supposed to be glad she's suffering. That's why I did all this. Came back here with my new face.

For revenge.

I look around. *The woods are lovely, dark, and deep.* The line from the Robert Frost poem suddenly pops in my head. It fits perfectly with the scene around me and my mood. Even though it's early morning, the woods are full of shadows.

I feel small standing here under so many tall, tall trees, but in a good way. Small like insignificant. Small like I'm just a tiny part of this big world full of growing things. *The woods are lovely, dark, and deep.* Small like I could get lost out here and no one would ever notice.

These woods already hold so many memories. Secrets too. It's lucky the thaw was early this year and the earth soft enough to dig into, I think absentmindedly. I pick at the dirt I wasn't able to wash completely out from underneath my fingernails. It's cold, but I don't pull out my gloves. Instead, I perch on a fallen tree and take out the notebook I keep in a zipped pocket in my coat.

Lauren was always better at words than me, but I dabble. Poetry mostly. Sometimes it's the only way to get the storms tearing up my head to calm the hell down. I start to write, and this morning the words are flowing:

Buried In the Wood
All the pretty, fragile things,
are buried in the wood.
Worms will nestle in your bones
beneath the earth for good.
Maybe God will be forgiving,
though for me, I never could,
and so in mimicked memory
I walk upon
what's buried in the wood.

THREE

LAUREN

Cuppa Cuppa
Saturday, March 31
Noon

Cuppa Cuppa's morning rush is over by noon. We go from every seat full to a half-empty room. Charlie is in the back running receipts while I restock the refrigerator. When my phone rings, I almost don't hear it in time. I dig it out of my pocket and am surprised to see the words *Kady's Mom* on the screen. For a second I consider not answering it. It's probably a pocket dial. But then I change my mind. It might look strange if I don't answer. To outsiders, Kady and I are still best friends.

"Lauren?" She sounds relieved. "It's Mrs. Mulligan. The Major and I are up in Duluth for the weekend, and we can't get hold of Kadence. Do you know where she is?"

I roll my eyes. Her parents can be really overprotective, but it only kicks in at weird times. Like, half the time they have no idea where Kady is and don't care, then all of a sudden they want to know her every move. Maybe it's because they had her late in life. Her dad was gone for most of her growing-up years anyway, and her mom is just, well...*old* and kind of tired all the time. They never expected to have kids, then it was like, oh hey, a baby. Okay, let's feed and clothe it, and occasionally pay attention to it. If Kady was the way she was...well, no one ever turned out the way they did by accident.

Though I have to say, her dad has been much more tuned in since our music thing took off. It was like he finally knew what to do with her once he could put her in some kind of category. She was a Talented Kid. He had the TV footage to prove it. And he could be a Proud Dad, talking to all his military buddies at the diner in the mornings about his little girl. Kadence was always going on and on about that, about how much her dad bragged about her.

Whatever.

"I don't know," I say, as I stock the bakery case with prewrapped sandwiches. "Maybe still sleeping?" It comes out as a rasp, so I clear my throat and say the words again, but they barely come out any clearer.

"Would you mind stopping by the house and checking on her?" Mrs. Mulligan asks.

I have to say yes, even though I don't want to. Sometimes I wonder if I am physically incapable of saying "no" to people. I *wonder*, because I've never actually tested the theory.

I hate to be mean, but being nice isn't so great either. It can make you feel like a doormat, you know? My grip on the phone tightens. Was that what I was to Kady all those years? Yes-girl Lauren—does whatever she's asked, writes the songs, plays the instruments, sings the harmonies like a good little marionette?

Not anymore. Never again.

But I don't say no to her mom. It's not like she'll understand the current state of my relationship with Kady, like how we haven't talked much at all in the last six months. I can't stop and explain all that to her mom, like how it would be completely awkward and painful for me to show up at their house after the huge fight Kady and I had last week. Or even after last night.

"Thanks," Mrs. Mulligan says with a relieved sigh.

I close my eyes and exhale through my nose. "I get off work at two o'clock. I'll stop over then."

"Oh, that late? Well, I guess that's fine." Though she doesn't sound like she means it. "I'll keep trying to reach her too."

I hang up as one of our regulars steps up to the counter. I give him my best Cuppa Cuppa smile and it feels almost genuine. "Double skim latte?" I ask because it's his usual, "or can I get you to try some rejuvenating green tea?"

He makes a scoffing noise. "Tried it. I'd rather lick the carpet."

"It's good for you," I urge, but I'm already frothing the milk.

Charlie passes behind me and sticks his nose into the conversation. "You're...what? Seventeen? Eighteen? What do you care about what's good for you?"

"Eighteen. And I'm *all* about what's good for me these days, Charlie. It's my new thing. I don't even swear anymore. And I'm telling you, too much caffeine is going to kill you. First it'll be migraine headaches, then brittle bones, and by the time you realize what's happening, they'll be carving your tombstone."

"Well, that's cheery." Charlie drops his ass down on a stool behind the counter and picks at his teeth. "If you don't like coffee, why are you working in my house of poison?"

His question catches me off guard. Maybe it's because I've been thinking so much about Kadence, but the question could so easily be turned: Why do you hang out with that girl if she's poison? *Did.* Why did you hang out with that girl?

"Call me a missionary. I'm here to convert. Give me a couple years and this place will be called Lauren's Tea House and Music Café. Where everyone plays great and stays late." I was teasing but—hey—I kinda liked the sound of that. Lauren's Tea House. That would be cool.

After I hand off the latte, I take the opportunity to slip into the back room and call Kadence. I'm going through the motions here, but I did promise Mrs. Mulligan. My call goes straight to voice mail. Good enough. I did my duty. But then, on impulse, I call Mason. I don't know why I do it because I'm kicking myself the whole time it's ringing. An hour ago this would have been like the last thing I wanted to do. Right before losing my fingers so I can't sing *or play* anymore.

Chalk it up to due diligence and all that because I haven't talked to Mason in over a week. Not since things got weird between us. Weirder than they already were, I mean. Still, he could swing by Kady's house and check things out for her mom.

In my nervousness, I knock over a stack of paper cups while waiting for Mason to pick up. Charlie yells, "Keep your mind on your work, girl," which is ironic because he's getting high in his office.

The phone is still ringing. I'm about to hang up when I hear Mason's voice on the other end. "Hey."

"Hey."

And then. Silence.

Neither one of us wants to hear each other's voice. I'm embarrassed. Scratch that. *Mortified.* He's obviously still punishing himself for what we did. I cut to the chase. "Have you heard from Kady yet today?"

More silence. Then: "Listen, Lauren, I don't think—"

"No, I get it." I feel my face heat. This is so awkward. "I'm calling because her mom's worried about her. I thought maybe you'd heard from her. Forget I—"

"Why is her mom worried?"

"Because she's not answering her phone."

"It's only noon."

"Yeah, I know." I wish I hadn't called. I feel like an idiot. I don't need to feel like *more* of an idiot with my sort-of best friend's boyfriend. I'd checked that off my never-to-do list a week ago.

"I was going to stop by her house after practice tonight," Mason says. "I wanted to clear some things up between us." Pause. He doesn't have to say anything more. I know what "some *things*" means. The memory of my first-ever kiss—godforsaken, horrible mistake that it was—has been relegated to just some *thing*.

Mason chews his lip. I only know this because I know him so well. That's what comes from watching someone, studying them really, for so long. It wasn't a coincidence that when Kadence insisted we write a song about Mason, I was the one who wrote all the best lines.

"Listen, Lauren. I'm sorry about what happened, but I wish you hadn't told her."

"I didn't say *anything* to Kadence. I swear." Is that what Mason thought? I mean, I don't think I could bear it if he thought I'd been actively *trying* to cause a fight.

"Yeah. Well." He doesn't sound like he believes me. "I gotta go." He hangs up. I stare at my phone a few long moments after the screen has gone blank, then grind the palms of my hands into my tired eyes. The whole situation with Mason had gotten so messed up.

I mean, yes, I was still trying to figure out who I was. Like, who I was without Kadence. But I never wanted to be *that girl*. But I *had* been that girl.

Not anymore. Never again.

■　■　■

I claimed I felt sick, and all it took was the threat of throwing up in front of Charlie for him to send me home early. Instead, I make my way over to the Mulligans' house. When I get there, I sit in my car for a full minute, just staring at their driveway and picking at my nails.

Kadence's car is there. Parked on the far left where it always is.

But the driver's door of her car is hanging wide open. It's as if she gave it a push but was too tired to give it the strength it required to latch. I bet her battery's dead now. She never did take care of all the nice things she had.

Kadence got her car from her uncle on her sixteenth birthday. She wanted a red Corvette like Jake Ryan in *Sixteen Candles*. Her parents refused, but her uncle gave her his beater. She used her birthday money to have it painted cherry red. *Fake it till you make it*, she'd said. That was always the way. Never satisfied with life the way it came, always pushing for more. And she always made it happen. It was admirable. Enviable, some might say. I might say, though I don't always like to admit it.

Right now the car door—the way it hangs open—looks like a sliver of fingernail broken off an otherwise perfect red manicure. I swallow the lump in my throat as I take a second to gather my courage. I knock on the front door and wait. Nothing. I knock again. Still no answer.

I feel weird about letting myself into the Mulligans' house, *creepy stalker weird*. But Mrs. Mulligan is nervous enough about Kadence that I know she'd want me to check things out for real. They keep a key stored in a fake rock in the garden to the left of the front door. I find it easily, unlock the door, and step inside the house.

"Kady?" I call uncertainly. My gruff voice echoes off the walls.

The Mulligans' house is military straight, just like Kadence's dad. The walls are a pale gray. No picture ever hangs crooked because no one ever slams the doors. Pieces of furniture sit at right angles to each other. The only hint of a blemish is a plaster patch on the wall—painted over with gray paint—where my elbow once dinged the drywall.

It happened after our first song reached a million views. We posted a few videos our sophomore year, got a handful of subscribers, then

BAM! When that millionth view came in, Kadence spun me around and around and around until I saw stars. She let me go, and even though my head said stop, my body kept moving and I staggered into the wall. I paid for the patch with my summer babysitting money. I thought Kadence would pitch in. If she hadn't let go...But it was always so easy for her to let go now, wasn't it?

As I walk through the house, I can't help but notice how quiet it is. That strange, waiting, breath-held kind of silence that a place gets when it's empty. If Kadence were here, I'm sure I would sense her. The movement of air, the groan of a mattress, the rhythmic beeping of an alarm clock being ignored. I go upstairs.

"Um, Kady?" I call again. There's an edge to my raspy voice now. I push open the door to her room.

Kadence's bed is made, but the clothes she was wearing last night aren't on the floor. There's no purse, no laptop. There's the antique chair by the window, the only piece of furniture in the whole house that reflects anything of Kadence's personality, but even it looks wrong. It takes me a second before I realize that it's missing the usual heaps of clothes hanging off it.

I look around the room, spinning in a circle as if Kadence is merely hiding—perhaps braced against the corner and the ceiling like a ninja, ready to jump down on me and give me the scare of my life. But my eyes confirm what I already knew. Kadence isn't here.

FOUR
KADENCE

Found Video Footage
Kadence Mulligan's Laptop
Date Unknown

Image opens.

Kadence Mulligan's face appears on-screen. Though she is obviously sitting on a bed, she is in full show regalia: tight purple dress with blue rhinestones lining the bodice, thick false eyelashes, bright pink lips. A glittery purple pashmina scarf is wrapped around her neck.

"Is this thing working?" Kadence smiles and waves. "Hello, my beautiful Kady-Dids! I'm trying vlogging for the first time! I know, I know, it took me forever to get with the program and try this. It's funny, as comfortable as I am on stage, I still feel shy on camera."

She ducks her head and runs a hand through her hair, then laughs nervously. "Wow, if Lauren heard me say that, she wouldn't believe it. Anyway." She sits up straighter and grins again. "Here we are. You, me, and only the tiny world of cyberspace between us. So, how are you, my lovelies?

"It's a cold January day up here in Minnesota." Little cartoon penguins dance across the bottom of the screen.

"Which is why I've got my super sparkly scarf on today. My boyfriend, Mason, gave this to me. I know"—she leans in as if conspiratorially—"don't you all wish you had boyfriends who had good taste like mine does? The secret is to find guys who love their sisters. Or at least are forced to go shopping with them all the time." She laughs.

"But seriously, guys." She holds up the end of her scarf. "To all my fellow songbirds out there, you've got to take care of your throats in winter. If Lauren's health issues have taught us anything, it's to be vigilant about taking care of ourselves." She shakes her head and looks off camera to the left as if lost in thought.

"Performing without her still doesn't feel right. It's only been a couple months, but...we've been singing together since we were twelve, you know." She closes her eyes and breathes out before focusing back on the camera. "But we've gotta keep thinking positive. She's still resting up and the doctors say that's all she can do right now. And I can't say enough how much we appreciate all your prayers and good wishes. *Seriously.*"

"Okay." She breathes in, sitting back and slapping her hands on her thighs. "Now I'm going to answer some questions from our Facebook page. I figure it's so much more fun to answer this way than in short updates, right?

"First question." She looks at her laptop. "When did you and Lauren start singing together?" A small frown tugs at her mouth, but she covers it quickly with a smile. "I was an army brat, so I'd moved five times by seventh grade when we landed in Pine Grove, Minnesota. But this time was different. Dad was retiring and we were finally going to stay in one place. I was so excited. Nervous too."

Kadence leans back, careful to keep her legs crossed as she gets into the retelling.

"With each new school, I had this *process.* A plan for infiltrating so

I didn't turn out to be a friendless loser. The key was confidence. You had to walk into each new place like you owned it. That and finding a best friend as soon as possible.

"But I was having a harder time than normal at this school. That is, until I finally got my schedule fixed so I could be in choir. I was a soprano but was sitting at the dividing line by the altos right by this girl. She was good. Like, really, really good. Our voices sounded amazing in harmony together. We were both grinning by the end of class, even though we hadn't said a single word to each other yet." Kadence sighs happily and leans back on her bed.

"It was one of those destiny moments, you know? We became best friends. Perfect timing too. She had this guy hanging around kind of stalking her when we walked out of the choir room together. A total Creepy McCreepster. I guess he'd been hanging around her for a while. She was too nice to tell him to get lost, so he'd been keeping at it. With me around though, he backed off. She had protection and we both had a new best friend. And the start of not only a life-long friendship, but this awesome music thing too."

Kadence grins. "Thanks so much for tuning into this episode of the Kady-Did Show and for all your questions. Continue sending your support for Lauren via our Facebook page or through hashtag #feelbetterLauren. I know she's moved by all of your love and support. Life is short, my darlings. Reach for the stars before they burn out!"

Kadence flashes double peace signs and the video cuts off.

FIVE

MASON

Jean-Paul Renaudin Memorial Hockey Arena
Saturday, March 31
6:00 p.m.

I hadn't expected to get a call from Lauren this afternoon. I half expected us to never speak again. Not that I blamed her for that. At least not entirely. Now everything is a mess. Kady hates me. Lauren hates me. *God*, even I hate me.

It's quiet here at the rink. The stands are empty. Everything echoes—from the scrape of my skate blades to the tap of my stick against the ice. I pull back my arm and take a slapshot to one of the pucks I've dumped out of a bucket. I send the puck flying into the open net. At first, I hadn't been worried when Lauren called, asking if I'd talked to Kady yet. I figured she was probably sleeping in on a Saturday, or maybe she'd gone off for a little while to work out her own shit. I was hoping that was it. I didn't know what I was going to do if she couldn't forgive me.

My mind flashes back to that day last week in the cafeteria. I should have stepped in when Kady and Lauren got into that fight. I'd never seen them go at it like that before, and definitely never in public. Girl fights are supposed to be hot, but this one didn't do anything for me. It was horrible and made even worse because I was the cause of it all. Me and that stupid kiss.

I take another shot, but it ricochets off the pipe.

Lauren should never have put that note in my locker. I should never have agreed to go to the fort with her. Lauren should have kept quiet and said nothing to Kady, just like we agreed. I should have pulled them apart before Lauren hit the cafeteria floor. *Shoulda, shoulda, shoulda.*

My dad always tells me not to *should* on myself. It's supposed to be a joke, but it's not very funny.

By the time I got to the rink this afternoon, Kady still hadn't returned any of my texts. And by then I'd sent plenty. Each one more pathetic than the last. I even used the crying face emoji. Maybe that's why she's not responding.

The beginner figure skaters are showing up for lessons. Twenty or so little girls in mittens and colorful sweaters. They remind me of my little sisters, which reminds me that I need to get home. I collect all my pucks and drop them in the bucket. Then I head for the locker room. The first thing I do there is check my phone. Still nothing. And now I'm starting to freak out a bit. Kady's never been quiet this long.

SIX

LAUREN

Cuppa Cuppa
Sunday, April 1
12:07 p.m.

A day passes. Major and Mrs. Mulligan have come home from Duluth. Still no sign of Kadence. They're out of their minds with worry. I'm a jittery mess. Maybe I have caffeine poisoning or something. Maybe I've been unintentionally ingesting it. Like breathing in caffeinated air or something at Cuppa Cuppa. Mom tells me to sit down. I'm making her nervous.

I jump online, looking for an easy distraction. Google Alerts tell me that someone has just tweeted about me and Kadence. Out of habit, I click on it to see which of our songs is getting some buzz. But they're not talking about a song, and they're not mincing words.

@MBlake96 WTF just heard Kadence Mulligan is missing??? One guess who's behind it. Payback's a bitch, Lauren.

A cold trickle of dread runs down my arms, and sweat prickles the back of my neck. Who the hell is MBlake96? Her profile pic is a yellow duck, and she's got no bio. I slam my laptop shut and get up from my chair so fast it topples over.

The noise makes Mom jump. "Holy—!" she exclaims, and then with a tone of exasperation, "Isn't there any homework you could be doing? You're wound as tight as one of your guitar strings."

Dad looks up from his book and his eyebrows come together, like he's seeing me for the first time.

"I don't have any homework," I say, and for once in my life I wish I did.

"Do you have *work*-work today?" Dad asks.

I shake my head and bite at a hangnail. I'm not scheduled to work again until later this week, but they're right. I can't just sit here at home. I need to stay busy. Mom always says, "Busy hands quiet the mind," but this time it comes out as, "Why don't you unload the dishwasher?"

I'm grateful for the suggestion and happily get to work. Maybe if I stay busy all day, I'll be able to sleep tonight. When I'm done with the dishes, I call Charlie to see if I can come in to work.

"You're not on the schedule, dumb ass." Coming from Charlie, that's a term of endearment. I roll my eyes even though he can't appreciate the effect.

"I *know* I'm not scheduled. That's why I'm calling." Dumb ass. "Can I, please?"

"Fine," he says, "come in"—because by now I am practically *begging* him—"but only if you promise you're not still sick."

For a second I don't know what he's talking about, but then I remember my little white lie. "I'm not sick," I say because I'm not. Not really. It's just that I didn't get much sleep last night. My mind kept replaying Friday night like it was on some perpetual loop in my head:

Kadence arrived at Cuppa Cuppa at six o'clock. She unloaded her gear. The place was packed. She sang; I held myself together. Afterward, she stuck around to watch me clean up. I thought we were going to talk out the Mason situation. We didn't.

She left abruptly, saying "Abyssinia!" which is an old-fashioned expression she picked up when she was going through a retro phase. Apparently it's 1930s slang for "I'll be seeing you."

I found her gone from her house the next afternoon. Abyssinia!

Repeat.

Repeat again.

Sometimes my mind wanders into more detail in the sequence. Like how, when she stuck around after everyone else left, she didn't say anything right away. How her silence made me fidget. How in my awkwardness, I said, "Great show."

"Thanks," she said like I was just anyone, just one of the many who came up nervously to say, "Great show," not knowing what else to say but desperate to make some kind of personal connection with her.

Kadence was always the less approachable of the two of us. It was probably because she was the showiest. It was the hair, I think. And the way she carried herself with her shoulders back. She was tall enough to look over a lot of people's heads. It was funny because onstage she would connect with the audience, but when the show was over, it was like a switch had been flipped. Enter diva mode.

Not me. I was always happy to talk to people about the music. They'd come up and say, "You have such a beautiful voice." *Had.* Had such a beautiful voice.

"This really is the coolest little coffee shop," Kadence had said finally. Maybe she was sincere. Maybe she was being patronizing. It was sometimes hard to tell. One thing was for sure—Kadence always had an eye for style and design.

She had redecorated my bedroom for my sixteenth birthday present. She'd said I had outgrown the little girl decor. The pink walls and pink chiffon curtains had been with me since I was four—so I could see Kadence's point—but there was history in the cotton-candiness of it all. My history. So it took me a little while before I finally caved.

My mom gave us free rein, and Kadence jumped in, clipping magazine pages of what she called "hip" and "glam" styles of the rich and famous. *Fake it till you make it*, she'd said.

She came over one morning with a gallon of paint that looked like melted chocolate, as well as a sky-blue comforter she bought at Bed Bath & Beyond. An early birthday present, she said. She even talked me into buying a used chandelier at Goodwill. It had about a hundred dangly crystals and probably belonged over a dining room table rather than my bed, but she spray-painted the metal parts blue, then convinced my dad to install it.

Later, I got some paint pens and wrote my favorite song lyrics all over the walls. Lots of Lennon and the Eagles. Communist Daughter and Trampled by Turtles. Some Damien Rice. I have to say the room turned out pretty cool, though it took me a solid week before I was comfortable enough to get a good night's sleep. Any bit of light caught the crystals and turned my room into a spinning light show. It was like sleeping under a disco ball. Kadence was all about the show. The Kadence Show.

Enough with the bitter thoughts already, okay? I rub both my hands down my face, feeling my calloused fingertips against my cheeks. I'm so tired. I got used to the room eventually, but how am I supposed to sleep in there now? Every inch of it reminds me of Kadence.

Looking back, I wish it had occurred to me to come up with something equally cool for Kadence's sixteenth birthday. Her parents would never have let me decorate her room (not that I had that kind of skill), but still. I could have come up with something on par with a bedroom remodel if I'd tried.

Instead, I went with the sentimental gift. Something that would remind Kadence of all we'd been through together. I spent days going through old photo albums, both books and online, until I found the perfect picture. It was of us the summer after eighth grade, right before we won the Washington County Fair Talent Show. We were so nervous, and you could see it on our faces. It was like we knew we were going to win, but would we really?

When I gave it to her in a Best Friends Forever frame, she said thanks, then sulked for the rest of the night. So, yeah.

Flash forward two years. Now we're both eighteen. Kadence's birthday was last week. March twenty-third, to be exact. I'd learned from my mistake and had plans to make it really special. Then I didn't end up doing anything because she found out that I'd let Mason kiss me in the F.U. Fort.

Let's just say, letting your best friend's boyfriend kiss you puts a damper on lots of things, starting with birthday parties. As I watched her pack up her guitar last night at Cuppa Cuppa, I wasn't sure where I stood with Kadence anymore. Were we even still friends?

I squeeze my eyes shut tight. I don't want to think about any of this anymore. It's all such a mess.

SEVEN

JUDE

Troy's Garage, Pine Grove
Sunday, April 1
2:30 p.m.

I climb out of the work pit underneath the Honda and nod to Rocky as I grab the oil dispenser line that hangs from the ceiling between the two workstations. Rocky's finished topping off the car next to the one I'm working on.

"Man, is this rush ever gonna be done?" Rocky complains, mopping his sweaty brow on his sleeve. "It's killing my Sunday chillax policy."

I laugh. "Okay, number one, never say 'chillax' again." Rocky is in his mid-forties. He's Native American and his name isn't really Rocky. I don't know what his actual name is, come to think of it. I just know he got the nickname sometime in the eighties because he's a big guy and used to be a boxer.

The slight hum kicks on as I start pumping oil. "Number two, if you wanted a chill shift, don't work Sundays. Everyone and their grandma thinks the weekends are the perfect time for an oil change. I'm already two hours past when my shift was supposed to end."

Rocky rolls his eyes as he tightens the fuel cap. "Well, that's because Troy's a dick who doesn't know how to schedule right."

I don't disagree, but I make it a habit not to talk bad about the boss while I'm at work. I stop the oil pump at five quarts, then pull out the line and set it back in the hanger. I check the levels and reattach the cap. Nothing's leaking. Good to go.

"So I'm having a barbecue this weekend. You should come," Rocky says. Then he laughs. "I know that my niece Dana would sure love it if you did." He bobs his eyebrows up and down. I shrug uncomfortably. Rocky laughs harder.

Most of the guys at the garage pretty much ignore me or refer to me only as "Junior." That's because Dad works here too, though we're rarely on the same shift. Rocky's different. He's decided I'm funny. Dana dropped by during my shift one time to get Rocky to change her oil at a discount, then hung around in the lobby, trying to talk to me when I took my coffee break. Rocky's never let me forget it.

"Shut up," I say as I shut the hood of the car and give him the finger.

"Oh Jude, you're so *fine!*" he calls after me as I round the car and get in the driver's seat. At least closing the door shuts off the sound of his voice.

"Jackass." I say it with a smile and a shake of my head though. I drive the little Honda back out to the parking lot. Rocky's a cool guy, and as much crap as he gives me, he's always going on and on about his kids. He has a ten-year-old boy and a five-year-old little girl. And they are the center of that man's whole damn world.

I hear this guy yammering about his kids all shift, and then I go home. To my dad. He never says anything when I come in the door. Curious, I once clocked how long it would take before he actually spoke to me. It wasn't until two days later. Forty-two hours and seventeen minutes. And what was the great nugget of wisdom he

31

shared when he finally broke the silence? *Hey, grab me a beer from the fridge.*

I'm still thinking about all this crap when I head into the office with the keys from the Honda. The waiting room is full of people out for their Sunday oil change. But that's not what catches my attention.

"If anyone sees my daughter, you need to call this number immediately." A man holds up a picture of Kadence Mulligan with the word *Missing* across the top in large black lettering. A teenage guy stands beside him, looking like he hasn't slept. Mason Sisken. The boyfriend. I look back at the flyer. Kadence's face grins out from the image, the perfect picture of small-town innocence.

I look back at the man standing ramrod straight in full military dress. This must be Major Thomas Mulligan. I know his name. I know everything about Kadence, made it my business to know once upon a time. But I guess I never realized her dad was so old. Like not normal parent old, but *old* old. He's got to be in his late sixties, maybe even seventy. He passes the fliers to my boss, Troy the Dick.

"The police won't take this seriously until it's been such-and-such hours"—the disgust is clear in Major Mulligan's face—"but this is *our* town and we look out for our own. I served this country with honor for thirty-five years and never asked for a single thing in return. Well, I'm asking now. Help me find my baby girl. Post these flyers wherever you can around town, and please, call immediately if you or anyone you know hears anything about Kadence." He swallows hard, then turns around in a swift about-face and leaves the office.

Mason follows behind him, carrying a giant stack of fliers and never having said a word. He doesn't seem to recognize me from school, but then he never looked up from Kadence's picture.

A couple women cover their mouths with their hands. Troy tacks one flyer on the bulletin board and starts taping another one in the window. I only realize that I'm still frozen in place when Robert, who mans the register, asks, "Are those the keys to the Honda?"

"What?" I swivel toward him, then look down at the keys in my hand. "Oh. Yeah." I hand him the keys. My eyes track back to the door that the Major and Mason just exited through. Kadence. Missing. I'm surprised at how little I feel at hearing the news. You'd think I'd *feel* something more, y'know?

Instead, all I have is an intense need to know how Lauren is reacting to it. She has to know. It's her best friend. And then my feet are moving. I'm by Troy where he's finished taping the last corner of the poster to the window. "I gotta go. I'm already two hours past shift and I'm late for something."

I don't wait for his response. I push through the employee door to the back to grab my coat and helmet. Then I get on my beat-up Harley and go.

The shop's a little outside of town. I appreciate the growl of the engine under me as I take corners a little too sharply and drive a little too fast. My head is a swirling mix of Kadence and Lauren, and dwelling on that shit will make me reckless, so instead I focus my thoughts on the machine underneath me.

My bike is the closest thing I have to a religion. I built her up from a stripped frame I found in this old lady's barn that her son paid me to clean out back when I was living at Mom's. It took me a year to buy all the parts second hand and rebuild the bike, with a lot of advice from Ben, this ancient guy at the garage where I worked.

I get to a straightaway and gun the motor, really letting her loose. It's April and damn-it-all freezing, but I appreciate the bite that slowly burns into numb, even through my thick gloves. I stay focused on the road, only slowing when I come into town.

The square is what some might call picturesque. It was nominated one of America's most beautiful towns in some useless national poll by a crap Internet magazine. I park the bike and stomp out the kickstand. Yeah, beautiful, my ass. Guess they didn't get the double-wides in that picture. Or the guys laid off from the factory.

Even as I'm walking down a side street to cut over to the coffee shop, I see a skinny homeless guy walking all hunched over, staring at the ground like he's hoping that his next meal or his next fix is gonna pop right up out of the pavement. He's got a bright turquoise and lime-green backpack on though, so you've got to give him points for style.

Soon enough I'm on Main Street and walking into Cuppa Cuppa. Lauren's probably not even here. She usually works mornings on the weekends. But here I am anyway. I scan the room.

And there she is.

There are a bunch of people in line, and I duck behind an especially tall, wide guy. I still have enough of a vantage point that I can watch her. Damn it, that sounds creepy. What the hell am I even doing here? Her back is turned to me as she reaches for a syrup bottle that's high on a shelf. She's so short that she can barely grab the thing. It makes my mouth twitch with an almost-smile as a rush of memories hit me.

When we were kids, she was always asking me to reach things for her. There was that long, lazy summer between sixth and seventh grade. I'd just had a growth spurt and was super tall all of a sudden. The acne was getting bad by then, but she never even mentioned it. She treated me the same as she always had, ever since we'd met in third grade when I'd asked her for a pencil. Instead of giving me one of her spare yellow number twos, she gave me a fancy mechanical one with an Iron Man graphic on the side. I thought, *Wow, what a cool girl.*

We were friends after that. So I'd ride my bike over to her house every day that summer. I had a pedal bike back then. She'd make us peanut butter and honey sandwiches and then we'd spend the afternoon under a tree reading for an hour or two, nerdy as hell, but we didn't care. She was reading *Les Misérables* that summer, the unabridged version. I was more into graphic novels. Then we'd go on long walks around her neighborhood or sometimes in the woods behind my house with my dog, Coco. We never actually went *into* my house. The inside of my place never felt like the inside of Lauren's.

Like with the peanut butter. It never ran out at Lauren's house. Her parents never forgot to go grocery shopping. Or to, you know, buy her new clothes when her old ones were too small. I think her mom still tucked her in at night, at least until sixth grade when she started complaining about it. I remember thinking how awesome that would be, since more often than not, I was the one pulling my *mom* off the floor and trying to put her in bed, or at least onto the couch. Dad was a pro by then at ignoring things, so it wasn't like he was gonna do it.

There's this one day that sticks out in my memory especially. It had been a bad scene with my mom the night before. I was only, what, twelve, maybe thirteen? But I could tell Mom was changing. Acting different than she did when she was drunk. Sometimes she'd come home giggling and laughing and wanting to dance, but she could turn mean and start screaming just as fast, or go quiet and get real, real sad. Then she'd cry and not stop.

That night she'd passed out on the floor, and when I moved her to the couch, she didn't wake up or even mumble like normal. It was like she was in a coma. I'd seen that on TV. I stayed up with her to make sure she didn't stop breathing. She woke up only long enough to vomit on the rug around three in the morning. I cleaned it up and spent the rest of the night so scared. I slept off and on, curled up on the recliner after the sun came up and Mom's snores became loud and more regular. Around noon I showered and biked over to Lauren's.

"What's wrong with you today?" she asked after half an hour when I wasn't as talkative as normal. I shrugged. Lauren was my best friend but sometimes I felt mad at her. Her house was so nice, her family so perfect. It made me want to punch things. That afternoon I wanted to go in her living room and start throwing all the ceramic figurines her mom had arranged so carefully on their mantelpiece. I wanted to see them shatter and then stomp on the tiny pieces until they were sharp shards lost in the soft carpet so her family would all cut up their feet.

Lauren rolled her eyes. "Sandwich time," she said and headed toward the kitchen. The little metallic latches on her overalls jingled as she walked. I followed. I always followed, because in my craphole life, Lauren was a bright spark. That day though, not even she could break through.

I shoved my hands hard in the pockets of my thin, threadbare hoodie, eyes on the ground as she got the bread and plates ready. I managed to ignore her until she went for the stupid peanut butter. She seemed to sense my mood or maybe she was pissed that I wasn't talking, because instead of asking me to grab it like she usually did, she pulled out the step stool and started climbing up to reach the top shelf of the pantry herself.

"Don't be dumb," I said. "I got it." I stretched out my lanky frame and easily reached the jar.

She grinned at me, and for once we were face-to-face since she was already up on the step stool. I turned my face away, embarrassed because I had a breakout of especially large acne constellations on my upper cheeks. I'd dubbed it Acne Majorus. The movement shook my shaggy hair over my forehead and I felt better then, hoping it was hiding my skin.

"Why don't you move the PB to a lower shelf?" I mumbled, moving back and sliding the jar along the counter closer to the bread where she was making the sandwiches.

She laughed, such an easy sound. God, it came so easy to her. "Why would I do that when I've got you around to grab it for me?" she asked, brushing by me and putting her hand on my arm for a brief moment as she went.

My whole body reacted to her touch. My heart rate doubled. Sweat broke out on my forehead. And then my stupid throat was closing up. Because yeah, ever since I started noticing how pretty she was, her touch made me feel a little horny. But it wasn't just that. No one ever touched me. She made me feel like I could actually fix problems. As if being tall and useful could compensate for everything else. That was it for me. I was done for. That was the day I totally fell for Lauren DeSanto.

My jaw clenches at the memory of what a fool I was, pinning all my hopes on a girl who would rip my heart from my chest only months later.

Now I have to look away from Lauren, who has just turned around. But it's too late. I've already caught a glimpse of her. She's still so pretty. For a heavy moment, the old shame hits hard. I want to duck and cover, hide my face. No one could ever want me. My breaths start coming short and heavy. Damn it. A panic attack is the last thing I need right now.

I step out of line and turn to put my outer coat on the large rack by the door, but then stop and ball my hands into fists, taking deep breaths...in...out. *In. Out. In. Out.* I probably look like an angry, huffing bull to anyone glancing in my direction right now, but I can't give a good goddamn. How can she still have the ability to affect me so much?

I'm not that stupid son of a bitch writing unrequited love letters any more. I've taken back the power. I got my payback. I mean, things might have gone a little farther than I planned, maybe even gotten completely out of hand...I scrub a hand down my face. But at least there's no more reason to still feel like that shamed, ugly, awkward kid around her.

I take another deep breath. I shake out my shoulders to loosen them and stand up straight. Right. Fuck 'em all. I smooth my hands down my leather bomber jacket. It's slim enough to fit underneath the thicker coat I gotta wear when I take the bike. I never leave home without it. It's as much armor as it is a signature piece. This is who I am now.

I turn around and rejoin the line that's slimmed down considerably. Time to see how well Lauren's doing now that Queen Bitch is missing from the picture. Just one person between her and me, and she finishes with them right as I stride up.

She's just handed the last customer his change, and I speak before she can look up.

"I'll have an espresso, three shots, straight up."

She starts scribbling on her pad. "Is that all, sir?" She glances up and her breath catches. "Nathan," she whispers.

This is the first time I've spoken directly to her since I came back last August. I wasn't sure if she'd even recognized me. No one else did, except Kadence, but that was only after I told her who I was. Then again, Lauren and I weren't exactly on speaking terms when I left at the end of sophomore year. So maybe she's known it was me this whole time and just didn't know what to say.

I want to swallow but instead stick on a smooth smile. "It's Jude. I go by my middle name now."

She keeps staring at me, her pen frozen over the little pad.

"Jude," she finally echoes, as if trying out my new name on her tongue. "Nathan Jude Williams."

It does things to me, hearing her say my name. Especially my new name for the new me. She says it with her voice all low and raspy, like she's been a smoker all her life. I know it means she can't sing, and the sound of it sends another mix of emotions pounding through my skull. I'm turned on, happy in her misfortune, then deeply ashamed, then just sad for both her and me.

"That's going to be hard to get used to," she says. Then she asks,

"What are you doing here?"

I smile my most confident grin. "Getting coffee." I tap the pad where she wrote down my order, almost brushing her hand. She yanks her hand back and I hide a smile. I'm unnerving her. Good. Her best friend is missing and then her good ol' buddy, ol' pal Nathan, who she stabbed in the heart, shows back up in her life. All in the same day. Must suck to be Lauren.

"Right." She looks flustered. "I'll just get this made for you."

I know other customers often sit down and wait for her to call out their orders, but I lean my hip against the counter and watch her as she tamps down the espresso and sets up the shot. The machine growls to life as she puts the little cups underneath to catch the dark brown liquid that pours out.

"You been working here long?" I ask, even though I know the answer right down to the day.

She shrugs, setting up the next shot as soon as the first one finishes. I can tell she'd rather avoid conversation with me. Her neck is red and splotchy. It always does that when she's nervous. The thought makes me smile internally, though on the outside I play it cool. This, I've learned, is the key. The appearance of indifference. Cool Guy 101. Looking like you don't give a shit. Most the time I actually don't. Except when it comes to Kadence and Lauren.

"I think I saw you working a couple nights ago at the show when your friend was singing."

She shrugs again, pouring the shots into a cup and popping on the lid. I pull out my wallet as she comes back toward the register.

"Didn't I hear something about you two, like, being a thing on the Internet a while ago?"

She cringes. "Yeah, something like that," she murmurs, not meeting my eyes.

I hand her a five-dollar bill. She quickly makes change and I toss it in the tip jar. She's about to move away, but I reach out and grab her hand.

"Hey," I say, my voice softer. Damn, I don't even know what I'm doing, but being this close to her, seeing her warm skin and not touching her, is killing me. A few strands of hair are stuck to her cheek, and it's all I can do not to reach up and brush them behind her ear. "It's good to see you again, Ren."

Her eyes widen in surprise at the old nickname. "You too, Na—" She stops herself, pulling away from my touch. "Jude." She shakes her head and looks me over. "You look good." She smiles, but there's a tinge of sadness in it. Maybe it's me reading into it, but I feel like I can see everything that we had and lost, all in that one expression. And it suddenly strikes me—what if more than the bad feelings keep me coming back to Lauren? What if part of this compulsion is about all the good memories too? Hate, I know what to do with. But the other stuff?

"You've got a James Dean thing going on," she says.

I cross my arms and lean with my back against the shelf by the counter. "Yeah? Am I a rebel without a cause?"

She smiles again. My chest constricts painfully, like a horse just back-kicked me. Damn it, why does she have to be so pretty, so...so *Ren*?

I grab my coffee before she can say anything else. "See y'around," I call over my shoulder. Then I get the hell out of there.

EIGHT

KADENCE

Found Video Footage
Kadence Mulligan's Laptop
Date Unknown

Image opens.

Kadence Mulligan strikes a pose as she sits on the very edge of her bed and arches her back. She's wearing skin-tight jeans with rhinestones running down the seams and a cropped Jimi Hendrix T-shirt.

"Hello, my lovely Kady-Dids! And it's another beautiful, frosty afternoon that I'm greeting you from up here in the frozen north. But"—she gestures down at all her bared skin—"it's gonna take a little more than subzero temperatures to get Kady Mulligan down." She laughs easily and sits up on the bed, bouncing on the springs several times in excitement and clapping her hands.

"As you can see, I re-dyed my hair"—she shakes her long magenta hair around—"so it's nice and vibrant again. Nothing to chase away the winter blues like a bright, happy hair color. Though lemme tell you," she says, laughing, "the Major—that's my dad—was less than impressed the first time I came home from the salon like this." She makes a mock stern face and deepens her voice. "'Young ladies should only have hair the color God gave them.' So I tried explaining that in the twenty-first century, God gave the world hair dye and salons."

She laughs again. "He only stopped grumbling about it when our music started doing well and I explained it was part of my signature look. Like Marilyn. Or Madonna. Or Gaga. That helped. At least I'm not wearing a meat dress, right?" She shakes her head, rolling her eyes but still smiling.

"Okay. So, on to the questions! I got a great one this week, sent in by a Twitter follower. @Kadydid_4_life asks, 'When did you and Lauren first know that you had something special? Was there a moment?'"

Kadence looks upward at the ceiling as if she is thinking. "Well, now that I think about it, there really was. Lauren and I were best friends and had been for a year, but it wasn't until eighth grade when we entered this school talent show." She puts a hand over her eyes as if embarrassed. "I know that might sound dumb now, a little, dinky school talent show. But it was this *huge* deal back then. I mean, Lauren and I even got to go into the principal's office and announce the talent show over the loudspeaker. Which felt so big at the time." Kady rolls her eyes at herself.

"I know, I know. We were soooooo cool." She laughs. "Lauren and I spent every waking minute together—singing, writing songs together, and practicing some more. Lauren was great with lyrics, but she didn't know much about how to exactly"—Kadence waves a hand, her brow furrowing as if trying to figure out how to explain—"own a stage or really, you know, give the music a *soul* in that moment with the crowd there. She was killer at the technical stuff, but sometimes she treated music a little like math.

"So then we get to the night of the talent show. Lauren was so nervous." Kadence laughs fondly at the memory. "We were second-to-last to perform. A few acts before us, there was this girl who was really, really good. She brought down the house, and people backstage were saying she was the best of the night and no one was gonna be able to beat her. So that didn't exactly help Lauren's terror!

"Which is why I had to literally drag her out on stage. Like, I had to grab both of her wrists and tug her out there! If I hadn't, she would have run the other direction. But you know, I had this totally Zen thing going on. I had this inner calm"—Kadence closes her eyes—"like I knew somewhere deep inside that this was the beginning of something huge. That this was our moment.

"I set up Lauren's kick drum and plugged in both of our guitars. She was shaking like a leaf so I got her settled on the stool and put the guitar strap over her head. I made her look in my eyes. I said, 'Lauren, look at me. Don't see anyone else. It's just you, me, and the music. That's all that matters. You, me, and the music. That's all that ever matters.' And she nodded. I'd really gotten through to her."

Kadence looks back up at the camera. "Then we played. And it was magical. The entire auditorium was spellbound. I don't even remember what the song was about. It was one of our earliest attempts obviously, something Lauren had written about a childhood friendship she had lost, I think.

"It was just her voice and mine and the strum of our guitars echoing in the totally silent auditorium, and it was, God..." Kady shakes her head in wonder, as if reliving the moment. "I'm getting goose bumps just remembering it." She rubs her arms and gives a small shudder of delight. "Anyway, Lauren and I weren't the only ones who felt the magic. It's funny, we didn't even get first place in the talent show. They gave it to that other girl who'd sung several people before us, Mary something or other. But Lauren and I were who everyone was talking about at school the next week.

"And that was it. That was the moment I knew we were going to be something. I knew it was the start of something important. I didn't know what. I didn't know how big we'd become or how incredibly blessed we would be to have all of you amazing fans. But I felt the magic that night, guys, and that is what music is all about.

"All right, time to sign off for the episode." She kisses her palm and holds it out to the camera. "Life is short, my darlings. Reach for the stars before they burn out!"

NINE

LAUREN

Sheriff's Office
Monday, April 2
10:15 a.m.

You know how the police in TV shows always say, "Sorry, ma'am, we don't deem them to be a missing person until they've been gone at least twenty-four hours?" That is *not* a joke. They really don't—at least when that person is an adult (even if just barely).

Which is why the county sheriff didn't send someone to talk to Kadence's parents until late yesterday afternoon. Too late by Mr. Mulligan's estimation, since apparently he'd already plastered the town in missing person fliers. I guess they asked Mrs. Mulligan for a list of Kadence's closest friends. Which is why I'm sitting at a table in the middle of a cinder-block room, biting my nails down to the nubs.

I know they're going to be talking to Mason too, but I don't know if it's already happened or not.

I sit back in my chair and let my arms hang down, though my foot is bouncing against the floor. It takes me a second to realize I'm beating out the rhythm to Nicki Minaj's "Anaconda." I have to put my hand on my knee to quiet my mind.

The room they put me in is painted blue like the chandelier Kadence made for my birthday. I suspect the color was chosen on purpose because someone read that it had a calming effect. It's not working. My palms are sweating.

I hum-sing a line from a new song I'm working on. I know I'm not supposed to do that, but it calms my nerves even though the sound comes out rough and scratchy. *Metamorphosis, you make me change my dress. My shoes, my face, I am such a mess.*

I wonder what Kadence would do in this situation, and I try to channel her. A kind of What Would Kadence Do? moment that tells me that Kadence would smile.

I smile.

It feels all wrong. *This* is all wrong.

The chair across the table from me is empty. Behind the empty chair, there's a mirror. I'd bet a hundred dollars there's someone watching me on the other side of it. I watch CSI reruns. All three cities.

My parents are outside in the hallway, waiting for me to be done. They wanted to be in here with me, but one of the unexpected perks of turning eighteen is you get to fly solo when interrogated about your best friend's disappearance. I'm glad my little brother, JJ, is at school and doesn't know what's going on. Better he be wrapped up in all the usual junior-high drama than any of my own.

Man, Kady, I wish you were here. The thought hits me unexpectedly. It shouldn't. It's what I've been waiting to feel all this time. It's just that sometimes, like at a funeral, the reactions everyone *expects* you to have are delayed. And you feel guilty, wrong even, for not feeling the way you know you should.

I've always been that way though. My emotional reactions to things can get a little disjointed. Like in first grade, when Billy Thompson killed a frog during recess, poking its guts all over a rock, I didn't start screaming until the middle of class a few hours later. I didn't calm down for another forty-five minutes, and then only when my parents came to pick me up. And yet...when my dad took me deer hunting a few years later, I was fine.

A blond man walks in holding a Styrofoam cup and a tiny tape recorder. His broad shoulders strain his shirt. He sets the tape recorder on the table and gestures at me with his cup. "Can I get you something?"

The vending machines I passed in the hallway didn't have anything remotely organic. I was bummed at the time because I didn't get breakfast, but maybe it's a good thing I took a pass. Is this guy hoping to trick me into giving up a DNA sample? Or am I being crazy paranoid? I feel more sweat break out on my forehead. At least now he won't go mining for my saliva in a half-eaten Hot Pocket.

"No, thank you," I say and sit up a little taller. What would Kadence do? A small part of me recognizes the irony in trying to emulate Kady when only days ago I was swearing that I was done with her forever. The other part of my brain is telling me to shut up because all I want right now is to get out of here.

My fingers feel twitchy. I wish I was holding a guitar. People don't realize it, but guitars are like shields. They provide a layer of separation between you and the crowd. From anyone who wants to ask you questions.

"I'm fine." I add, "All things considered."

He shrugs, sits down, and pulls a yellow pad out of the desk drawer and a pen from behind his ear. He hits the Record button.

"My name is Detective Kopitzke. Let me start by saying that you are not a suspect."

I nod.

He tips his head. "Is something funny?"

"No," I whisper. Was I smiling?

"We asked you to come in here today because we understand you are one of Kadence Mulligan's closest friends."

I arrange my mouth at the last minute into some kind of expression, I'm not sure what.

"As you know, we're trying to find your friend, and we're hoping you can tell us if there's somewhere special she likes to go. Is there anywhere you like to go with her?"

The question gives me pause. Kadence always made me feel like I could follow her anywhere. That if I didn't, I would miss out on something awesome. Most of the time she was right. When someone asked, "What's going on Friday night?" ninety-nine people would answer "I don't know," but Kadence would say, "So, so much! I can't decide!"

But then there were other times too. Times when she took off by herself for her little "camping trips." The first time she did that, we were only thirteen. Mrs. Mulligan called our house, asking if Kadence was there. Apparently Kadence had told her we were having a sleepover, but that wasn't true. She had other plans, and she never thought twice about lying to make those plans happen. That night, her plans had included camping out in the woods along the creek. She said she needed a break from her parents sometimes. I understood that, but *camping*? Alone?

Detective Kopitzke leans back in his chair, and I realize I've forgotten to answer his question out loud.

"She used to go on these little camping trips," I say. "She'd take off overnight. Sleep in the woods or a tree house or someplace."

His eyebrows go up. "She doesn't strike me as what you'd call the camping type."

48

I feel a prickly sensation at the back of my neck. "I know. She was pretty high maintenance. Is," I say when I realize I'm thinking of Kadence in the past tense. I have to stop that. I can't do that out loud. Not with big, blond Kopitzke taking notes. "Is high maintenance. Not that high-maintenance girls can't camp. Just that it's hard to understand Kadence going anywhere she can't plug in a flat iron. But then, maybe that's why she always camps alone. God forbid someone should see her without full makeup."

I'm rambling. I laugh a little, embarrassed. "That's not my line, by the way. It's Kady's. 'God forbid someone should see me without makeup!' She says that a lot. I don't know anyone who has seen her natural face since eighth grade, including me." I sit on my hands as if this can make me shut up.

"When's the last time she went on one of her camping trips?"

"I don't know. When we were sixteen? At least that I know of."

Kopitzke scribbles my answers on his yellow pad. "And how long would she be gone?"

"Usually just overnight."

"Does the fact that she's been gone three days worry you?"

"Yes," I whisper, staring down at my lap. Does looking down make me look shifty? Guilty of something? I quickly look up and meet Detective Kopitzke's gaze. I smile again, but my cheeks feel tight. I imagine tiny hairline cracks running across my face.

"Do you miss her?" Kopitzke asks.

I don't answer right away. There was that little twinge I felt a few minutes ago when I wished she was here. But aside from that, the most honest answer is no—I don't miss her. The moment she announced she was going solo, I understood more about our friendship than I'd cared to admit to myself. I was Kady's friend only as long as I was useful to her. It was a good six-year run, but it's over now.

Detective Kopitzke leans forward across the desk at me. "You're hesitating."

"I don't know," I whisper, voice cracking. "We haven't been spending a lot of time together. It's hard to miss what you don't have."

"I understand you used to perform with Kadence, that the two of you were like a band or something."

"Or something." My eyes drop slightly to his jacket lapel where there's a coffee stain. I wonder if Mrs. Detective Kopitzke didn't have time to take in the dry cleaning or if it's from this morning.

"But you can't sing anymore."

I try to keep my teeth from grinding. "Not now. No."

"How does that make you feel?"

Oh, so now he's a shrink? He wants to know how it makes me feel? A tremor runs through the muscles in my arms. I cannot allow myself to feel anything. Not here. I cannot show this man how humiliated I am for letting Kadence run my life. How I'm the lowest of the low for kissing Mason, but even lower for how I treated Jude. That's something I try not to think about too much, but lately—ever since I saw him at Cuppa Cuppa—he's back front and center in my thoughts.

Kadence used me, turned me into someone I'm not, and even though losing my voice and not being able to sing totally sucks, at least it gave me the chance to step back and reevaluate my life and what's good for *me*.

Do I miss Kadence? No. No, I don't.

But I don't tell him any of that and just shrug. It makes me look like a brat, but I'm pretty sure smiling looks worse. I'm totally stuck. I don't know how to act, how to look, how to sound. I tell myself to act naturally, but I've lost my grip on what that feels like. I shift in my chair and roll back my shoulders, hoping to reconnect with my body.

Detective Kopitzke studies my face for several long seconds. Then he says, "We understand you were the last person to see Kadence Mulligan on Friday night."

Something about the way he says "last person to see her" sets off alert buttons in my head. Suddenly I can picture them hooking me up to something that measures how much sweat I can produce in an hour. I mean, sweat equals guilt, right? I think I read that somewhere.

Kadence would never let the pressure get to her.

"I don't know if that's true," I say. "She stuck around the coffee shop for a little bit after the show. It was just me and her for a few minutes, then she left. Went out the back door, headed for the parking lot. I don't know who she might have seen back there. Obviously she managed to get herself home though. Her car was there."

I'm rambling again, but I'm proud of myself too, because that's a fine piece of logic if I ever heard one. Kopitzke makes some kind of note. I try to read it, but it's at a bad angle and he's too far away.

"We understand that you and Kadence got in a pretty big fight recently at school."

My body goes rigid and I swallow loudly. Did Mason tell him that? Why would he? He had to know how that would make me look. For a second my temper flares, but I get it back in check. I mean, even if Mason had said nothing, the story would have come out. There were plenty of witnesses. Like a whole cafeteria full. Better walk carefully on this one.

"It wasn't that big."

"Then tell me how you would describe it."

I roll my eyes. "It was a couple days before spring break. People were getting antsy. They were happy for any kind of excitement. Trust me. As cafeteria drama goes, it wasn't that big of a deal."

"I understand the fight was over a boy?"

I sit back in my chair and cross my arms. I'm afraid the posture makes me look sullen and oppositional, but I can't help myself. That's exactly how I feel. "Kadence was paranoid. She accused me of hooking up with her boyfriend."

"Mason Sisken."

I don't respond.

"Was she right?" His pen is poised to write down whatever I say.

"She was misinformed."

"What would make her think you and Mason were together?"

"I don't know." My eyes glance over at the wall with the door. "You'll have to ask her."

"Well, Lauren, we can't exactly do that now, can we?" He leans back across the table, his hands folded like he's begging me to come up with something that he can use. "Think. What would make her accuse you of something like that? Were you alone with him at some point?"

The memory of the kiss hits me hard in the gut. Mason and I had gone to the F.U. Fort, a rotted plywood lean-to that got its name from the words spray-painted on the outside wall. It's in the woods behind the high school, and it's held together with bailing twine, chewing gum, and the prayers of blunt-smoking dropouts.

As little kids we thought it was really scandalous. We whispered about it. The big kids drank sloe gin back there. Mason and I hadn't been drinking when we went. I don't even know how we ended up there. I mean, not exactly.

"Lauren?"

"I'm sorry. What was the question?"

"Were you alone with Mason at some point? What would make Kadence think something had happened between you and him?"

I suck on the inside of my cheek. "I don't know. Maybe because that's the kind of thing she would do with someone else's boyfriend, so it was easy for her to assume that someone would do it to her?" Snarky.

I sound snarky, and I doubt it's helping.

"Kadence fooled around with other people's boyfriends?"

"Sometimes."

"Can you give me any names of those other people?"

"There was this one girl? Mary? She moved to a different school though."

"Did Mason know about any of this?"

I pause and hold my breath, weighing my words. I'm not such an idiot that I don't see my opportunity when it comes. Mason had no trouble pointing the finger at me by telling the detective about the fight—that is, if he was the one who told. Well, ever heard of payback? I could do the same to him. Who doesn't like a jealous boyfriend as the prime suspect? People eat that tabloid crap for breakfast.

But...I can't do that to him. I tried to tell him once about Kadence cheating, but he never believed me. Mason is sweet and a little naive. If he's the one who told Kopitzke about the fight, I'm sure he wasn't being malicious. He probably thought he was being helpful.

I shake my head. "No. I don't think so."

"So what happened in this fight between you and Kadence?"

I toss my arms up in the air, and they fall into my lap with a slap. "I told you it wasn't a fight. We were friends. She yelled at me in the cafeteria for a bit, then it was over. I apologized."

"Apologized for what? I thought you said nothing happened."

"I apologized for whatever she *thought* had happened. That was how it was between us. She got upset about something, and I apologized to smooth things over. Then we moved on."

"Some of your classmates said she pushed you."

"She didn't." Even as I say the words, I remember the feeling of staggering backwards, tripping on a stool. Banging my head against the floor. I sway a little in my chair.

"Was there any physical contact between the two of you?"

"She might have put her hands on my shoulders."

"What did you do in response to that?"

"I twisted away. Like this." I demonstrate. *Crap.* I'm doing that thing again, letting him lead me down that road I was talking about before. I've already said too much. I need to stop. If I wanted to hurt Kadence, it wouldn't be because she grabbed my shoulders and shook me around on Taco Tuesday. I have *wayyy* more material to work with than that.

"But she didn't push you. Not even by accident?"

"Well, maybe by accident. When I was trying to twist away from her, maybe I got knocked off balance."

"That sounds pretty physical. Putting her hands on you. Are you sure there was nothing going on with you and Mason?"

I stare him down. This guy would not let up. "I told you. There was nothing going on between me and Mason. There *is* nothing going on between me and Mason. Are we done yet? Can I go home?"

"As I said, you aren't under arrest. These are just some friendly questions. You are free to go whenever you want."

"Then I'd like to go now." I push my chair back and start to stand.

"One more thing." He raises a hand, and a second later a woman in a white shirt and black low-rise pants comes in. She has a badge hooked to her waistband. She sets a clear plastic bag on the center of the table. The bag is marked EVIDENCE with a bunch of numbers, and there's a piece of wide yellow tape with the words DO NOT BREAK SEAL printed on it. But more than any of that, I am transfixed by what is inside the bag. It's a green Cuppa Cuppa uniform shirt.

Slowly, I sink back into my chair. "Where did you get that?"

"From the garbage bin at your house," the woman says.

My eyebrows shoot up. "You can't go through our garbage." I'm impressed by how calm I manage to keep my voice, but my heart is crashing against my rib cage.

"Actually," she says, "we can."

I stare at them both. They've got to be kidding me. Why is this happening?

The woman leaves and Detective Kopitzke flips the bag over. There's a bloodstain on the shirt. It's not big, but it's enough. My forehead prickles as I break into a cold sweat.

"Do you mind telling me how this blood got on this shirt?" he asks. "And while we're on it, how it ended up in your trash?"

I can tell that they've already determined it's Kadence's blood. My mind scrambles to explain it convincingly. "It was an accident," I say, my already fragile voice shaking.

"*What* was an accident? Exactly."

My hand trembles as I raise it to my mouth and bite at a hangnail. "Kady cut her hand packing up her gear when she left the coffee shop Friday night. I said I'd get her a paper towel but"—I swallow loudly— "but she just used one of the old uniform shirts that were piled up at the end of the bar. Charlie wanted me to trash them when I finished closing because we got a new color for spring, and they'd just come in. I only took the shirts home because the...um...the dumpster at work was overflowing that night."

"So what's the color of the new spring shirt?" he asks, cutting me off, and I can tell he doesn't believe me.

"Um...I don't know." Then I add, "Yet."

When a look crosses his face that tells me I'm confirming all his suspicions, I start talking fast. "That's only because Charlie screwed up the order, and the logos were all wrong. He had to send them back." Damn that pot-smoking dumb ass Charlie. If I'm in trouble because of him...so help me...

"Your boss...That's Charlie Horn?" Detective Kopitzke writes his name down on the notepad.

"Right."

Detective Kopitzke's mouth torques. "Do you know what Kadence cut her hand on?"

"Not exactly. It happened in the parking lot when she was loading her car. An amp or something? Some loose piece of metal? I don't know."

"Well, that sounds like a perfectly reasonable explanation."

I can't tell if he believes me or not. "Yes, it is. Can I go now?"

"Yes, you can go. Please stay in town though. We'll likely have more questions." He looks at me in a way that makes my stomach sour. "Oh, and Lauren? Kadence's parents have asked for a press conference this evening. Are you willing to participate? I'm sure it would be a great comfort to them to have you there."

After all he's practically accused me of, I can't imagine why he'd want to have me there, but saying no doesn't sound like a good idea, and as always, yes came more easily. "Yeah, sure. No problem."

When he escorts me through the door, Mom and Dad are sitting on the bench in the hallway. They both stand together like they've been propelled from their seats.

"Is she done?" Dad asks. He wraps his arms around me, and I have a flicker of calm.

"I hope she was of some help," Mom says.

I roll my eyes and pull out of Dad's hug. "I'm hungry," I say, which makes them all turn their heads toward me with the same strange expression. Why do I keep saying exactly the wrong thing?

"Of course, honey," Mom says. "You're all worn out. She hasn't been sleeping." She addresses this last comment to Detective Kopitzke. I want to kick her. What will he make of that? "She misses Kadence so much," Mom adds.

Detective Kopitzke and I exchange a look. "Six o'clock," he says. "Be back here by then."

"What do you want me to say?" I ask.

Detective Kopitzke stares at me for a few seconds. Then he says, "When someone is missing, most people ask the viewers to call in with any tip or information they might have. In some cases they ask for their loved one's safe return."

Oh, I think. *Duh*. Why didn't I think of that? Detective Kopitzke's looking at me like he's wondering the same thing.

TEN

MASON

Sheriff's Office—The Interview
Monday, April 2
11:00 a.m.

I pull into the parking lot outside the sheriff's department. It's one place I never thought I'd have reason to be. I wasn't even sure how to get here at first. I turn off the ignition and put my keys in my pocket. Even though I'm alone, it's humiliating how bad my hands are shaking. I need to be strong for Kady.

The thought of someone touching her makes my stomach turn with the same sour spin it's been doing since I left the rink two nights ago. Going around with her dad, handing out fliers yesterday...it felt like I was at least *doing* something. They need to find her. I need to find her.

I get out of my car and a gust of air lifts a greasy hamburger wrapper from the floor of my otherwise immaculate truck. *Brady*, I think. *Goddamnit, Brady.* My friends know they aren't supposed to leave their food garbage in here. Sometimes I think they do it on purpose just to get me worked up. Normally I'd be pissed seeing that wrapper flutter around, then settle on the seat, but right now I can't think about anything but Kady.

Once inside the sheriff's department, I am directed to a small room. There's a table. And a tiny tape recorder. It looks old.

"I'm Detective Kopitzke," says a short, muscled man. He directs me toward a chair on one side of the table. "I'm going to be asking you some questions."

He pushes the record button on the tape recorder and that's when it begins. Though the way he talks, I have this terrible feeling that it's already the end. *Kady*, I think. *Kady*.

Kopitzke: When did you first meet Kadence Mulligan?

The question is so basic, so inconsequential, that I'm not sure how to answer. Did anyone ever just meet Kady? More like, everyone knew who she was the moment she walked into a room. It wasn't like there ever needed to be a formal introduction.

Mason: How does this help us find her?
Kopitzke: It helps to have a full picture of who she is.

I take a deep breath and give him the benefit of the doubt.

Mason: We met two years ago during our sophomore year.
Kopitzke: At school.
Mason: Not exactly. I met her in my little sisters' playroom.
Kopitzke (laughing): Not what I was expecting.
Mason: It was a Saturday morning. I was playing tea party with my little sisters, Annabel and Meredith. They're twins...

The detective raises his eyebrows at me, and I bite my lip. Heat rushes into my cheeks at the memory because that morning I was dressed in my usual Saturday morning clothes: a floppy, pink hat and a feather boa.

I was the only sophomore on the varsity hockey team back then. If any of my older teammates had seen me, I would never have lived it down. Still, I did whatever I could to make my little sisters happy. Translation, tea parties.

Mason: Then Mom woke up and came into the playroom…

I can picture her so clearly. Her bathrobe was cinched tightly around her waist, and her hair looked like birds had been trying to nest in it all night.

Mason: That's when the doorbell rang. Mom answered it. A few minutes later she came back and said, "You have company." And it was Kady.
Kopitzke: Had Kadence Mulligan ever come to your house before?
Mason: Never.
Kopitzke: That must have been an interesting morning for you. I don't think any girls ever spontaneously visited me when I was in high school.
Mason: With Kady, things are always interesting.

In fact, thinking back, it had taken me a second to process what Mom was even saying. Kadence Mulligan was at our door?

My first thought was *Why?* But then I remembered something my lab partner said during biology when the varsity roster was posted: *You being the only sophomore on the team is going to get you a lot of tail. Girls eat that crap up. And you know who loves a high profile more than anybody.*

Who? I'd asked.

He'd narrowed his eyes at me. *I'm just saying, if you get Kadence Mulligan's attention, you're set for life, my friend.*

I thought he was blowing smoke up my ass. Not that I'd had any trouble with girls in the past, but Kadence Mulligan?

I swallow hard. Why haven't they found her yet? What are they doing to find her? I think Kady's dad might be right. They're not doing enough. They're not taking this seriously enough. These questions are pointless. They don't even have modern recording devices. But I don't say any of that to the detective.

Mason: Yeah. Kady's like on another plane from the rest of us. Another stratosphere.

Kopitzke: Oh, come on. A good-looking guy like you? Smart. Athletic. Nice too? I've done my homework. Asked around. One girl we talked to called you the "total package." I'm not surprised Kadence Mulligan would be interested in you.

I shake my head and once again fight back the blood that's rushing into my cheeks. Kopitzke has it all wrong. I'm not all that, and I was completely surprised by Kady's interest. From the moment I saw her leaning against the door frame to my sisters' playroom, I was like, call it a day, signed, sealed, DE-livered. I was all in for this girl. I think my mouth may have even been hanging open.

I can still remember exactly what Kady looked like, standing there in that doorway, and I swear my heart knew it was in serious trouble. Because there I was, wearing a feather boa and holding a teacup to my lips. Pinky out.

ELEVEN

JUDE

Pine Grove High School
Monday, April 2
1:30 p.m.

"Hey, man, you heard about that DeSanto chick?" Elliot asks as he takes a long drag on his smoke and offers it to Ari, an Asian girl who dresses like a goth-meets-anime-gamer chick. Black lipstick and heavy eye makeup crap, but then with pigtails, short skirts, and knee socks. Elliot's a big fan of the short skirts, though most the time he's not dumb enough to say this within her hearing.

A small group of us, maybe eight or so, are out here in the woods. We're all skipping class for a smoke break. I don't know any of them well enough to call them friends, but they're cool enough to hang with.

Elliot's question catches my attention, but I'm careful not to let anyone see. Ari takes the smoke from Elliot, all the while giving me her best *do-me* eyes from where she's leaning against the wall of the F.U. Fort. I ignore her.

The F.U. Fort's the best place to go when you need a smoke away from the prying eyes of teachers. It's total BS, since most of us are eighteen and a couple months away from graduating. But hey, whatever makes this purgatory pass quicker, right?

I take a slow drag of my own cigarette and wait for Elliot to say more. I like the way the smoke warms my lungs. My mom's always telling me these things will kill me. I think it's the hypocrisy of *her* telling me not to dump chemicals into my body that makes me smoke just to spite her. If she stays clean three whole years without any relapses, maybe then I'll stop. Or maybe that's just an excuse and by then I'll blame it on an addictive personality. Which I also inherited from her. Nice how that works, ain't it?

"Oh yeah." Ari jumps in. "Heard she totally offed her friend. Lost her voice and it made her go all psycho bitch." She raises her arm and starts making the discordant *Psycho* music noise as she slashes downward several times.

"Shut up, guys." My spine is stiff as I look around at the others. Only a few other than Elliot and Ari look my way.

"Chill out, man." Elliot laughs. "Everyone's been talking about it. Have you been skipping *all* your classes? I know you like to keep your head down and do your whole loner thing, but *dude*. It's all anyone is talking about."

I clench my jaw and force myself to keep calm. Damn it. What's wrong with me? This is good. Couldn't have worked out better. Kadence is out of the picture, and Lauren's being blamed for it. I shift uncomfortably and toss my smoke to the ground, grinding it under my foot. Then I scrub both my hands over my face. Everything feels wrong.

"What are they all saying?" I ask.

"Rumor is that Lauren was the last one to see Kady before she disappeared," Ari says, perking up. For a goth chick, she's just as into gossip as most girls I've ever met. I'd swear she's about to start leaning in and flipping her hair. "And that they've been total rivals since Lauren lost her voice. Then there was the big blowup in the cafeteria about Lauren trying to steal Kady's boyfriend. Were you there that day?"

"Heard about it. Wasn't there." I take half days on Tuesdays and Thursdays to go work at the garage.

"Oh man, that fight was epic." Elliot laughs. "Too bad there wasn't mud and a wrestling ring, because then it would have been totally *hot*." He arches his back and rubs down his chest slowly, then makes his voice high-pitched and breathy. "Oh, Lauren, you've been such a naughty girl, stealing my boyfriend like that. Come here and let me *spank* you."

"Shut up," Ari and I say at the same time. Ari smacks him hard on the shoulder for good measure. I wince a little because all those chunky rings she wears might as well be brass knuckles.

Elliot and Ari bicker as we head back for the last couple periods of the day, but all I can think about is what they've said. I listen to the whispers as I make my way through the halls instead of putting in my earbuds. Elliot was right. Everyone *is* talking about Lauren. Saying she had something to do with Kady's disappearance. But they're just a bunch of idiots at school. I try to shake it off.

For once I've been trying *not* to think about Kadence and Lauren. Like maybe this is a chapter I should finally put behind me. The things that I wanted when I came back have been accomplished, even if they happened in ways I didn't always expect. The two girls who tormented me are now all fucked up themselves. That should be enough, shouldn't it?

When I get home that evening, I flip on the TV while a frozen pizza cooks in the oven. I kick into Coco's half-full dog bowl. Damn it, I told Dad to take care of this.

I reach down to move the bowl, but the local news comes on the TV, and right there on the screen is the girl I've just vowed to forget.

Lauren's standing beside an older couple. Kadence's parents. I lean closer and turn up the volume.

A young female reporter, with teeth that seem too white to be natural, faces the camera. Her back is to a large crowd gathered around a podium. "The Washington County Sheriff has called a press conference this evening regarding the disappearance of local teen Kadence Mulligan.

"She was discovered missing a little over forty-eight hours ago. Friends and family found her car door open, but it appears as if she never made it inside the house. Her purse and backpack containing her laptop and schoolbooks have not been found. Police believe she went missing in the early morning hours of March 31 after a very well-received concert at Cuppa Cuppa, a local coffeehouse. Anyone with any information is asked to call the tip line below." A phone number runs at the bottom of the screen.

The camera focuses on Kadence's parents, who are stepping up to the podium. The Major stands with military bearing as he makes a similar plea to the one he did at the garage. "Please," he says at the end, swallowing so hard his Adam's apple is visible on-screen. "We want our baby back home. We—" He breaks off and looks down.

Kadence's mother is crying as the camera focuses on her. She has white hair and looks to be in her sixties. She begs for anyone who has seen Kady to please call the sheriff's department.

The camera zooms out. Lauren's right there, standing beside them. Mason too.

A thin woman in a tight-fitting button-down shirt and dark pants puts her hand behind Lauren's back and directs her to the podium. Lauren nods slightly. I wonder what she's thinking. She looks nervous.

Lauren leans into the microphone and says a word that sounds like *Abyssi*-something. She flinches a little, as if she's surprised by the sound of her voice in the speakers. Her eyes flash around the crowd, then she glances down at the podium. "Um...I mean..." Then she looks up and nods. "I'll be seeing you, Kady."

My eyebrows shoot up in surprise. Lauren seems to hear how weird that sounded too, because she winces before the camera cuts away from her. I shake my head. *What the hell are you doing, Lauren?*

The news switches stories after that, and I turn it off. The oven timer beeps. I go back in the kitchen to take out the pizza. Dad comes in the door just as I'm slicing it.

"Hey," he says, grabbing a beer from the fridge. I put slices of pizza on a couple paper plates and slide one across the counter toward him. I give him a head nod, then take my own paper plate and head to my room. The TV turns on behind me, and Dad flips the channel to some game or another.

Yep, that's about the usual extent of our nightly interaction. He goes to work, comes home, drinks a few beers and watches TV, goes to bed, same thing over and over except Friday and Saturday night, when he can put away a whole twelve-pack by himself. He's a loner too.

See how I can blame everything on my genetics? None of this is actually my fault. The acne too. That was genetic. And the depression. The term "loner" might actually just be a nice way of saying "god-damned depressed."

I stare out my window. The sun has almost set. I haven't turned on the light in my room. I'm still just standing here in the semidarkness, holding my plate in one hand.

I put the pizza on my desk, but I still don't sit down and eat because while I'm staring out the window, I'm thinking of Lauren. She must be feeling horrible after that train wreck of a press conference. She's probably playing that stupid phrase over and over in her head. *Um, I'll be seeing you, Kady. Um, seeing you. Seeing you. Seeing you.*

I used to be the king of the awkward conversation. If there was a way to put my foot in it, I found it. A memory flashes so clearly that I'm back in the room, smelling the engine grease and oil that's soaked into the concrete. Eighth grade shop. Four guys taunting me and blocking my way while the teacher was out of the room. "What, pizza face? You want something?"

I stood, furious, staring at the floor and wishing it'd open up and drop these jerks into a pit to be eaten by a monster with giant gnashing teeth. No such luck. "I need to get my tools," I mumbled.

The ringleader, some douche named Steve—because weren't they always named Steve or Brad or some other douchey name like that?— started cracking up. "You hear that guys? Zitzenstein wants to grab my tool! Shoulda guessed you were a fag along with being a stalker freak."

They all laughed and then one of the others shoved me back into the wall before Douche was like, "No man, don't touch him. He's probably contagious. You see that face? Don't want to catch the plague."

Around that time the panic attacks started. I could never say the right thing and just wanted to go back to being invisible. But no, Kadence Mulligan had insured invisibility was no longer an option for me. I stopped talking to people altogether.

It's only been since my face cleared and I've put on this new persona that I have my voice back. I've got the armor, the jacket, the new face, the blue eyes—eyes that only last week a girl told me were like deep Caribbean pools she could get lost in for*ever*, because chicks say dumb shit like that to me now. But I remember. I'm really still that other guy underneath this mask.

And then, without really thinking it through, I'm shrugging on my leather jacket and then the thicker coat on top of it. I'm out the door and kicking my bike to life. It growls and spits gravel as I speed out of the double-wide's short driveway and onto the road.

The DeSanto house looks like I remember it. That seems unfair. Everything else has changed, but there her house sits, looking the same as it always did on those hot summer days when I was a kid half in love. Who am I kidding? Half in love? I was totally gone for that girl.

One of her parents' cars is in the driveway. I drive past the house and park down the street. As I make my way back to Ren's place, I kick at the hardened slush with my steel-toed boots. I don't give myself a chance to question what exactly the hell I'm doing here. I just walk around to the back of her house until I get to what I hope is still her bedroom window. I don't bother with pebbles or any dumb crap like that. It's a one-story house. I knock on the window.

Nothing happens for a long moment, so I knock again, using our old knock. BUM. Dramatic pause. Ba-BUM. Wait three seconds and repeat.

After another moment, the curtains whip open and Ren stares at me through the window, eyes wide. Her dark brown hair is pulled into a loose ponytail. She's wearing thick-rimmed hipster glasses and what must be her pajamas—a spaghetti-strap tank top that's so tight over her chest, it's a struggle not to stare.

She seems to realize at the same moment how little she's wearing because she races away from the window and comes back covered in a thick, fluffy turquoise robe. "What are you doing here?" she asks through the window. I can't hear her voice, but it turns out I'm pretty good at reading lips. Her lips.

The window hasn't been washed in a good long while, but with the half-moon for light, I can still clearly see her face. She's been crying.

Christ. It hits me in the gut, seeing her hurting. What the hell? Wasn't this the point? To get my revenge? To make them hurt as bad as they hurt me? But Lauren's not Kadence. And enough's been done already. Too much. And suddenly I don't want to be this person anymore, with only anger and hate to wake up to each morning.

Without thinking, I put my hand, palm up, to the glass like I always used to. I could never stand it when Lauren cried. Just like she used to, Lauren lifts her palm and meets mine, only the window separating us. My heart is suddenly galloping two hundred times a minute.

"Let me in. I want to talk," I say.

She drops her hand and looks down. Her ponytail falls forward over her shoulder, and for a long moment I think she's going to shut the curtains and turn away from me.

But then she flicks the locks and heaves the window upward. She doesn't get it very far. It sticks after only a few inches. She must not open it very often. I lift from my side, and together we get it all the way up. I make a move like I'm going to climb inside, but she stops me with her hand.

"What are you doing here?" she asks.

Right. Guess she's not down with a guy from her past randomly showing up at her window in the middle of the night. Good on her. "I need to talk to you. It's important, and"—I look around and blow into my hands—"it's really cold out here. Can I come in? Just for a second?"

"You could talk to me at the coffee shop. Or at school."

"This can't wait." I'm BS-ing right now, but first and foremost it seems important to breach the first barrier and get her to let me inside.

Again, she hesitates and glances toward her bedroom door. She's probably worried her parents will hear.

"I won't stay long," I say. "Please."

She exhales and says, "Fine. But just for a second." It's clearly against her better judgment.

"Thanks," I say as I climb over the windowsill.

She stands silently a few feet away, watching me as I right myself. I drop my heavy coat to the floor and close the window behind me so the cold April air doesn't cool down her room too much. When I turn to face her, her big brown eyes are fixed on me.

I glance up toward the ceiling. There's a crazy, blue chandelier hanging over her bed. It never used to be there. I sense Kadence's influence and grimace. Lauren turns her back on me and fusses with a framed picture on her dresser. It's of her and her dad during deer-hunting season six years ago. I know the photo well. Father and daughter with an eight-point buck. Her first kill. She was so proud. I never really got the whole bonding-over-dead-animals thing, but whatever.

"So what is it?" she asks.

I put my hands in the pockets of my jacket. "I was watching the press conference, and I heard what everyone was saying at school and..." I trail off. Her guitar and a few scattered sheets of paper are lying across her bed. She must see what I'm looking at because she picks up the guitar and leans it against the wall. Then she sits down heavily on the bed and puts her hands over her face.

Crap, I'm not saying anything right. Doesn't help that I don't know what I even came here to say. But I move over to the bed and sit beside her, careful not to sit too close or crowd her.

"Look, I know you didn't have anything to do with it. Those idiots can accuse you of hurting Kadence, but I—"

She looks up at me, stricken. "Is that what they're all saying?"

I'm not one for sugarcoating the truth. "Yeah, that's what they're saying."

"Then why are you so sure I'm innocent?"

I meet her eyes, suddenly conscious of the fact that even though I'm on one end and she's at the other, we're sitting on the same bed. It wouldn't take too much for me to move so that our thighs were touching. It's dark in her room with only her small bedside lamp on. Like she was getting ready for bed. It's so intimate. And I'm probably going to hell for thinking about all this when she's upset and has obviously been crying.

Then again, who am I kidding? There are plenty of other things I've done to send me to hell, so I might as well look. Her lips are so full and pink, but it's a dark pink, like berry or plum or something. Something fruity. Something sweet.

"Nath—" She catches herself. "Sorry. *Jude.* How do you even know? Why should you believe me?" she asks again.

My attention snaps back to her eyes. "It's high school. Idiots saying dumb crap because of the fight you two had in the cafeteria. You know people eat that shit up. I guess that's maybe why I came over. I kept thinking about you, knowing you must be feeling bad." As I say it, I realize that it's true. That *is* the reason I'm here. Damn. Just because I've decided I might be done hating her doesn't mean I can forget the past either. But then I'm talking again before I can think too deeply about any of it.

"It's total crap that everyone's going on and on at school about how wonderful Kadence was. The cheerleaders are planning a freaking candlelight vigil for her. They're all trying to make out like she was this sweet girl who no one would ever want to hurt." I can't help scoffing. "The police need to be making a list of all the people she's screwed over through the years."

Lauren shifts beside me on the bed. She hasn't said anything and I realize I've been monologuing. Which is probably weird. A dude she hasn't talked to in years shows up at her bedroom window, then goes on and on about what a bitch her missing best friend is. *Smooth.*

"Yeah, but right now they're focusing on me." Her voice is quiet in the dim room. "They asked me all these questions today. I felt like I was in one of those cop shows. I get so stressed out in situations like that. Lord, not that I've ever *been* in a situation like that before. It was just awful."

She shivers and I can feel the vibrations through the mattress. She's edged closer in my direction, probably unconsciously, but I'm aware of every inch. I don't know why she's opening up to me. She probably doesn't either, except that I'm someone outside the situation so maybe that's the reason she can.

"Well, maybe *we* could look into it. Take some action instead of waiting around." The words are tumbling out of my mouth as soon as they pop into my head. No filter. No thinking them through. "Like ask around on the down low. It's not like anyone is going to volunteer to tell a bunch of cops, 'Oh yeah, she was a total bitch to me and I hated her.'" The words ring a little too close to home, and I wonder if Lauren sees through me. I glance at her anxiously.

She swivels her body so she's facing me, her eyebrows furrowed. I stiffen, waiting for her to call me on it. But instead she asks, "Just, what? Go up and start asking random people if they hurt Kady?"

I laugh with the relief of tension. "No. More like we make a list." My eyebrows draw together as I work through it. "I can think of a couple people to start with. Like that guy, Jeremy what's his name? The pep rally guy who made a fool of himself saying he loved her up onstage. Elliot told me all about it and how Kadence led him on. Then she cut him off cold and ignored him like she'd never met him before."

While I'm talking, I see out of the corner of my eye that Lauren pulls her pillow to her chest. I'm not sure if it's meant to be some kind of subconscious shield against me or against the things I'm saying.

"Jeremy Atkinson, " she says. "Jeremy was just a big fan. And Kady never led him on."

I roll my eyes at her. At least now we're back on firmer ground. "Oh, come on, Ren. You know her better than anyone. She cheated on Mason all the time. Mason might have been too blind to see it, but you weren't."

She looks away again and tightens her grip on the pillow. Then she suddenly looks back at me with narrowed eyes. "What makes you think you know Kadence so well?"

This time it's me who looks away. Crap, she's not supposed to know I'd been watching, that I know things about Kadence, about *her*, that I shouldn't. It was mostly back when I first moved here, while I was still on the medication. The depression, the unhealthy fixating.

When I'd finished the full course and stopped taking the little yellow pills around Christmas time, the fog in my head cleared. I looked back at the notebooks full of my scribbled handwriting. The times and dates. Tracking movements. It wasn't normal. Even *I* was freaked out by it, but there it was in my own handwriting. Everything was so messed up. Still is. What the hell am I, of all people, doing in Lauren DeSanto's bedroom?

But then Lauren lets out a tired sigh, and all my attention is back on her. "Kady *could* be secretive sometimes," she says. "You could never tell what she was thinking. She'd disappear for hours at a time, sometimes even overnight. Then when you'd ask why she wasn't picking up your calls, she'd act like you were the crazy one. She'd pretend you hadn't even called her when you had it in your call history."

I frown. "Did you tell the cops all that?"

Now it's her turn to roll her eyes. "Yeah, because that would go over so well. How is it going to sound if I try to describe the real Kadence Mulligan when everyone else they're talking to is like, 'Oh, Kady is the best. Everyone loves her!' They're already suspicious of me. Telling them the truth is only going to make that worse."

I stare at her a moment. All this time she hasn't said anything about actually missing Kady. I mean, I know why I don't miss Kady, but I was never her best friend.

I think about the accusations everyone was talking about at school. The fight in the cafeteria. Then again, sometimes Lauren is hard to read. It was one of the things I liked about her back in the day. She was shy and socially awkward too. There was the way that everyone expected you to act—and then there was Lauren. She was always in her head, focusing on a problem from one angle at a time and only one angle.

Like at the press conference. Her mind was obviously somewhere else. Maybe she'd been thinking she should just reach out and talk to Kady like she normally would. Even though that was totally inappropriate for the actual moment.

As I'm staring and trying to puzzle her out, she says, "I'm scared, Nathan." I look into her big eyes and feel bad for the thought I had moments before. She's not trying to be selfish. She's scared. Really scared. I can see it.

Unless I'm wrong, and she's learned more from Kadence over the years than how to overcome her stage fright.

"See?" I push away the thought. "This is why I came over. I still know you. I knew you'd need a friend right now, someone you could say anything to without judgment. Whatever happened between us before...that's in the past." I swallow down the lie and force myself not to think about any of it.

Instead, I reach out and put my hand over hers. I don't interlace our fingers or anything like that. I just cover her hand with mine, and immediately my mouth goes dry again. Her skin is so soft. My eyes close involuntarily. When we were kids, we'd hold hands when we went out to pick spring wildflowers together, in that unself-conscious way kids have.

No one has held my hand in a very long time. Not since Ren herself actually. Damn it, my eyes feel wet. My goddamned eyes are wet. No tears or anything, thank Christ, just a little more moist than normal. But I don't move my hand. More importantly, neither does she.

"So what do you say?" I ask. "Do you want to make a list and ask around? Talk to some people?" I don't look over at her. I can't quite bear that, not while our skin is connected. Part of me is still that kid, afraid of seeing disgust in her eyes at touching me, at touching the monster.

"I can't," she whispers, so softly I barely hear it, and then her hand slips out from under mine. "I'll just let the police do their job."

And then she asks, "Jude, why are you offering any of this? Why would you help me? Why are you even here? We haven't talked in years and when we did..." She lowers her eyes. She's clearly ashamed.

This was the moment I wanted all those years. For her to apologize. For her to get on her knees and beg my forgiveness. For her to explain how she could do what she, my best friend, did to me. My best fucking friend. Everything is happening too quickly. I was afraid she was about to accuse me, then she was holding my hand, and now I'm getting an apology.

Or not.

I sit and wait for it. But she doesn't say anything else. She just sits there with her head bowed, looking at her hands in her lap. She pushes her glasses up her nose. Crap, I love a girl in glasses. Again the mix of emotions is too much, too fast.

I stand up, not able to share the same space with her anymore. I walk to the window. I should leave without another word. I should tell her that I'm glad the precious friend she chose over me all those years ago is missing now, and I'm glad they're accusing her of it. But my tongue's a stupid traitor and won't form the words. My mouth's too dry. My chest feels tight too. My hand shakes as I reach up and run it through my hair.

"Nathan," Lauren whispers, her low voice sounding even more raspy than it usually does. When I look back over at her, I see a tear tracking down her cheek, illuminated like a streak of silver in the shaft of moonlight coming through her window. "Jude, I—"

I wait again for her apology, but it still doesn't come. And I can't bear standing here and waiting for it another second, no matter how much I need it.

"I just came for old time's sake, Ren. But it's fine. I get it," I say, not as much to acknowledge her words as to get myself back under control. *Fine. This is all fine.* I tug the collar of my bomber jacket up. *Shields up, mask in place.*

I stand and give her my best cool-guy chin nod. "Good to see you again." I head toward the window.

But then I commit a cardinal sin. I look back. And she looks torn. As if she wishes I wasn't going.

Just like that, she's blasted through all my shields or armor or whatever other stupid-ass metaphors I ever thought could protect me from this girl. I manage one more chin nod, then I've got the window open and one leg slung over. I hope this looks like something other than what it really is—me fucking fleeing. I hear only the barest echo of her "good night" before I'm out into the night air.

TWELVE

LAUREN

DeSanto Residence
Wednesday, April 4
3:15 p.m.

I didn't go to school after my interview was over on Monday, but I tried to go yesterday. Jude warned me that it might be tough, but school sounded like the most obvious place to find exactly what I needed. A little normalcy. I couldn't have been more wrong. It was a disaster. I might as well have had the plague for as close as people were willing to get to me. And that included Mason. It particularly included Mason.

We hadn't spoken since the day everyone realized Kadence was missing—not even at the press conference. The way things were going, I didn't expect him to speak to me ever again.

Every hallway was filled with whispers. Suspicious eyes followed me long after I passed. Twice, girls made a point of "accidentally" knocking into me in the hall, spilling my books. Even the teachers looked at me with a mixture of pity and misgiving. Some kid I've never even seen before blocked me and quoted my idiocy from the press conference: "I'll be seeing you, Kady." The girl he was with wrinkled her nose. "Seriously, Lauren. Your best friend is missing. It's nothing to joke about."

I skipped lunch and spent the last period hiding in the bathroom, the one by the home ec room that smells like burnt pumpkin.

When I got home, Mom lifted her eyes from the page of her magazine. "How was it?" she asked as if she already knew the answer. The look in her eyes set my chin trembling again. A second later I was curled up in her lap, which was something I haven't done since second grade.

"Baby," she said, and I can't even begin to explain how good it felt to hear her call me that. "Today didn't stand a chance. It was going to suck in every possible way."

"You know what people are saying about me?" I asked in a small voice. The thought of it crushed me. It was like the most heartbreaking song I'd ever sung, and the weight of it pressed down on me until my chest hurt and I gasped for air.

She nodded. I could tell she was hurting for me.

"I can't believe this is happening," I said.

"Your dad and I, we're praying that Kady'll be found safe and soon, but, honey, we're also very worried about you."

"About me?" I asked, sitting up and wiping my eyes.

"We were never 100 percent sold on you girls putting your music on the Internet, using your names. It's too easy for some psycho fan to find you. If that's what's happened to Kady—God forbid—who's to say you aren't at risk too?"

"It's not a psycho superfan, Mom."

Her eyebrows pulled together. "And what makes you so sure?"

I couldn't answer that question. I returned my head to her shoulder and wrapped my arms around her neck. She rocked me like I was her little girl again. It felt so good, but it couldn't make things right. I knew, deep down, that no matter how this ended, things would never be okay.

"One more thing," she said, stroking my hair. "We think you may need a lawyer."

That was yesterday. Today I stay home and watch TV, flipping channels between *The Price is Right*, HBO, and *House Hunters International*. Picking my calloused fingertips over the strings on my guitar...

Playing goes against doctor's orders. Just *thinking* about our songs causes my vocal cords to flex and rub involuntarily. But I can't stand not playing at all. Sometimes I have to break the rules. It's either that or lose my mind.

I work out a chorus for the song I'm working on, though the bridge is still a mess. Something about the G chord doesn't sound quite right. Or maybe it's just my ears. Maybe I'm too sleep-deprived for my senses to work properly.

If that's it, too bad, because I don't see the situation improving anytime soon. Every time I close my eyes, all I can see is Kadence.

I take a really long shower. That kills a nice chunk of time. Really, that's what I've been doing all day. Killing time. And chewing my fingernails down to the nub. But I'm way past the nub now. Tiny bits of blood seep from the tears in my skin.

I eat lunch in my bed and leave the plate on my bedside table.

I wish that I could take back what I told Detective Kopitzke. I do miss Kadence. I miss the protection her persona gave me. Who was going to mess with Kadence Mulligan's best friend? No one. I miss how we used to laugh together. Man, could we laugh. Kadence could get me to laugh so hard I cried.

Those happy memories possess me to log on to the Internet and pull up our videos. Maybe I'm looking for the comfort of seeing her face, hearing our voices blending together. Once again I find myself wishing that I could go back in time to last summer when we were still at the top of our game.

I scroll back through a year's worth of comments. There are hundreds upon hundreds of them:

rayraysay6 1 year ago
Kadence and Lauren, I love you.

lluvhboo 10 months ago
Lauren, your voice is amazing!

martinvb7 9 months ago
How do you get your hair like that Kadence? #jealousmuch

monkeymay22 9 months ago
あなたはすばらしい

Damonatorgeo 8 months ago
I wish you guys went to my school.

sadie_92 8 months ago
I'm singing your song TWISTED for our school talent show. K? Please say that's okay. I'll post a link. K?

bellechanson71 7 months ago
France loves you!

pinky72466928 5 months ago
OMG! Lauren I'm so sorry you're sick. Get better sweetie. K?

claudia051 5 months ago

Es tut mir leid zu hören, Sie krank sind! Love from Germany.

ifitsbaditsBrad 4 months ago

I miss you guys singing together. Stay strong, Lauren. Things are going to get better.

geocache4life 3 weeks ago

It's not the same without Lauren.

43 likes

yayigotsnow4nutcracker 3 weeks ago

True dat. Is Kadence even going to be able to perform without Lauren? No offense to Kadence cuz she's awesome but isn't Lauren like the real, real musician of the two?

Lemonadeyummm 3 weeks ago

They're BOTH awesome.

Beetsbearsbattlescars 2 weeks ago

Are there going to be any more music videos?

cadydid_4_life 2 days ago

What? News is saying that Kadence is missing??????????? #OMG #Kady-Dids #KadenceMulligan

reeltreble321 2 days ago

What's going on?

BlairIsHilare88 2 days ago

(((Hugs))))

godisgood4000293 2 days ago

This is terrible. I can't believe it. Praying for you both.

2 likes

JulieSmith0623 2 days ago

Bring Kadence back. I've got all your songs playing on repeat. Love you guys. Can't believe it.

But as of yesterday there is an abrupt shift in the tone of the comments. I know I should stop reading, but I can't help myself. It's like watching a train wreck, except that I'm on the train. And still I can't. Look. Away.

No one whispers on the Internet. The anonymity lets people not only look on with suspicion, but play judge and jury. Some are already sharpening the ax.

My stomach is in my throat. Tears coat my eyes, and my tongue feels so thick I can't choke down the ugly cry building inside me. It's out before I can slap a hand over my mouth.

OzGirl1994 1 day ago

I just heard that Lauren killed Kadence. #notsurprised

523 likes

Bloated72 1 day ago

Heard that too.

Caseyjoquinn 1 day ago

I don't know. That doesn't sound right. I can't picture Lauren doing something like that.

GirlzJustWannaHavFun01 1 day ago

Unbelievable. True colors come out.

Raven_B 1 day ago

Saw that coming.

14 likes

ThugLyfe98 7 hours ago

Bitch.

jellybean77123 45 mins ago

I hope you go to hell for what you did to Kadence. #Kadydids4ever

And that is just a sampling. There are at least a hundred more like those. Some good. Mostly bad. I feel sick thinking about Kady being dead, and these so-called fans toss the idea around like it's nothing. They don't know me. They don't know Kadence either. Tears prick at the back of my eyes, but I know I have no right to cry.

This is all cosmic retribution for my sins. I am no better than any of these people who changed their allegiances with the flip of the switch. *Jude*, I think, his new name filling my mind. I did the same thing to him. Called him a stalker, got him suspended when he was still just a little boy. Kadence made the suggestion, but I went along with it. Little lemming. The "yes girl."

I deserved all the nasty names Jude called me back then.

I choke on the sob that's building in my throat. I wish he were here with me. I wish I could talk to him. He'd understand. At the very least, he'd listen. He's changed so much, and not just in his looks.

It took a lot of guts to come back here after how people treated him. How Kadence and I *taught* people to treat him. But as strong and capable as he looks now—especially climbing through my bedroom window and telling me everything is going to be all right—I can sense that something is broken in him. Something isn't right.

I might still be trying to figure out who I am without Kady, but that's the kind of healthy person I want to be. Someone who helps put people back together instead of tearing them apart.

And what about Kady?

I stare at the floor. I don't even know what I think about her anymore. My memories are too much a mix of the good and the bad. I want to cry and laugh and scream. I squeeze my eyes shut and put my hands against the sides of my head. All the emotions are building like steam in a teapot. Except it feels like there's no release valve and I'm going to explode.

I take a few deep breaths. By now it's four fifteen. Mom and Dad are still at work, and because it's Wednesday, they won't be home until about seven. JJ is in his bedroom. Minecraft music seeps under his closed door.

I flip off the alt radio station I've been listening to and turn on the eleven-inch TV on my dresser. Then I flop down on my bed and click through the channels. It's mindless and it's numbing, and gradually the tension leaves my body. Which is, of course, the point.

I've barely fallen asleep when I hear someone saying my name. At first I ignore it, but then I hear it again. I open my eyes to mere slits and look toward the door, thinking JJ is calling for me. That's when I realize it's the TV. Saying my name.

I blink blearily and twist my neck toward my dresser. That's when I catch a glimpse of Kadence on the screen.

Wait. What? I sit up in confusion. Is there news about her? I grab for the remote, still not comprehending. Kadence is on the news?

The TV shows a young blond woman standing in front of the

Washington County Sheriff's Department with Kady's picture in the upper left corner. The woman looks familiar. I blink again. Underneath the picture is a bulleted list:

- Tip line: 651-555-TIPS
- Missing: Kadence Mulligan
- 5'9" 120 lbs.
- Magenta hair, blue eyes
- Last seen leaving Cuppa Cuppa coffee shop, Pine Grove, Minnesota, evening of March 30
- Reward: $10,000
- #HelpFindKady

I finally find the remote at the bottom of my bed and turn up the volume mid-sentence: "...into Kadence Mulligan's disappearance continues as troubling new evidence comes to light," says the blond newscaster, eyebrows down in what I can only assume is her attempt at a serious face. Somehow she's still managing to flash her teeth, because at the same time, I swear it looks like she's smiling.

"We here at KLMN Minneapolis now have confirmation from inside sources that Mulligan's music partner and best friend, Lauren DeSanto, is a suspect in the investigation."

What? I shoot off the bed so quick I get my feet tangled in the sheets and almost fall over. I know people at school have convicted me, but who are these inside sources? Things look bad, yeah, but I told Detective Kopitzke about Kady's camping trips. They've got to check out every lead. They can't just say it's me.

"Drops of Kady's blood were found on her driveway, and even more on the shirt DeSanto was wearing the night of the disappearance," the woman continues.

Wait. What? That's not right. They got that wrong! I was never wearing that shirt they found.

"Insider crime-scene investigative sources reveal that while DeSanto claimed the bloodstains on her clothes came from Kady scratching herself on her equipment from the night's performance, no blood was discovered on any of the aforementioned equipment. DeSanto was also the last person to see Kadence Mulligan before her disappearance."

I sputter in outrage. All the emotions I managed to calm earlier are suddenly back, but ten times worse. Who's watching this? *My God*, my parents could be watching this! Someone could have this on at work. They could be calling my parents down the hall to come see it.

"DeSanto's future singing career has been stymied by health problems since early last November. I spoke to fellow classmates at Pine Grove High School earlier today to get a better picture."

The screen flips to a mic being held out to Cynthia Johnson, a girl at our school who was always trying to hang out with Kadence and me back in the day. Kadence used to make fun of her and call her and her kind "Desperation Nation"—the people who wanted to feel famous by hanging out with famous people.

"Lauren hasn't been right since she lost her voice," Cynthia says, shaking her long brown hair. "And then there was that fight the other day in the cafeteria because Lauren hooked up with Kady's boyfriend."

"There was a physical altercation between the two girls?" the reporter asks.

"Oh my gosh, it was *bad*. It started with Kady pulling Lauren's hair and screaming at her, then Lauren went down *hard*. But I mean, who wouldn't have been upset? Kady and Mason have been together for years now. For her best friend to have...And now Kady's missing..." Fat tears stream down Cynthia's face.

I want to throw my socks at the screen. Cynthia. Freaking

Desperation Nation. How many people did she have to shove out of the way or trample to make sure she was the one on camera? I bet she's kept those fake Bambi tears up all day and can produce them on command. All so she could get on there and make it sound like I... Like I—

I press a hand to my chest. God, I'm breathing too hard, too fast. I'm barely getting anything in. I blink hard, feeling light-headed.

The video switches from Cynthia's face to a full screen of one of our music videos, a fan favorite. Last time I checked, it had more than 750,000 views. Kadence is in her full glitz-and-glam show getup, with that bronzer she always dusts her body with before every take because she swears it makes her *practically glow* on camera. She's grinning like crazy as we sing. I have to admit that I look like a dull, flannel-clad sparrow beside her.

It never bothered me before, but now I wish I'd taken Kady's advice and brightened my look up a bit. I always thought it was more important to put the focus on the lyrics rather than what I was wearing. Now I'm not so sure. I doubt anyone watching their TV right now is listening to the lyrics.

The camera zooms in on my face and freezes the frame. Oh man. I wasn't expecting that. The video doesn't do that normally. The news show must have edited it that way, and I see what they're trying to do. I glare at Kady in the freeze-frame, my eyebrows drawn and my mouth turned down. "No arrests have been made at this time," the reporter says as the video minimizes, still locked on that shot where I look pissed off and guilty as hell, obviously their intention even though they haven't out and out said it. Talking about our fight, and then this—

"That's out of context!" I yell at the screen, finally gulping in a full breath.

The only reason I was looking at Kadence like that was because she'd changed the lyrics in the middle of a performance. She can't do that! How many times do I have to tell her she can't change the lyrics, especially when we're onstage? It's completely unprofessional.

"Our inside source was unable to provide more information except to say that the investigation is ongoing," the reporter continues. "Certainly all eyes in Pine Grove, all of Minnesota, the Internet, and the world beyond will be following this story to see that justice for Kady is found."

Without missing a beat, the reporter flashes a blinding white grin. "Kristi Clemens reporting."

I flip off the TV and, with a shriek, throw the remote against the wall. It leaves a small indent in the paint.

What just happened? How did it all move so fast? Kadence has only been officially missing since Sunday night and the press conference was only Monday. But then again, I saw the fans turn on me, and I didn't do myself any favors at the press conference.

And Kady...and Kady...Suddenly I can't breathe again. I gag and barely manage to keep from throwing up. Then I roll over on my bed and scream into my pillow.

But that's not enough and suddenly my hands are scrabbling at my sheets. I rip the comforter and blankets off the bed, then the sheets, then shove at the mattress itself but don't move it very far before letting out a frustrated huff. I turn away and pace my floor like a caged animal.

What do I do? What do I do? I can't sit here and do nothing.

That's when my phone rings. It's an unidentified number. I shouldn't answer. It will be more of the same from school. Maybe it's a reporter. I pick it up anyway.

"Hello?" I whisper, running a hand through my wild hair.

"Ren?" It's Jude. Thank God, it's Jude. I collapse on my mattress.

Then I hear him say to someone who's with him, "You guys go on without me." There's some chatter in the background, and then he asks me, "Are you okay?"

"How did you get my number?"

"Don't worry about that," he says. "How are you doing?" His voice is so sweet, so tender. He talks to me like I am something small and soft and in need of care. I don't think I can bear it, so I laugh more out of self-defense than any real sense of humor.

He doesn't understand. "What's so funny?"

"You shouldn't be so nice to me. Didn't you hear? I've already been convicted, no possibility of parole."

"Ren...people...people are assholes."

I don't think he knows about the TV show. He probably thinks I'm talking about people at school. I wish that was all it was. "Did you see the TV news—?" I begin to say.

"Yeah, people were Facebooking it. I saw the clip." He sounds apologetic, as if he's to blame for public opinion.

"Already?" I ask, disbelieving. "It was just on."

"It must have been on earlier too."

I don't say anything right away. My insides are coiling and recoiling. I look around my room for something more to throw. Anger I can handle. Sort of. Anxiety, maybe. But mix in fear, confusion, sadness, and guilt—and it's all too much. I might spontaneously combust. That's a real thing. People can actually do that.

"Hey," Jude says. "The whole world isn't out to get you. I know you didn't do anything wrong."

"Yeah." I laugh with even more incredulity. "And why is that exactly?"

"Why is what?"

"Why should you think I'm not capable of hurting my best friend? You know—better than anybody else—how capable I am of doing *exactly that.*" I suck in my breath. I hadn't planned on being so blunt. So freakin' honest.

Jude doesn't say anything right away. I've made my point. He can't deny it. "Did you hurt her?" he asks, so maybe I haven't convinced him after all.

"No," I whisper, remembering all of Kadence's and my history. The good. The bad. And most of all, the ugly. That's when my tears, which had until now only been threatening to fall, become the Deluge. "No, I didn't."

Neither of us says anything for a while. Then Jude says very quietly, "Ren? You still there?"

"Yeah, I'm still here. You know that thing you said the other night... about starting my own investigation...Are you still down with that? I think you're the only one I can trust."

"Yeah, Ren. I'm still down."

And then I blurt out before I can stop myself, "Can you come over? Like now?"

He doesn't even hesitate. "Be there in five."

I look around my messed-up room and wince. "Cool. But maybe make it fifteen."

THIRTEEN

MASON

Sheriff's Office—The Interview Continues
Monday, April 2
11:25 a.m.

Kopitzke: Do you think Lauren DeSanto was capable of hurting Kadence?

I think about that. Sure, Lauren DeSanto may be like a wounded bird, but Kady wasn't the one who wounded her. There would have been no reason for Lauren to lash out at Kady over what happened to her voice. But then...Lauren isn't always rational about things. She got a B+ on an English test once and took it out on the lunch lady. Started yelling at her about the overuse of MSG in the Tater Tot hot dish.

When Lauren got mad, she never had trouble slinging arrows. What she needed to work on was hitting the target.

Kopitzke: Mason, I'm asking if you find Lauren DeSanto to be a credible person. Do you trust her?

How am I supposed to answer that? I mean, yeah, once Lauren tried to convince me that Kady was hooking up with other guys, but I don't think Lauren was trying to be dishonest. I think she was actually worried about me, even though I knew it wasn't true. Kady wasn't capable of that kind of dishonesty. Besides, she was with me so much she didn't have time for anyone else.

I think that's what's hurt me the most lately. Kadence has been so involved with her songwriting that we haven't had time to hang out like before. I've missed her. Without Kady I'm just me, right? Nothing special. Kadence made me special. She made everything special.

I'm feeling antsy. Shouldn't we be out doing something? Shouldn't we be organizing a search party? I don't like just sitting here and *talking*. But fine, if answering their questions is going to get them in action sooner, the quicker we're done with this, the better.

Mason: Yeah. Yeah, I trust Lauren.

Kopitzke: What about Kadence? Do you trust her?

Mason: She's my *girlfriend*.

Kopitzke: Yes, but is she dependable? Predictable? Would she ever do something like take off without telling her parents or you or any of her friends?

Mason: Never. If she even *tried* something like that, her parents would have her on lockdown forever. They worry too much about her health.

Kopitzke: How so?

Mason: Normal parent stuff. Kady's got a pretty bad allergy, so they monitor what she eats pretty hard, and they make her carry an EpiPen.

Kopitzke: Food allergies are rough. You have to be strict with yourself, no cheating allowed.

His statement brings me back to Lauren's accusation about Kady cheating on me. Lauren had been angry about it. She said she didn't like Kady treating me badly. I called Lauren a liar. I told her it was a pretty low thing to lie about and that she didn't need to take out her own personal unhappiness on me and Kady. For all I knew, she was trying to break us up just to make herself feel better.

Surprisingly, Kady forgave Lauren. But then that's the way Kady was. Is. She's loyal to her friends. All of them. And she's never one to carry a grudge. Lauren, on the other hand...

Kopitzke: Mason?

For a moment I've forgotten where I am. I look up, and Kopitzke is staring at me like he's waiting for an answer. I can't remember what question he last asked. I can't remember what I've already told him.

Do I admit that Lauren has the potential to get really angry? No. He wouldn't understand. Angry or not, I can't believe she'd actually hurt Kady. Though, who really knew what went on in that girl's head?

FOURTEEN

LAUREN

De Santo Residence—Lauren's Bedroom
Wednesday, April 4
6:00 p.m.

Jude makes me put his name at the top of the list. He says if we're going to do this, then we're going to do it right. *Thorough* is our mantra. If someone could have a motive to hurt Kadence, their name goes on the list.

I add mine below his. I'm already a suspect, and Kadence has hurt me too. Maybe not as directly, maybe not as viciously as she's hurt others, but sometimes the cruelest acts are the silent ones.

We're in my room because I don't feel safe anywhere else. I'm sitting at my desk, head bent over a spiral notebook. My laptop beside the notebook. My ukulele by my feet. I feel calm now. The momentary tantrum from earlier has passed. Tantrums, that's what Mom calls them. As if it's something I never outgrew from when I was a little kid.

Jude's sitting on my bed, on top of the blue floral comforter that I arranged perfectly back in place before he got here. When I glance over, I notice him looking at the dark smear across the dirty plate I left on my bedside table. "What the hell did you eat?" he asks.

"Hmmm? What? Oh. Organic black beans with a gluten-free tortilla."

Jude's face contorts and his eyebrows pull together. "Why would you eat that?" The way he's acting, you'd think I'd told him it was a pile of poo.

"It's good for me," I say. "I've been trying to go organic, caffeine free, even gluten free, but that one's pretty hard to stick to. I'm trying to do what's right for *me* these days." Mentally I add, *inside and out* and *for once in my life.*

Jude shrugs. "If you say so. But a life so free sounds pretty restrictive if you ask me."

"Well..." He has me there. I can't honestly say I get a ton of enjoyment out of black beans. "I didn't ask you."

The corners of his lips turn up, and his thumb and forefinger rub the satin edge of the fleece blanket that's poking out from underneath my comforter. I've had that blanket since I was a toddler. I remember rubbing the satin—self-soothing in the moments I was feeling most upset. *Are you good for me, Jude? Inside and out? Am I doing the right thing here?* And then I look away before the questions show up on my face. Because seriously. If Jude notices, he's perceptive enough to ask. I clear my throat and bend over my notebook.

Below my name, I write: "Mary." I have to pull an old yearbook out of my desk drawer to remember her last name. "Blake." I don't know how I forgot that. In ninth grade, Kadence called her "Blake the Rake" because Mary was tall and thin with buck teeth. It didn't take long for the whole school to catch on.

I remember thinking it was funny at the time. I feel bad about that now. Mary was actually pretty. She just had a slight overbite, and more importantly she was super talented. Easily the best girl in the freshman choir, and she beat me and Kady out at the eighth-grade talent show. Looking back, that's probably why Kadence went after her.

I stare at the name a second longer, and a memory tickles at the back of my brain. It takes another moment for it to settle in. @MBlake96. I pull up Twitter and scroll back through my feed, but I can't find it again. Doesn't matter. I remember the most important part. *Payback's a bitch, Lauren.*

"Oh yeah," Jude says, seeing her name. "I forgot about her. Why is she on the list?"

I turn my head toward him, eyebrows raised. "Kadence made out with Mary's boyfriend behind the bleachers after the last football game junior year."

"That was a long time ago for her to still be mad about that."

"It was pretty ugly," I say, looking back at Mary's name on the paper. "Mary ended up changing schools," I add, my voice fading out at the end. *Payback's a bitch, Lauren.* I frown in confusion.

Jude shrugs. "Okay. Good enough for me. Who else?"

"Justine Dow."

"Really? How did Kadence piss off Justine?"

"Called her out when she got her period on a day she wore white pants."

Jude shudders, and I laugh. It's funny to see a big tough guy get weirded out by periods.

"Moving on," he says. He gets up from the edge of my bed where he's been sitting and stands right behind me, leaning over my shoulder as he looks at the names on the list. I can feel the heat rolling off his body. His hair tickles my cheek. "Be sure to put Jeremy Atkinson down."

I nod, remembering that Jude had brought him up the day before. Jude had been accurate when he accused Kadence of toying with

Jeremy's emotions. I write down Jeremy's name, then add Caleb Morrissey.

Jude taps Caleb's name. "Kadence outed him to his dad, right? That was after I left too, but I still heard about it."

"Yeah," I say. "It was last year." I turn around in my chair so I can see Jude better, plus it makes him take a step back and I needed him to do that. Jude's physical closeness is unnerving. Exciting, but unnerving.

"Kady, Mason, and I were hanging out in Caleb's basement," I say, explaining how it all went down. "Kady invited this other guy to come over because she knew he was totally into Caleb. They drank a bunch of scotch, and Caleb and this other dude started making out. Kadence and I had gone upstairs to use the bathroom, but when I came out, she was telling his dad that there was something wrong with the TV downstairs, and he should probably come check it out."

"Shit."

"His dad's a trucker. Very old-school macho. When he came down and saw what was happening, he grabbed Caleb by the back of his shirt and hauled him out of there. Beat him within an inch of his life."

Jude's face sours. "Dammit, Ren. Why were you friends with her? She's vile."

"I don't know," I say, looking at the floor. What Jude doesn't understand and I can't even begin to explain is that there were so many good memories too. Kadence could be really sweet. She made me feel special. She told me her secrets, and it made me feel important. Which is lame. I know that.

"It wasn't like Kadence expected that to happen," I say. "She thought she was helping him get out of the closet and all that. I mean, obviously it was completely naive and wrong of her, and looking back on it, she should have minded her own business."

I hate the way Jude is staring at me. It puts me on the defensive.

"And that thing with Mary…" I hurry on. "Kadence was just talking to her boyfriend but he was macking on her, and the next thing Kadence knew, they were kissing." My shoulders flinch in reaction to my own words. Saying it like that reminds me of what happened between me and Mason. Am I as innocent in that kiss as I've been telling myself? "We were young. Stupid. Immature. I'd know better if it was happening today."

Jude sighs like he's really, really tired. So far we have four names on the list besides our own. There should be more.

"What about Kadence's boyfriend?" he asks. "Mason, right?"

I make a scoffing noise in my throat.

"What?" he asks. He obviously doesn't get it.

I roll my eyes. "Clearly you don't know Mason."

"Okay. Well, what about some psycho fan? We should look at your videos. Go through all the comments. Maybe someone threatened Kadence there. We could backtrack their IP address and find out who they are."

"Here. Take it. I don't want to read any more comments." I stand up and offer him my chair, and when I do, we find ourselves face-to-face. Our chests inches from each other's. He stares down at me, holding me in place with his eyes. I should look away, but I am transfixed by him. *Transfixed*, like some romance novel heroine. Or like a bird confronted by a snake.

I clear my throat and try to step around him, but we do that awkward simultaneous side-step thing. I feel like he takes up the whole room, and I'm suddenly feeling short on oxygen.

The moment is charged with anticipation. I feel like I can read Jude's mind—if only for a second—and I wonder why he's not moving, why I'm not *doing* anything. As good-looking as he is, I should be wanting to tackle him. I mean, my bed is right there. My parents are at work. This would be perfect if everything wasn't so absolutely... not perfect.

In that moment I have two thoughts. One, I want to write a song about this. Two, it doesn't matter how many names we put on the list.

Everyone, including the police, think I'm involved. I don't need to rain that misery down on Jude. How would it look if suddenly we were seen as being together? As in, *together* together? Someone like Jude, someone who looks like Jude...how hard would it be for the police to investigate him as an accomplice? He has to know this too.

"Ren?" he asks.

I'm absolutely undone when he calls me that. I swear my heart is fluttering like a bird caught in my chest. A lyric pops to mind: *Winged heart, you beat against me like a bird in flight.*

"You all right?" he asks.

"Fine," I whisper, my face heating up. "See what you can find online. I need to clear my head." I bend down and scoop my ukulele off the floor, then sit on the bed and pick out a couple chords. Fingers busy, that's better. So much better.

He looks at me with worry and compassion. I can't recall any of my other friends ever looking at me like that. I sit cross-legged and strum a few bars while simultaneously watching Jude work. The music has the same effect on me as that old blanket did when I was a kid. The more I work the strings, the more the worry and stress eases.

I know, I know. I'm not supposed to play. But extreme circumstances call for extreme measures. I slide my fingers down the fretboard, and for just a moment, the world feels righted again.

Jude scowls at the screen, his eyebrows drawn together. His leather jacket hangs off the back of my desk chair. His T-shirt is tight around the shoulders and arms, and the muscles in his forearms twitch and flex as his fingers work the keys. He's trying so hard to help me. How could I have ever been so cruel?

Yes, he said all those nasty things to me in eighth grade, but he backed off right away. It was really only the one time. I didn't need to tell the principal he was stalking me. I didn't need to lodge the complaint that got him suspended from school. I didn't need to retaliate by calling him names—names that I knew would hurt—and I really didn't need to encourage the rest of the school to do the same.

I don't deserve his forgiveness. It almost makes me feel worse. *Winged heart, you should leave me. My soul's torn apart.*

After about twenty minutes, Jude turns in the chair and rests his back against the wall. "I'm coming up with nothing. You want to go visit Caleb?"

My eyes go wide and my palm slaps flat against the strings. It's one thing to make a list. Quite another to actually go confront these people. "I don't remember where he lives."

"I googled it."

"You want to go now?" I ask, hoping for the answer I know I'm not going to get.

"Lauren, I want to help. I don't like the idea of people accusing you like this. It's not right."

How could I argue with that?

Jude goes out my window, and I meet him down the street, a block from my house. He holds out a spare helmet for me to wear. I laugh when I see it. "You came prepared."

"It wasn't like you were going to chicken out," he says with a grin. Sometimes it's weird how well he knows me.

He pushes the helmet down over my head. Then, for the first time ever, I'm flying down the street on the back of a freakin' Harley. More importantly, I'm on a motorcycle behind *Jude*—correction, *straddling*

Jude—with my arms wrapped around his waist and the heat of the engine underneath me.

It is the most amazing feeling, and I wish I could write down all the lyrics that are racing through my head. Ones that have already been written, like *born to run* and *free falling* and *My restless hands are grabbing for a time that's never there.*

Then some that have not yet been written, like *Redemption comes in pieces, but you assemble them with care* and *I'm riding on a feeling that I didn't want to bear.*

There's wind and cold and warmth and fingers clutching leather. And then soon, way too soon, Jude is pulling to the curb and all the music in my head grinds to a halt on a dissonant chord.

That was quick. This town is way too small.

I'm staring at Caleb Morrissey's house through the visor of the helmet, and it's like, *crap on a cracker*, we're actually doing this. Are we seriously doing this? Every wild and wonderful thought leaves me. Now, with the engine below me cooling and stilled, I really, really, *really* do not want to do this.

"Let's do this," Jude says happily, looking over his left shoulder at me.

Reluctantly I take off my helmet and dismount. I don't want him to notice that I'm scared, so I smooth my hands through my hair. In part because it hides the fact my hands are shaking, and in part because I think it's important for some reason to look my best when I talk to Caleb about the worst night of his life.

Jude rings the doorbell before I have time to chicken out.

There's silence for a long time before we hear shuffling feet on the other side of the door. Then the door swings open and Caleb's dad looms in the doorway. He's in his fifties with iron-gray hair and several days' growth on his cheeks. He eyes us up and down. "I'm not buying no raffle tickets or magazine subscriptions."

He moves to close the door again, but Jude holds up a hand. "Sir, we're here to talk to Caleb. Is he home?"

If possible, the man's mouth turns even farther down at the corners. "That fairy don't live here anymore."

"Can you tell us where he moved to, sir?" Jude asks swiftly. I'm glad he's managing to ask the questions, because I'm officially struck dumb and standing here like an idiot. Caleb doesn't live here anymore? Oh no, surely it's not because...Not because of what happened that night...

"Please, sir," I say, using Jude's tone of deference. I hate it even as I use the term of respect, but suddenly I have to find Caleb, and not just for our list of suspects. I never thought he'd get kicked out of his *home*. "Please, we need to talk to him."

The man stares at us for another nerve-racking second, then finally wrenches his thumb over to the right. "End of the street," he growls. "Last house on the left. Red door. Lives with his grams." With that he turns on his heel and slams the door in our faces.

Jude turns toward me. "Friendly guy," he deadpans.

It's only a half-minute ride down the street to the end of the block. Jude walks up to the red door and knocks like none of this is a big deal.

I bite my lip, praying for a nice old lady to answer the door and tell us, "Sorry, but Caleb isn't home." When the door opens, however, we see the hulking shoulders of Caleb Morrissey himself, six foot two and wearing a camo hunting jacket. As soon as his eyes narrow in on me, the easy expression on his face falls to a sour scowl. "What do *you* want?"

I step back, unconsciously moving myself slightly behind Jude. What were we thinking? That we'd just show up and say, "Hey, where were you the night of Kadence Mulligan's disappearance, and did you by chance have anything to do with it?" Yeah, because that was going to work.

Again, Jude saves the day.

"Hey, man," he says and sticks out his hand. "I'm Jude Williams. Nice to meet you. I take it you already know Lauren here." He gestures at me.

Caleb stares at us both, his eyes hard. Caleb was more Kady's friend than mine, but he was always nice to me. For such a big hulking guy, he was a sweetheart. He was never feminine, not like some of the stereotypical gay guys you see on TV. In fact, I might never have known if Kady hadn't told me he'd confided in her, or if I hadn't seen him making out with that one guy on his couch.

Of course that was the night it had all gone to hell, the one time he'd let himself be *himself*, uncensored.

And then when he showed up at school with two black eyes and a broken nose, I never said anything to him about it.

"What do you want?" Caleb asks again, his voice harsher now, and I realize I've been staring at him as these memories of the past fly through my head. But all I can do is continue to gape. He's looking at me like I'm the squishy residue of a bug on the underside of his boot. Which isn't undeserved.

"Well, have you seen the news lately?" Jude says, filling the silence, his tone light and almost jovial. "Our girl Lauren here's being called a murderer."

Caleb nods his chin once, his attention on Jude now. "Yeah, I saw." Meanwhile I stare at the ground, totally mortified. What is Jude doing?

"Well," Jude says, clapping me hard on the back, "of course she didn't actually murder Kady, but the whole thing has got her looking back on all the shit she and Kady pulled. And she's wanting to make amends. She might not have done anything to Kady, but she knows they both hurt a lot of other people along the way. She's on what you might call an amends tour. Like they do in twelve-step programs."

My mouth drops open and I stare at Jude. But when I glance at Caleb, he no longer looks like he wants to slam the door in our faces. Close it, maybe, but not slam it.

He eyes me critically, so I nod. And even though I want to stomp on Jude's foot with the heel of my pointy boot, in a way, he's not wrong. I do wish I'd told Caleb I was sorry. I *do* owe a lot of people apologies.

"So can we come in?" Jude asks.

"No," Caleb says. I can feel the waves of hostility coming off him again, and I'm about to turn around and head back to the bike when Jude says, "Hey, cool tea set."

"What?" Caleb asks.

Jude pushes past him into the house, dragging me along with him.

"Hey!" Caleb says as Jude casually picks up a teapot that's sitting on a doily on the end table beside the sofa. He lifts off the lid and turns it around in his hands. Meanwhile I stand nervously clutching my hands together, glancing back and forth between Jude, Caleb, and the door.

"Dude, put that down," Caleb says. "That's my grandma's. You'll break it." He takes the teapot from Jude and gently sets it on the end table. "You can go now."

"Give us a second," Jude says. That was the line Jude used on me when he stood outside my bedroom window. I'd let him inside. I doubt Caleb will give in so easily. Not with me standing here.

"Say what you need to say then and get out," Caleb folds his arms in a no-nonsense gesture.

"We're here to talk about Kadence," Jude says.

Caleb's eyebrows shoot up. "I thought she was here to apologize." He gestures at me.

I swallow hard. "Yes, I am. I had no idea what Kadence was planning to do to you, but I saw it happening, and I didn't stop her. In a twisted way, I thought she was doing it out of friendship. I'm sorry. I had no idea of the consequences. Please believe that."

At this, Caleb's jaw goes so taut that the veins on his neck and forehead stand out. "Is this some kind of joke?"

"Caleb," I start to say, but he interrupts me.

"No. Don't even." He laughs a low, bitter grumble. "You know what? Kadence told me the same thing about you. A few weeks after it happened. She came up to me, mascara running down her face, crying me a river and saying how it was all your idea, how she came out of the bathroom and saw you sending my dad downstairs. She kept saying it wasn't your fault, because you were only trying to help. That you thought it wasn't right for a father and son not to be open with each other and that you never meant for what happened to happen."

I stare at him for what feels like minutes. My mouth is hanging open, and by the time I process what he's saying, I'm sputtering. "But—but that's not true! Kadence was the one who told your dad to go downstairs."

Caleb interrupts me again. "I don't even care. Do you understand that? It doesn't matter to me which one of you did what. I was the one who got beat up that night." He pounds a hand against his chest. "Both of you little girls ran back to your homes with your nice parents and got tucked into your little beds. I was the one who had no home, no bed to sleep in that night. I was the one whose father said he had no son anymore.

"So I don't care about all the stupid little games you and your friend like to play. I don't care that you feel sorry now." He's all but yelling and each word is making me wince. I hate confrontation, and no one has ever out and out yelled at me before. And he's not nearly finished.

"Because I bet you barely even do feel sorry. I bet all this is you feeling bad because finally your perfect little life isn't so perfect anymore. People are calling you bad names on the TV. Boo-hoo. Poor little Lauren DeSanto. Kadence Mulligan isn't around to be your shield anymore. You lost your voice and suddenly you aren't so special anymore. Now Kady's missing and everyone's blaming you. Again, boo-hoo for you."

I step closer to Caleb. He's still got over a foot on me, so I'm sure I don't look too threatening, but it's time to start fighting my own battles, and his sarcasm is making me mad. "You sure have a lot of anger built up towards Kadence and me, don't you, Caleb? In fact, the way you are talking right now, it sounds like between you and me, you're the one who had the most reason to wage a vendetta against her."

"What the hell are you talking about?" He looks at me like I'm crazy, then over to Jude.

"Oh my God," Caleb scoffs, staring at me in disbelief. "You're not here to make amends at all, are you? You're here to accuse me of having something to do with her disappearance."

None of this is going the way I thought it would. Not that I really thought out exactly how it *would* go. But I've come this far, so I go ahead and blurt out my next question.

"Where were you on the night of Friday, March 30?"

"Are you serious right now?" He looks over at Jude. "Is she serious right now?"

Jude gives his trademark easy smile and shrugs.

"Tell me if you have an alibi, and then we'll go," I say, unwilling to give up at this point.

Caleb shakes his head in a mixture of disbelief and disgust. "I cannot believe the balls on you. You and your friend destroy my life, and now you come back here and try to pin some huge crime on me?" He drags his wallet out of his pocket, still shaking his head. After flicking through some bills, he pulls out a concert ticket stub and waves it in front of my face. He stills it long enough for me to see that it's for a concert in Minneapolis on the thirtieth. The headline act started at nine thirty. "Me and my friend Jake went to this concert together and then stayed with his cousin in St. Paul overnight. We stayed all weekend."

I reach for the ticket stub to get a better look, but he snatches it away before I can. "No way," he says with a laugh. "You think I'm going to let you steal the evidence of my alibi so you can try to frame me for whatever you did to your friend? I always knew the pair of you were twisted. Should've known it would end up like this one day. Got to say though, if one of you was going to end up in the ground and the other with blood on her hands, I'd have put all my bank on Kadence coming out on top. Guess you never know. Gotta watch out for the quiet ones."

I take a step back and my breath shoots out of my lungs as if I've been punched.

"I think that's our cue to leave," Jude says, stepping over and putting his hand at the small of my back. He gives a nod to Caleb as we pass and then leads me to the front door. We leave the house without another word.

Before he turns the ignition, Jude looks over his shoulder at me. "Do we try to find Mary now?"

"No," I say. I still don't quite have my breath back. "I'm beat. I don't think I can do this again. Not today anyway."

"That's fine," Jude says. "Hey, are you okay?"

I don't have an answer. I don't really know how I feel about anything anymore, except that I think I might throw up. Please don't let me throw up in front of Jude.

He looks at me uncertainly, his eyebrows furrowed. I get the sense that he's studying me. "Well, if you still want, we can pick this up again tomorrow. I can do a little checking on my own at school too, if that's okay with you."

"Yeah. Whatever. Just get me home."

"Ren." His voice softens. "Close your eyes. Try to enjoy the ride."

Thirty minutes later he drops me off in front of my house. I run to the door but turn in the doorway as he drives away. I watch him until he disappears around the corner.

■ ■ ■

Later that night, I think about telling Jude to forget this whole thing. Anyone else we talk to is going to be more of the same. I mean, seriously. What were we thinking? But before I can pick up my phone, I hear a sound. It's small. And muffled. And I've heard it before, though not often and not in a while. It's a sound that makes my heart twist and my hands soften.

I creep down the hall to JJ's room. I know if he hears me coming, he'll cover up the evidence, so I push his door open slowly and wait for him to look up.

Not surprisingly, I find him sitting on the floor with his back against the side of his bed. His room is a disaster, littered with clothes, game controllers, and old Pokemon cards he bought at a garage sale. I am prepared for all of that. What I am not prepared for is the angry red welt under his left eye.

I drop to my knees in front of him and push the dark hair off his face. "What happened?"

He twists away from me, turning his head. "It doesn't matter," he says. "Go away."

"Don't tell me it doesn't matter. Did somebody hit you?"

That's when JJ looks at me. Like really looks at me. There's a sheet of tears over his eyes. He doesn't blink. God love him, he doesn't blink. "I went to the park after dinner. People were saying things about you. I handled it."

"You handled it?" I rasp, then, "You handled it? How is getting hit *handling* it?" Righteous anger is building up in my gut. There is no way this sweet kid is going to suffer for me. I might be many things but being above taking down a middle schooler is not one of them. "Who was it?" I demand.

"I said it doesn't matter," he whispers back.

"I said, 'Who was it?'"

JJ hits the power button on his game console. The familiar Minecraft music comes on, and that's the end of our conversation. Stubborn kid.

"Fine," I say. "Put some ice on it."

"I will. After Mom and Dad go to bed."

Before I leave, I turn and say, "I hope the other guy looks worse."

A small smile creeps over JJ's tear-stained cheeks, but he doesn't take his eyes off his game. "He does."

So I guess JJ did handle it, though there's nothing there to celebrate. It's not like I feel all warm and fuzzy about my little brother using his fists to defend my reputation.

I go back to my room and throw myself across my bed. Maybe I don't have to take out my frustration on a punk playground kid, but I know one thing for sure. I won't be bailing out on Jude. Next chance we get, we're going to hunt down Mary Blake.

Jude wants to deflect the attention off me for *my* sake. I don't care so much about that, but this will be the last time my family pays the price.

FIFTEEN

KADENCE

Found Video Footage
Kadence Mulligan's Laptop
Date Unknown

Image opens.

Kadence sits like a queen on her throne in a high wing-backed antique chair in her bedroom. Her magenta hair is elaborately curled and clipped back in the front like a fifties pinup girl. She's wearing a vintage halter dress and has on heavy cat-eye makeup with cherry-red lipstick.

"Hello, my Kady-Dids! A lot of you have been groovin' on my Instagram and Tumblr pics, asking about my new style. Yeah, so admittedly, I'd been going through a bit of a rhinestone phase for a while there." She puts up a hand, wincing a little. "I know, I know, every girl's gotta try to find herself through a little fashion experimentation. Don't sic the *Go Fug Yourself* girls on me!"

She gestures down at her halter-top dress that's fitted in the bodice with a full flared skirt in a strawberry print. "Now, we're going rockabilly, baby! See, fashion's got philosophy behind it. That's what people don't get. This vibe fits a lot better with the new world of indie musicians." She scrunches her forehead. "I think I'm categorized as indie folk or indie pop or maybe both on the download sites. They can't make up their minds where to put me." She laughs, then sobers, tilting her head to the side.

"But, you know, that's fine with me. I think I like being indefinable. Music should be in a world without labels."

She grins. "Okay, now to the question session. Question from @blueangel21: how did you start your YouTube channel and get viewers? Me and my band only have like fourteen views. Frowny face."

Kadence bobs her head with a sympathetic expression. "Well, blueangel21, believe me, I know your pain. It was not easy at the beginning. We were in tenth grade when I got the idea to put our music online. Lauren and I were coming up with this great material. It was time to start sharing it with the world. But we were in school and it wasn't like we could go on the road or book gigs in bars, which is how most musicians do it. So I got to thinking, let's go to the Internet! Maybe no one will click on our videos. That's fine. We would have put it out there at least. We would have done *something*.

"But just like I had to drag Lauren onto that stage in eighth grade, trying to get Lauren to do something new and adventurous like this was like pulling teeth." Kadence lets out a breath of frustration. Then she laughs, as if shaking it off.

"Anyway, eventually Lauren agreed, and she was onboard once I convinced her all she had to do was just show up and play the music. I would take care of all the rest of it. But of course we were on a budget." She grins slyly. "Well, I can be a smart cookie when I need to be. And if there's one thing I'm good at, it's encouraging people to catch my vision.

"I talked the brother of a friend of mine into helping. He was in college getting an arts degree and had access to quality AV equipment.

He got us sessions on the college's soundstage and recording equipment and then used the footage as class projects. Total kismet!

"But just because we'd jumped one hurdle didn't mean we were done yet. Not by a loooooong shot. We had some videos made for a few of our songs—"Twisted" and "Calliope" and "Sweet Regret"—then put them on YouTube. And...nothing. They just sat there. And *sat there*. We had around ten views the first week.

"I was so bummed! I'd told myself that I had only wanted to put it out there, and it was fine if no one watched it. But I guess, deep inside, I'd really hoped people would see it. I didn't care about them clicking 'like' or leaving comments or anything. I just wanted them to hear, to partake of the magic, you know?

"Still, I believed in our music, and I wasn't going to give up. All my favorite musicians talked about having such a tough time in the beginning. So I learned how to do the whole social media thing and how to reach out to other artists and support them. I really went after it, hours online after school every day, treating it like a part-time job. The Major is always talking about *diligence* and *discipline*." She lowers her voice to imitate her father on the two words. "So I worked my tush off. Lauren was certainly no help." Kadence rolls her eyes.

"Sorry, I don't mean to be unkind. It killed me because she didn't *get it*. She didn't see what I was doing for us. How our numbers were growing and what that visibility could mean for us." Kadence lets out a huff of breath as if trying to get herself under control and then smiles again. "But whatever, it was fine.

"And then, one week, all because of you guys, it happened. We went viral." Kadence shakes her head and leans back in the chair. "*Viral*. It's a word that people say all the time, but the experience of it is something entirely different. It's this wild, insane thing. Over a couple weeks we went from having one thousand and two thousand views overall to getting, like, five thousand views a *day*. I still try to figure out what happened," she says with a laugh, throwing her hands up.

"It was so amazing. You're always hoping for something like that, but it seems like the kind of thing that happens to someone else, not to you. But there it was, happening to us. It was insane. So wonderfully, awesomely, exhilaratingly insane." Kadence laughs and puts a hand to her forehead as if caught up in the memory of those days.

"Anyway, from there, we got all kinds of new attention. The local news somehow heard about us, maybe because of the Major. Sorry"— she laughs even as she puts an embarrassed hand over her eyes"—that's my dad. I keep talking about him like you guys know him. Anyway, he's this rough-and-tough army guy, but...it was the first time in my life where I felt like he finally, really noticed me and understood what I was doing. He was so proud. It felt really good.

"He'd go and have coffee with all the other military guys every Saturday morning and brag about his daughter, even though I *begged* him not to!" She tilts her head to the side, a crease appearing between her eyebrows. "That just—" She breaks off, looking down. For a moment, an expression other than that of the polished performer appears on her face—what seems like an unintended flash of vulnerability. "Well, it meant a lot to me."

When she glances back up, her bright grin is back in place. "Love you, Daddy." She presses a hand to her heart.

"So anyway, the local news picked up on the story. Even Lauren was into it all by this point, although she'd been a total Debbie Downer throughout the whole process and thought I was wasting all my time online. But I think when the news crew got involved, even she started to get that this whole thing was a big deal." Kadence raises an arched eyebrow. "And yes I may have told her 'I told you so' a feeeew times."

Kadence laughs. "But it was all good. More and more, we kept making music. Any artistic differences, we were able to work through. And then"—Kadence gives a dramatic pause—"we got the call from *America's Talented Kids*."

She clasps her hands together and bounces in her chair like a little kid who can barely contain herself. "In spite of everything else, nothing could've prepared us for getting the call from a national talent show saying they wanted us to come on and perform live for them." She presses a hand to her chest again. "I thought I was about to have a heart attack while I was on the phone with the producer. I mean *seriously*!

"We filmed last summer and it aired in November as part of sweeps week." Kadence's face falls a little. "Of course, it was bittersweet to see ourselves on TV because Lauren had started having trouble with her voice by then. But we both hoped her illness would be a short-term thing, so when it aired"—Kadence brightens—"I went over to her house for the big viewing, since my dad, tough army guy, doesn't exactly like popcorn kernels getting stuck in his couch cushions.

"So I was at her house with her parents, and they made giant bowls of popcorn for everyone and ice cream sundaes too—you know, the kind with bananas, whipped cream, the whole nine yards. And then there we were on-screen. It was different than being on the local news, because you knew the entire nation, all of *America*, could be watching you at this moment." She takes a deep breath, filling her lungs. Then she shakes her head, as if trying to find the right words to explain it.

"It was weird, watching ourselves on TV and remembering what it was like to be there in Hollywood, taping it in that huge auditorium filled with people. Lauren wasn't the only one nervous that time. I was shaking too. But both of our voices came across so pure that I couldn't have been happier with it. And then our three-minute song was over." She laughs, as if at herself.

"It's funny how so much angst and excitement goes into a three-minute clip! But of course it wasn't just about those three minutes. There was a giant resurgence of interest in all of our videos online and a ton of new subscribers to our YouTube channel.

"That made Lauren and me want to keep making music, but she couldn't. Because of her voice. I had to make the hardest, most difficult decision of my life to continue on as a solo act. I kept trying to discuss it with Lauren, but she didn't want to talk about it much. She finally sat me down and told me to do it. She said we hadn't worked this hard and come all this way to stop now. And that one day, she truly believed her voice would be better, and we'd be singing together again."

Kadence takes another deep breath. "Phew, guys, I don't know if I've ever really talked about all this. I swear, these videos are like therapy sessions for me." She smiles at the camera, her eyebrows knit together and revealing the earnestness in her expression. Then, what she'd said jovially in her past videos comes out quietly this time, like a whispered prayer. "Life is short, my darlings. Reach for the stars before they burn out."

The image goes dark.

SIXTEEN

JUDE

Pine Grove High School
Thursday, April 5
12:40 p.m.

I walk down the hall after lunch and glance at my phone.

Lauren: Did you talk to Justine yet?

Without breaking stride, I text back.

Me: Yeah. Non-starter. Said she barely remembers it.

What I don't say is that Justine seemed far more interested in flirting with me than talking about any of it. She kept leaning in and running her hand up my arm. Since I was aiming to get information out of her, I went with it. I tilted my head and gave the half smirk that girls seem to eat up. Add the half-eyebrow lift and they're goners. If it weren't so sad, it'd be funny how easy it is to manipulate people. Justine was all but a puddle at my feet.

My phone pings again.

Lauren: Are you sure? She could be hiding it. Did you ask her about Kadence being missing?

Me: Yeah, she was just concerned like everyone else. It seemed genuine.

Lauren: Okay. So Justine's off the list. Who's next?

I imagine her typing on her phone, and I wish I could skip school too so I could be with her. I'd do it in a heartbeat. But that would be weird. We've only been back in contact for a few days. Even if all I want to do is spend every waking minute with her. Damn it. I'm not back to the fixating. I'm *not*.

I close my eyes, lean back against a bank of lockers, and think about riding on the bike with her yesterday. She was scared and she clung to me with every bit of her body. Her arms, those freaking thighs. She's not one of those pencil-thin bony chicks either. Girl's got *curves*. I let out a long, shuddering breath and bang my head back against the lockers. Christ, I don't know if what I'm feeling is normal or obsessive. How the hell am I supposed to know the difference?

My phone pings and I force my concentration back to where it needs to be.

Lauren: Jude, you still there? Or did you have to go to class?

I glance at the clock on the top of my phone. Crap. I've got like one minute to get to class. I type as I jog in the direction of gym.

Me: Jeremy's next. Got gym with him now. Txt when class is over.

SEVENTEEN

MASON

Sheriff's Office—The Interview Continues
Monday, April 2
11:37 a.m.

Kopitzke: I understand Kadence and Lauren DeSanto got in a pretty big fight not that long ago.

I hesitate because I'm not sure how much he already knows, or how much I should say.

Mason: Where did you hear that?
Kopitzke: We've been talking to people at your school. They say the fight was over you.

Well, that's just awesome. Denial is on the tip of my tongue, but I can't help thinking that I shouldn't hold anything back. The fight was stupid, but if it helps them find Kady...and still...I don't like the way he's looking at me. Like he's judging me. The detective must sense my indecision.

Kopitzke: Do yourself a favor, Mason, and tell me what happened.

Mason: Well...you see...it was last hour on the Thursday before spring break. We were all...beat, you know? I had three midterms plus this really big project that was due the next day. I know Lauren had been killing herself all week over some big English poetry project.

So anyway I got to my locker and there was this lime green Post-it note near the handle. It said: *Please. Need to talk. Meet me by the flagpole?* L

I knew "L" meant Lauren, so I waited by the flagpole and sure enough she showed up. She asked if I wanted to take a walk, so that's what we did.

We didn't say much right away, which was strange because I thought she needed to talk so bad. It was as if she was waiting for me to start things, which made it kind of awkward, like, was I supposed to know what we needed to talk about?

Kopitzke: Sometimes girls assume guys can read their minds.

I stare at him for a second, and he stares back. The corners of his mouth turn up. I can tell he's trying to be buddy-buddy so I keep talking. Whatever. I've already started. There's not much point in stopping now.

Mason: So anyway, we kept walking—first out toward the athletic fields, then down one straightaway on the track, then onto the cross-country course. From there we took the path that runs through the woods and so we ended up at the F.U. Fort.

Kopitzke: The what?

Mason: Oh, it's this old junker place in the woods. It's been there forever. It's not huge, only enough room inside for four people, maybe six if you really crammed them in. There was this old couch in there to sit on. Pretty gnarly but it was either that or the ground, and since the snow had just melted, it was still pretty muddy. So we ended up sitting down and we talked.

I hesitate as I remember our conversation. We mostly talked about Kady. Lauren had been really sad all winter, what with her voice and not being able to sing, and Kady having gone all hermit on her (and me) with her writing and recording. We missed her. We wanted things to be like before. Without Kadence, it was like we'd had a massive power outage and were trying to light our lives with little battery-operated candles. That's how Lauren put it, and that sounded about right to me.

At some point she started to cry and she laid her head on my shoulder. And that was that. Something about having her curled into my side, her dark hair falling over my chest...it was complete instinct. It wasn't like I thought about what I was doing, but the next thing I knew my fingers were under her chin. I tipped her face up to mine, and... then I kissed her.

I mean, it was all on me. I kissed *her*. At first, she didn't even kiss me back. But then, yeah, after a bit she got into it.

The whole time I was kissing Lauren, I was thinking, *Stop. Stop, you idiot.* And when it was over we were both like, *crap*, that did not just happen. I remember the first thing out of Lauren's mouth was, *We cannot tell Kady. Please don't tell Kady.* Which was fine by me. That was the last thing I wanted to do.

Because this would kill her, Lauren said.

Mason: Anyway, I don't know how, but Kadence found out about me and Lauren being in the fort together, and the next day at lunch, she stormed over to where Lauren was sitting and yanked her up by her hair.

Kopitzke: Her hair?

Mason: I know. Lauren yelled something like, "What the hell?" and Kadence went all ballistic. She yelled, "You slept with my boyfriend?" super loud. Everyone heard it. I was like, *Holy crap*. And Lauren was like, "Are you insane?" Because we hadn't done anything close to that. And Kadence was like, "I know everything!" She was devastated. It was tearing me apart inside.

Kopitzke: Then what happened?

Mason: Then Lauren turned her back, and Kadence grabbed her around the shoulders and spun her around. I don't think Kadence pushed her exactly, but Lauren went down hard. People were yelling "Fight! Fight!" because two girls fighting is pretty rare, and those two best friends fighting...

I glance down at the tape recorder and stop talking as my thoughts go someplace dark. I should have stepped in. I should have manned up and owned my part in the whole thing. I shouldn't have left Lauren alone to defend herself. The trouble was, I didn't know who I was supposed to go to. Was I supposed to rush in and comfort my girlfriend? Or was I supposed to help my friend, who was lying on the floor?

I remember some guy was standing behind me in the doorway to the cafeteria. He nudged me in the shoulder and said, "Dude! Did you really sleep with Lauren DeSanto?" And it froze me solid, right in the spot where I was standing.

Kopitzke: Did Lauren fight back?

Mason: No. She stood up and walked out of the cafeteria like it was nothing. It was almost eerie how calm she was. And the whole time, Kadence stood there crying. Some girls went up to her. I wanted to go to her too. *I really did.* I wanted to tell her that it was all a big misunderstanding. But I couldn't talk to Kadence. Not there in front of everyone. So...anyway, I tried to talk to Kady after school, but she wouldn't give me the chance to explain. We hadn't talked at all in the days before her show at Cuppa Cuppa. That's why I didn't go.

Kopitzke: I was going to ask you about that.

Mason: I thought it would be too upsetting for Kady to have me and Lauren both there. I didn't want all our shit to distract her from putting on a good show. But if I'd known...if I'd known it was going to be my last chance to see her...Please! I don't care about anything else. I'd give anything to see her again.

EIGHTEEN

LAUREN

Mary Blake's Residence
Thursday, April 5
5:00 p.m.

It took me and Jude over an hour to track down Mary Blake. She wasn't listed on the White Pages, and I had to call around to a bunch of old friends—by which I mean Kadence's friends, many of whom wouldn't even speak to me—before finding one that had Mary's new address and was willing to share. Even now that we've driven an hour out of town, I'm not 100 percent sure we're at the right place.

The house looks a lot like mine: a 1960s ranch with shutters on the large picture window. I can predict the layout inside. Living room at the front, kitchen to the back. Three bedrooms and a bath to the right. I wonder what else Mary and I have in common, and I wonder if it even matters.

I'd hoped maybe we could avoid coming here, but Jude's chat with Jeremy was fruitless. Apparently the guy was still a huge Kady fan despite how much she embarrassed him at the pep rally last year. That was Kady for you. Inspiring devotion and loyalty. How did she do it? Why did we all fall for it?

Jude sets the kickstand on his bike and kills the engine. It seems suddenly too quiet. At first it scared me to be so overpowered by a machine, but Jude makes it feel safe. He never goes too fast or banks the corners too tight, though sometimes I still have to close my eyes. He seems protective of me.

"Stay on the bike," he says as he removes his helmet. I take mine off too. "I'll be able to see you the whole time, but I should probably talk to her alone."

It's nice to know we're on the same page. After what happened with Caleb, clearly I am not an asset to this investigation. As I asked Jude before we set out, who on our list is going to admit any guilt when the perfect scapegoat is standing right in front of them? You'd have to be an idiot, and I don't remember Mary Blake being an idiot.

Jude had said not to worry, that he had a plan. He'd revved the Harley to life before I could ask anything else.

"What are you going to say to her?" I ask now that we've stopped in front of Mary's house. I pull my jacket tighter around me.

"I'm going to thank her." He takes off his gloves and shoves them in his pockets. The bike rocks under us as he shifts his weight.

"Thank her?" I ask to the back of his head.

"Yeah. I thought of it too late when we were talking to Caleb. It might have worked better with him, but I'm going to thank her for doing what I wasn't brave enough to do myself—taking care of the Queen Witch for good. Then I'm going to sit back and see how she responds."

"Be ready to duck," I say.

"Huh?" he asks with a halfway glance back.

"You're a stranger. You're planning to go to her door and thank her for offing somebody? You're going to be lucky if she doesn't punch you in the face."

"Yeah, okay," he says with a quiet chuckle.

I put my helmet back on. Anonymity is my friend.

I watch Jude walk up the sidewalk. Last year's brown grass fills the cracks. A part of me wishes Jude had parked his bike farther away, or that we'd brought a car. I feel vulnerable and exposed sitting out here in the open, alone at the curb. I glance over one shoulder, then the other.

The street is quiet.

Jude knocks on the front door and glances back at me with a confident smile. A minute passes. No one answers, though I think I see some movement at the curtains on the picture window. He knocks again. Another minute.

I'm about to call, "Hey, let's go," when the door opens and a tall, blond girl is standing in its frame. She's wearing jeans and an oversized, shapeless sweatshirt. Her long hair hangs forward, shielding her face.

I can't hear her very well. I assume she says, "Yeah?"

If it really is Mary Blake, her teeth look good. At least as far as I can tell from the curb. I wonder if she got braces. I don't think she recognizes Jude, but then nobody does. She has to be wondering who this hot guy is standing on her doorstep, but she doesn't flirt or even smile. Her face is absolutely flat. If anything, I detect a hint of fear.

Jude shifts from one foot to the other, and I assume he's trying out his plan to build rapport—one victim to another. As he talks, Mary's face takes on a look of incredulity, then there's a flash of pain.

She looks past his shoulder to where I'm sitting. I'm tense. Spine straight, shoulders stiff. I'm dwarfed by the size of the bike and must look like a nervous little kid.

I sense an intake of breath. Whether it's hers or mine, I can't tell.

"*You!*" she screams, launching herself from her doorstep. Jude swings sideways like a matador dodging a raging bull.

I don't have a second to process what's going on before she has crossed her front yard. I feel hands on my shoulders, then the next moment I am sailing backwards, looking at the sky. I have a weird slow-motion moment where I consciously think about how nice the clouds look, and then my helmet bounces off the concrete. BOOM! *Boom. boom.*

I slide on the ground and feel the roadway digging into my back. A second later the helmet is ripped from my head, wrenching my ears.

"Ow!" I cry, and the response to my pain is a sharp slap across the face. So I guess Mary Blake can be taken at her word. Payback certainly *is* a bitch.

"Hey!" Jude says. "Get off her!" Mary is pummeling my body with her fists. I cover my face, deflecting the blows as best I can because this girl is fighting like a Class A freak.

Jude wraps his arms around Mary and pulls her off me. Her legs kick and swing, circling in the air like she's doing some elaborate dance routine meant to maim me.

"You bitch!" she screams. "How dare you come here?"

"*Settle down!*" Jude yells. "*Settle* DOWN!" But it doesn't look like his words are having any effect on Mary, who must be having some kind of psychotic break because I've never seen anybody use their body like that—every part of her working independently to wound me.

"You ruined my life!" She's still screaming, completely enraged. I crab-walk backwards, then scramble to my feet.

"I didn't do anything to you!"

"Bullshit!" She spits at me, but misses.

Jude is still holding her back. "Lauren's not who you're mad at, Mary."

"Like hell she isn't," Mary says. "She stole my boyfriend and ruined my life."

"Not me," I say, holding my hands up, ready to defend myself if Jude loses his grip. "Kady. Kady did that."

"Kadence?" she asks. It's the first time I see any drop in her hostility. But then it's back. "You probably killed her, and now you want to blame all your sins on her? You're disgusting! How can you live with yourself? Why are the police letting you walk around like this?"

"Mary," I say, doing my best to keep my voice level. "You've made a mistake. Or well, not a mistake. You've just been led to believe the wrong thing."

"You don't get to tell me anything. You don't have the right to say a word to me. You stole Nick from me, and then Donny Mikkelson...He... he..." A ragged sob rips up and out of Mary's throat. Tears snake down her cheeks in little rivers.

Jude and I exchange one confused look. I feel a little sick hearing Donny's name. Neither of us understands what he has to do with anything, but our shoulders slump simultaneously because we both know who he is. Donny graduated last year and infamously got kicked off the hockey team when he was a junior for unnecessary roughness. The *hockey* team of all things. There are other rumors about him too. He's never been charged with anything, but I wouldn't want him left alone in a room with anyone I cared about. Any girl anyway.

How have I never heard any of this before? The look on Mary's face answers my question. She can't believe how close she's come to admitting the truth to us. Here. Now. This is why she changed schools. The R-word hangs heavy in the air between us. I feel sick to my stomach. I try not to fill in the blanks of what happened to Mary. I don't need that mental image. It's horrible enough that Mary lived through it.

Mary lets out a feral scream and thrashes in Jude's arms.

He lets go of her immediately, his hands in the air. "Easy," he says, positioning himself between me and Mary. He faces her. She stumbles back from him, heaving in deep gulps of air. She wraps her arms around her middle. My hand goes to my mouth. She's like a wounded animal.

This is not the girl I remember. Mary Blake, who could give Kadence Mulligan a run for her money as far as confidence and showmanship on stage.

Jude continues talking, his voice gentle. "I won't touch you again. I just didn't want you to hurt Lauren. I'm sorry about what happened to you, Mary. So sorry." His compassion is genuine. I spent enough time around Kadence to know the difference. "But it's not Lauren's fault."

"It is completely her fault," she says, reaching around Jude and poking me hard in the chest. "I only went out with Donny to get back at Nick. I never would have done it if not for you."

"I didn't do anything with Nick," I protest weakly. "It was Kady." Mary looks at me with such accusation, such hatred.

"Nick told me it was you," she says.

"Well, then Nick lied," I feel the heat creep into my face.

"Why would he lie?" she asks.

Before I can put together an answer, Jude steps in. "Maybe he had something to lose if he didn't go along with Kady's lie."

"Lie?" Mary asks.

"If Nick told you it was Lauren, it was because Kadence made him lie," Jude says. His confidence in me is surprising, but I'm as thankful for his trust as I am for his explanation.

"It wasn't me," I say again, hoping I sound as believable as Jude does. I want to cry but then feel like I don't even deserve to. Mary is the only one entitled to tears here. After all that's happened to her...

"Kady?" Mary asks, like she's struggling to make sense of everything she thought she knew.

"I'm really sorry," I say. My words don't do justice to what I'm really feeling. How do you even begin to apologize for something like that? Is "apologize" even the right word? "Sorry" is an inadequate word too.

Maybe all words are inadequate. Even for a wordsmith, language fails in moments like these. "About everything," I continue lamely. "But do you have any idea what happened to her?"

"What?" she asks, looking back and forth between me and Jude. "Kady? No. No. Should I?" Her eyes settle on me. I can tell it's going to take her a long time to see me any differently than she has for the last year.

Behind us, the front door opens and a thin woman with permed hair calls out to us. "Mary? Oh how nice, you have friends visiting! You know your father and I've been saying that you should invite people over more. Well, don't just stand out here, invite them inside! I just frosted a pan of chocolate chip bars."

"They're not hungry," Mary calls to the woman who I assume is her mother.

"Actually, I'm famished," Jude says.

I look at him incredulously.

"You see!" the woman says, waving us toward the house. "Come in. Come in."

Jude smiles and leads the way while Mary and I exchange a look of sheer discomfort. I'm pretty sure the last thing Mary Blake predicted when she woke up this morning was that she and I would be eating cookie bars together at her kitchen table. When we get inside, Jude is already sitting and Mary's mom is pouring milk.

The three of us sit in relative quiet except for Jude making *nom nom nom* noises. Boys. Nothing ever interferes with their stomachs. Mary picks at her chocolate chip bar with her fingers. I stare out the window at their bird feeder.

Out of nowhere she says, "I was going to be like you."

"Huh?" I ask, taking my eyes off the birds.

Jude stops chewing.

"I was going to be like you and Kadence. I loved to sing."

"Yeah, I remember," I say, smiling. "You beat us for first place at the eighth-grade talent show. You sang that Adele song. "Set Fire to the Rain," right? We weren't even a close second."

"That's because I had been training. You guys were still just playing around back then."

"I didn't know people trained for junior-high talent shows," Jude says. Both Mary and I look over at him.

"Not for that," Mary says. "That was just this little thing I did. I was training for something bigger. By the fall of our junior year, I'd made it through two rounds of auditions for a new Nickelodeon TV show. It was like a sketch-variety show. All the kids had to be triple threats: dancers, singers, actors. Singing was my strong suit, but I did pretty good with the others too."

There's a beat of silence, then Jude asks, "Who told Kadence?"

Mary shifts uncomfortably in her chair. "I did. I thought she'd think it was cool. That we had something in common since you guys were starting to record your songs."

"You bested her." Jude's eyes are full of sympathy.

"Only for a minute, I guess," Mary says.

"What happened with the auditions?" I ask.

She shrugs. "After everything that happened, I asked my mom to call the producer and withdraw my audition tapes. I wasn't interested anymore. I just wanted to stay home."

"Kady stole your dream," Jude says.

"I don't know," Mary says with a sad little laugh. "It's not like I was ever offered the job. I probably wouldn't have made the final cut."

By this time, Mary has decimated her chocolate chip bar. It's completely destroyed and lies in a pile of crumbs at the center of her plate.

Jude tosses back the rest of his milk, then pushes himself up from the table. "That," he says, pausing for emphasis, "was good, but we should get going now."

"What?" I ask. That's it? We're leaving?

"It's getting late. Some of us have homework." He looks down at Mary, his expression softening, but without condescension or pity. "It was nice to meet you."

"Oh, okay then. I guess we're going," I say, but something more needs to be said. "Mary," I start again, but then I pause. I sense that words are going to fail me again. "It was good to see you. I'm sorry for...everything."

I try not to visibly cringe at how stupid that sounds. But then I ignore my own discomfort. Sometimes it doesn't matter how awkward a moment is. I'm reminded of the same thought I had last night with Jude: I want to be the kind of person who helps put people back together, not the kind who tears them down.

"I don't know what's best for you—maybe you never want to think about any of us ever again. But if...maybe...you do want to talk to someone, someone who was there, someone who knew what Kady could be like...or just about anything...I'll leave you my number."

Mary makes a *hmpf* sound through her nose. I think it might have been a laugh. "Not likely." But there's a small smile on her lips. "Thanks though."

I scribble my number down on the back of an envelope that's lying on the kitchen table, then I quickly pluck a large crumb of chocolate chip bar off the plate and pop it in my mouth.

When we leave, Jude helps me onto his motorcycle, but he doesn't get on right away. I stare at the house, wondering if Kadence thought out all the ramifications of the little games she played with people's lives—the games I sometimes played along with her—or if the consequences never really mattered to her at all.

"I was really proud of you in there," Jude says, pulling me out of my thoughts.

"Why?" I ask. I replay the conversation in my mind, but nothing sticks out to me as being particularly valiant.

"You were sweet to Mary. She needed someone to be sweet to her. I like seeing that side of you again. I thought maybe it was gone forever. I'm glad to be wrong." He reaches up and pushes a lock of hair behind my ear.

"You're really pretty too," he says, and I can tell he's surprised himself by saying it out loud. I don't really know how to respond. "I always thought so," he adds.

"Yeah, well...you need to get out more."

"I don't think that's it." Then without any real reason, he draws me into his arms. It's warm there, pressed against his chest, and I think I may never want to leave.

I slip my hands inside his jacket, laying them against his chest. I scrunch the fabric of his T-shirt in my fingers. My cheek is pressed against his sternum. The tears I kept in at Mary's house spill over my cheeks. And then. Very quietly. I fall completely and utterly to pieces.

When was the last time I was this close to someone? I can't remember allowing myself this kind of vulnerability in all the years I've been friends with Kadence. I've never noticed before how careful I'd always been, how I'd walked on eggshells, afraid to show any weakness because I knew how Kadence treated the weak.

With Nathan...with Jude, I remember what it feels like to be loved—not that Jude loves me, but still, that's what it feels like—to be cared for, not because of what someone wants from me but because of what someone wants to give me.

I hear Jude take a deep breath, and then he says, "Do you remember what we promised each other?" One of his hands cradles the back of my neck, holding me firmly against him.

I know what he's asking. It was September, the fall of seventh grade, a month before Kadence moved to town. We took a class field trip to an apple orchard. We had wandered away from the group. I was so short—even shorter than I am now—and he laughed at me because I could walk under even the lowest branches on the apple trees. I put a rotten apple down his shirt. He fished it out and threw it at me, missing me on purpose.

I'd never kissed anyone. Neither had he. We were teetering on that awkward line. Not exactly kids anymore, but not knowing what to do with the crazy mess of hormones rushing through our bodies. I could feel the tension, strange and buzzing like a loose power line. Did he feel it too?

Nathan swung under a branch and found me standing on the other side. Our eyes met. Our faces inches from each other. I remember holding my breath.

That's when Joe Rice stepped into view.

"Well, well, well. If it isn't pizza face and the midget girl. Wait. What's going on here? Oh hey, Nathan, is the midget your girrrrrrlfriend?"

I was humiliated. Humiliated and heartbroken. I meant to lash out at Joe, but it backfired onto Nathan. "I'm not his girlfriend," I yelled.

The look on Nathan's face ripped my heart in a jagged line. I think about that day every time I eat an apple.

Jude's thumb strokes against my hair now. "Do you remember?" he asks. "After Joe left, we promised we'd never be mean like that to anyone. Most of all, we promised we'd never hurt each other."

His hands drop to my shoulders, and he takes one step back so he can see my face. "We've both broken that promise but, Ren, this is me making good on it. I'm starting fresh with you. I'm letting you start fresh with me."

"Thank you," I say because there is no better way to say it. He pulls me in to his chest again. For a second, I wonder why he's willing to forgive me. I don't deserve it, but I don't ask him to explain himself. I'm too relieved. I feel like I can breathe for the first time all day. I keep expecting him to let go but he doesn't. I clutch him back.

I take a deep breath and let it out slowly, the lyrics for my new song flooding my mind again:

Winged heart,

you take me by the hand and fly me home.

To a time and space that I could never find,

never find, alone.

NINETEEN

JUDE

Outside Mary Blake's Residence
Thursday, April 5
6:00 p.m.

Christ, what am I doing? I should let go of Lauren. I feel too much, and there's no way she's feeling the same toward me. But her body feels so good pressed against mine, and she's not pulling away. She smells so good, *feels* so good. Damn it, I've got to get myself under control. This was never part of the plan.

I force myself to pull away while keeping my face calm. A small crease forms in her forehead. I look away. *Don't let what you're feeling show on your face, Williams. Don't you dare. Play it cool or she'll bolt.* Coaching myself only sort of works. I think I've got my mask mostly in order, but if she looks close, she'll see the sheen of nervous sweat over my forehead in spite of the fact that it's getting chilly out here. Not to mention my heart, which is thumping like a roadrunner sprinting to get free. Christ, I gotta clear my head.

Out of habit, I pull a smoke from the pocket of my leather jacket and go to light up, but before I can pull the warm blast of nicotine into my lungs, Lauren wrinkles her nose. She grabs the cigarette from my lips and grinds it into the dirt before going to hop on the bike. Not a shocker that she doesn't think smoking is hot. Lauren isn't the kind of girl to buy into any of this new cool guy shit. No, she sees me as the kid I used to be. She puts the helmet over her head, but I can still feel her eyes on me.

I stand there blinking for a second because it hits me then—that *that* was the guy she let hug her—the boy she used to know. A second ago all I wanted was distance between us, but now I want to rip off her helmet, grab her, make her look into my eyes, and say, see *me*. I don't care what you call me—Nathan, Jude, whatever—just see *me*, like you always did. See the darkness too and don't be afraid.

I exhale hard, expelling the last bits of air from my lungs. Because *could* Lauren look at the real me now and not be disgusted, even scared? She and I have both changed. But the things I've done, if she knew...

I scowl and stride the last two feet to the bike, throwing my leg over. I jam my own helmet on my head. Lauren barely has time to lock her arms around my waist before we pull away from the curb, spinning a few pieces of stray gravel into the air behind us.

Lauren's warmth is so sweet at my back. The road spreads out clear in front of us, and in spite of all of the shit that's wrong, I don't want this moment to end. I want to drop my hand from the handlebar and grip Lauren's thigh possessively. I want to wrap her so tight around me and never let her go.

On impulse, I take a left-hand turn instead of going straight back to Pine Grove. I've come out this way before. Whenever I need to get away from the crap in town, I pick a direction and start riding. I take whatever nowhere roads I can find just to get lost for a little while. Being around trees and nature instead of human beings is a necessity sometimes. Makes me feel less homicidal.

The sun is getting low in the sky now, already turning pink. Lauren has her head laid against my shoulder. I don't think she's noticed my detour. At least, she hasn't asked where I'm going, not that I'd really hear her between the helmets and the roar of the bike.

I drive a little farther and then pull a left onto a dirt road that cuts through a thickly forested area. Branches hang low over both sides of the one-lane road. We hit a deep rut and Lauren lifts her head. A second later she's tapping me on the shoulder. I wave my hand at her to signal that everything's fine and I know what I'm doing. I speed up a little so she can't get any ideas of trying to jump off the bike, and like I intended, she wraps both arms around me again. Gotta stay on this train until it stops.

I hope she's not too freaked out. That isn't my intention. Only another minute to go. Finally, I bring the bike to a stop on a secluded stretch of road by a tall pine tree that I always use as a landmark. The tree is still just a baby, nothing like its huge, old-growth ancestors. But one day, maybe. I like to think about that, how it will grow so tall, like they did back before people came and cut them all down. This is the place I want to share with Lauren.

I plant my feet on the ground while we both take off our helmets.

"What are you doing? Where are we?" She sounds a little upset and I'm sorry about that.

I pop the kickstand and turn my head. "Sorry, Ren. Couldn't talk while we were on the bike. I wanted to show you something special. Remember how we always used to do that? If we found a special place, we'd save it up to show it to the other person?" I'm talking fast but I just want to explain it to her so she's not afraid of me. Christ that's the last thing I want.

"I found this place last summer right when I got back. Since we were nearby, I wanted you to see it. It's been a rough few days. I figured you needed a little break. A little bit of something beautiful to take your mind off things." She still looks uncertain. Crap, maybe I've done the wrong thing bringing her here. "But look, we can head back to town if you'd rather."

The hard look on her face softens. She hesitates for another moment, then gets off the bike. A small smile tips the edges of her mouth and she takes my gloved hand in hers, urging me off the bike too. "A little bit of something beautiful, huh?"

I grin. I'm suddenly as excited as when I was a kid and she agreed to go on adventures with me. Even if our "adventures" back then were only playing in the woods with my dog, Coco, or collecting aluminum cans so we could turn them in for change to buy little plastic action figures from the quarter machines.

I get off the bike, not letting go of her hand. I lead her away from the road and into the woods. The brush is thick underfoot, but I glance down and see that Lauren's wearing winter boots. She follows me with a quizzical smile on her face. She's got the cutest nose. It's shaped like a little ski slope and I want to trace my finger down it. Then I want to breathe in her hair. I think that's what makes her smell so good. Her hair always looks really, really soft too. A rush of feelings washes over me so intensely that it's all I can do not to start trembling like some goddamn preteen holding a girl's hand for the first time.

"Jude, is this private property?" She pauses and looks around with a frown. "Are we going to get in trouble?"

I blink, coming out of my mini-daydream about her hair. Right. Private property. "Do you really care?" I waggle my eyebrows at her in that way that always used to make her laugh.

She stops and drops my hand. Her frown deepens. "Considering the whole country thinks I murdered my best friend, it's probably not the best idea to get brought up on trespassing charges too."

"Hey." I touch her cheek with one of my gloved hands. Wish I didn't have the glove on. I want to feel her skin. "We're fine here," I assure her. "This is all state park land. No trespassing, I promise."

Her cheeks are slightly flushed as I grab her hand again and start forward. This time she comes with no hesitation. I like that. We head farther into the woods even though there isn't a cleared path. I lead the way, pulling branches aside for her.

"Are you sure you know where you're going?" she asks as we step over fallen logs and rotted leaves.

"I told you. I've been here before. Not even that long ago. It's a good place when you need somewhere quiet to think." What I don't tell her is the content of those thoughts that filled my journals. Vengeful plans against her and Kadence. Was that really only six months ago? I was so angry back then. Nothing at all like what I feel now walking beside my Ren, her hand so small in mine even with gloves on.

It feels so good out here. Clean air, clear mind. Healthy. Whole. I can do this. Put the past behind me. Let go of the monster and become a new man.

"Come on, it's just a little farther." I say.

I lead her down a rocky hill and into a ravine that's beginning to run with water again. The thin trickle is an offshoot of the larger stream we're heading toward, but it means we're going the right direction. I can even hear the rush of water up ahead.

"Good thing I wore my boots today," she says, smiling up at me. Unlike all the smiles she's given me the past couple days, those fake, forced ones—the kind you put on when you're afraid or when you feel the need to make other people comfortable—this one feels real. This is my old Ren, smiling at me because out here, I've made the rest of the world fall away for her. It makes me feel ten feet tall.

I grin back, afraid if I say anything it will be the wrong thing and I'll ruin the moment again. I hold back the branch of another pine tree so she can pass. I make an elaborate bow and wave her through saying, "My lady."

She smiles even wider, and it's like we're twelve again, but even better because we're both older. She's almost a woman, and I'm almost a man, and when she looks back over her shoulder to make sure I've gotten past the tree okay, there's something more in her gaze than simple childish happiness. It's a spark, a sizzle, an *awareness*. I move up close behind her, my chest all but touching her back, and put my hand on her hip. I whisper over her shoulder. "There. Up ahead."

She steps away from me to climb over a fallen tree. She stops and gasps. I grin again and move to stand beside her. The sun is just dropping below the horizon and the stream is wide enough to cause a break in the trees, letting in the purplish-pink light of the setting sun. It illuminates the five-foot waterfall perfectly, making the water splashing at the bottom light up like flashing diamonds.

"Oh Jude," she whispers, one hand clutching her chest. With the other she reaches blindly toward mine. I grasp it hard and bring it to my own chest. We stand like that for a long time, watching the sun set on the waterfall. It's the most peaceful, perfect moment of my entire life.

That is, until Ren turns toward me, leans up on her tiptoes, and brings her lips to mine. I hardly have time to take a breath.

Her lips taste like caramel and the barest hint of green tea. It's the softest touch, and I'm so shocked, so terrified that she'll pull away any second that I'm all but frozen. Then I come to my senses and start kissing her back, because damn, she could pull away any moment and I can't bear to miss an instant of it.

But the gentleness only lasts a few seconds more anyway, because then she pushes me up against a nearby tree and kisses me hard. I don't know if everything she's been going through is just bubbling up right now or if it's really because she likes me, but Christ, I've got so much heat in my veins for this girl, I don't care. I'm sure as hell going to show her that I mean it.

She's taken the lead so far, but now I'm the one wrestling for control. I rip off my gloves, needing to have more of my skin on hers. I cup her cheeks in my hands. She's even softer than I suspected. I wanna freaking groan. I pull back for a second so she's forced to look into my eyes. She's panting and wild-eyed and looks like she's about to say something, maybe about how this is a mistake, but I don't let her. I crush my lips to hers and flip our bodies so that her back is against the tree.

And it's not just kissing now. It's a hunger. On both sides. Not just me. I've made out with girls before, at my other school, but it's never been like this. Nothing like this. Her hands are in my hair, tugging frantically. My other hand slides down the back of her thigh, and I sling her leg around my waist as I pin her against the tree. Oh Christ. Ecstasy is pressing against her body, even with all our clothes on. We continue to kiss in an animal frenzy until she's frantic and tugging at my jacket and my shirt. I've kissed down her neck and to the top of her cleavage before I realize what we're doing and some semblance of sanity sinks in again.

"Wait," I huff out, blinking and trying to get air and a sane thought back in my head. "Ren, wait. We can't. Not here." Even though a big part of me is screaming: *Shut the hell up! Of course you can! Right here. Naked on the ground. Naked, naked, naked.*

She blinks up at me, looking equally dazed. She looks around us. It's getting dark now. I have no idea how long we've been making out, but I guess the sun's gone down. She suddenly covers her face in embarrassment. "Oh!"

I laugh and hug her before she can go into full freak-out mode. "Ren, stop it. It's fine." I tug her hands from her face.

She peeks up at me, her face completely red. "But we just made out like crazy...on government property."

"It's fine, Ren," I hug her even harder, laughing a little. "Everything's been crazy." I take a step back, though it half kills me. I only manage it because it's the right thing. For her. She still looks embarrassed. I attempt to force my mind off the obsessive repeat that I should be trying to get at least some part of her naked right now.

"Besides, it's not like you can resist this." I open my arms wide. "I mean, not to quote JT and all, but"—I shrug nonchalantly—"I do bring sexy back."

I finally get the response I want and she starts to giggle uncontrollably. "You...did not," she gasps between laughter, "just...say that!"

I dust off my bomber jacket and lean back against a tree with my arms folded in an exaggerated sexy model pose. "What?" I give her a chin nod. "S'up?"

This sends her into a whole new bout of laughter.

I push away from the tree and grab her around the waist, planting one more kiss on her lips, but only a quick one this time. I finally tamp down the voice in my head, though it makes one last attempt: *Okay, so maybe not naked, but what about pushing her back against the tree? Her body, your body, cement them together, then add friction*—I'm biting back a groan, remembering all too well how good she felt just moments ago with those sweet legs wrapped around me. Yeah. Not sure how well I'll be sleeping tonight.

"Come on, time to get back," I manage to say, and here's hoping she doesn't notice my voice is a little lower than normal. There's just enough light left and I've come here enough times that I know the way back to the bike.

The smile fades from her lips and she hugs me back, hard. "Do we have to?" she asks, her voice getting all croaky and raspy at the end. I wince, all dirty thoughts doused. I've kept her out too long.

"Yeah." The levity is gone from my voice now too. "But I'm with you now. You're not alone anymore."

She nods into my chest and doesn't say anything. I hug her tighter in a way I hope she'll take as reassurance. But it's for me too. She's in my arms. This really happened. We didn't say the words, but I think after tonight, she's mine now. Lauren DeSanto is finally mine. Everything I ever wanted, even when I thought I hated her, is finally here within my grasp.

Now if only I can get away with never mentioning the one thing that could fuck all this up: the truth.

■　■　■

The ride back to Lauren's house passes too quickly. Now that it's dark, it's cold as a witch's teat out here, probably in the upper forties. The wind cuts through my coat and jacket even though I keep my speed relatively low. I can feel Lauren shivering behind me even with her heavy down coat on. I barely notice the chill. I'm still flying high with the pressure of her arms around me and the memory of her lips on mine. I'm so caught up in her and paying attention to the road that I don't notice the two cop cars parked outside her house until the bike rolls to a stop at the curb.

Lauren immediately jumps off and yanks the helmet from her head, shoving it against my chest. At first I don't understand why she's moving so fast, but then I see her mom running down the front walk. She sweeps Lauren into her arms with an "Oh, thank God!" She squeezes Lauren hard, then glares over her shoulder at me with a look of fear. "You stay away from my daughter!"

"Nathan Jude Williams, down on the ground, hands over your head."

"What the hell?" It's one of those sensory overload moments. I'm being shouted at from all sides. When I look around, I see I'm flanked by four cops with their guns trained on me. Guns? I feel like I've stepped into some crazy twilight zone version of my life.

"Down on the ground, hands over your head!" One of the cops is shouting at me louder now. These guys are serious. This is no joke.

So I do what they say. I drop to my knees, then lie down on the lawn and put my hands behind my head. The next second someone seizes my wrists. I feel the cold bite of metal handcuffs cutting into my skin. Then I'm wrenched to my feet and a too-bright light is flashed in my eyes.

"You are under arrest for the abduction of Kadence Mulligan. You have the right to remain silent. Anything you say can be used against you in a court of law. You have the right to an attorney. If you cannot afford an attorney, one will be appointed for you..."

The officer goes on with the familiar script, the same one you always hear on TV. I look over my shoulder as they drag me toward one of the squad cars. Lauren. Where's Lauren? I can't see her. Is she watching this? What is she thinking? Oh, Christ, no. Not now, after our perfect night together. A deputy shoves me by the shoulders down into the backseat, and before I can think of a single thing to shout out to Lauren, the door to the cop car is slammed shut.

TWENTY

LAUREN

DeSanto Residence
Thursday, April 5
11:52 p.m.

I am a fool. And apparently that's never going to change. I wrap my pillow around my head and squeeze my eyes tight. Then tighter. *When will you ever learn, Lauren?* When will you ever learn?

I've always said yes to everyone, to *everything*. Always so willing. It's made such a mess of everything, and now I'm going to make that same mistake with love? A sob rips up from my throat, and I smother it against the mattress.

Forget it. No more. *I am a rock. I am an island.* And Paul Simon's perfect lyrics hold me—most assuredly—as I cry myself to sleep.

TWENTY-ONE

JUDE

Sheriff's Office
Friday, April 6
1:00 a.m.

I turned eighteen a month ago. Usually that's a great thing, what everyone's looking forward to. Being an adult, getting the hell out of high school. Buying smokes without any hassle. Yeah. Except for the part where the first time I ever get in trouble with the law, I end up in the county jail on a Thursday night.

I'm dragged in, stripped, searched—and when I say searched, I mean *searched*, which is just as unpleasant as it sounds. They give me new clothes—an undershirt and these sky-blue hospital-like scrubs to wear. Then there's the fingerprinting and mug shot. The entire time I'm thinking, *This is not happening to me. This is someone else's life, or I've watched too many COPS episodes in a row before falling asleep and this is just a seriously vivid dream.*

No such luck. I am booked. Officially booked. Fingerprints permanently on file, forever. Then they ask me weird questions, like for a handwriting sample, and if I have a job, along with the basics of where I live and who I live with. But they don't ask a single thing about Kadence.

They say that these are all normal booking procedural questions. I mention a lawyer and they say yes I can have a public defender, that I will be appointed one tomorrow if I want. I ask for my phone call, but when I call my home phone, Dad never picks up. Shocker. We don't even have an answering machine.

I wonder if he'll come by tomorrow when news gets around at the garage that I've been arrested. I wonder if the disappointment will hit me fresh when he doesn't. But maybe Rocky will come by. Christ, that's fucking pathetic, hoping someone else's dad will come when you're dumped in jail.

By the time I'm processed, it's one in the morning and they're leading me to a holding cell. Which is when I see I won't be alone for the night. Well, I'll be alone in my cell, but I'm led by five other barred rooms, and it's classy in here, lemme tell you. Some dirty bastards probably picked up for being drunk and disorderly and one guy who's strung out on something because he's muttering crazy crap to himself in the corner. Most of them are quiet, but a couple call out to me as I pass. Things about how I've had sex with my own mother. How they want to have sex with my mother. How my mother must have had sex with a dog and that's how I was born. Why are mothers always dragged into this?

"I know why you're here," says the loudest one as the guard leads me past, "and they all know it too." He tilts his head toward the other winners in the cells around us.

And suddenly my mask fails me, all this BS calm I've worked so hard for. The new man I'm trying to become. As if I could actually change who I am. Jude the cool, the collected, full of hatred but outwardly impervious. It's fucking shattering.

Because people are staring at me again. I'm Nathan the stalker, Nathan the monster freak. And I'm flung back to the day it all happened. Fall of eighth grade. I'd been so stupid. All the previous year and that summer, I'd thought, I'd hoped, if I could only get through to Lauren, if I could make her see that we could still be friends, then everything would be okay again.

Sure we'd never go back to being as close as we'd once been. No more afternoons of peanut butter and honey sandwiches. I got that. But it would have been nice if she would acknowledge me in the hallway or maybe talk to me sometimes. I was so lonely. I didn't have any other friends. At all. It was social suicide to be friends with the guy with the exploding face, and I wasn't exactly putting myself out there after Lauren ditched me. I wasn't especially good at school, so not even the nerds wanted to be around me. Self-preservation mechanisms kicked in, and isolating myself was doing the trick. Except for the super-lonely part.

But I missed Ren so bad. I would have taken any scraps she'd thrown my way. She was the one person I believed could still look past my face and see *me*, just like she always had. So I was going to make a grand gesture, like in the movies. It was going to be so sweet and so thoughtful that there would be no way for her to keep ignoring me.

If I could write her a letter explaining everything perfectly, the way I never could in real life, then she'd see. And I'd make her something too, something beautiful and meaningful. She always kept these small keepsakes on top of her dresser. Snow globes and miniature porcelain swans and other knickknacks, but always classy things. Not junk. If I wanted to make something she'd remember me by, it had to be of the same caliber.

So I had this great idea. Origami. But not some crap little crumpled-paper kindergarten project. No, it would have to be intricate and delicate and personal. That would prove to her everything she meant to me and, along with the letter, would make her realize that we were the kind of friends who could never lose each other.

I got a bunch of books from the library and mowed lawns to save up money to buy the fancy origami paper from the craft shop. Then I practiced and practiced and practiced. I decided to make a design from the advanced origami book, this supercool firebird phoenix. Lots of colors, hundreds of intricate folds to imitate the feathers. It would symbolize our friendship: rising from the ashes. Just by looking at it, Ren would have to see how many hours I'd put into it. And therefore how much she meant to me.

The thing took me three weeks to complete. I'd finished half of it before realizing I'd done a bunch of the folds the wrong direction and the wings wouldn't fit on the right way. I had to scrap everything I had. But I didn't get mad or start cussing or anything. I just brushed what I'd done into the trash and started over.

There's this whole philosophy behind origami. Like Zen and crap. After all the hours of folding those tiny pieces of paper, trying to make them all uniform with my big, clumsy teenage guy hands, I realized pretty fast that I could either get so frustrated there'd be no way for me to continue, or I could get super chill about it all. Because of my end goal, getting Ren back as my friend, I was able to go the chill route.

I could put up with paper cuts and hours of messing up and working with a magnifying glass trying to fit the tiniest pieces of paper together until my eyes were so strained I could barely see straight. I didn't mind. The suffering made it better even. It proved my devotion. She would *feel* it all, just by looking at my finished creation.

Finally, twenty-two days after I'd started the phoenix, two and a half months after I'd started learning origami, I was ready. The phoenix was perfect. It looked as good as the one in the book. I grinned down at it, then grabbed a spiral notebook from my bag. I wrote my note.

Ren, I made this for you. I want us to be friends again. I know you have other friends now. That's cool. But maybe we can talk sometimes. I miss hanging out with you.

I frowned down at the note, chewing on the end of the pen. I felt like I should try to say more, but I didn't know what. Lauren was always so much better with words than I was. Like, sometimes I could put thoughts down in my notebooks, but this was different. This was to *her*. But I was confident the phoenix would say everything I couldn't. I signed the note and tore out the page. Then I folded it twice and slid it into my pocket.

I put the phoenix in an old Pop-Tarts box so it wouldn't get crushed on the way to school, then went to her locker. I knew Ren had history first period and didn't go by her locker because it was on the other side of campus. The halls were busy so no one noticed me sidle up to her locker.

I quickly rolled the tumbler to her combination and opened the locker. I was an office aide and had looked up Lauren's combo when the secretary wasn't looking. At the time, I didn't think of it as being creepy. I was still thinking in terms of grand gesture.

When I had Lauren's locker open, I pulled the note from my pocket, smoothed it out, and then grabbed the phoenix from the Pop-Tarts box. I set it all up on the tower of books in her locker where she couldn't miss it. Then I clicked the locker closed with a wide grin on my face. Grand gesture accomplished. Now it was time to wait for Lauren to come to me, amazed and overcome at my super thoughtful gift, and we could go back to the way things were.

So I waited.

And I waited.

And waited.

A week later I heard Lauren's voice saying my name. But she wasn't coming up behind me, putting a hand on my arm, and gushing over the phoenix.

No, it was her voice saying my name over the loudspeaker...to the whole damn school.

"Man, Nathan is such a stalker *freak*. You should have seen that nasty note he put in my locker last week. How did he even know my combination? It was soooooo creepy."

Her friend Kadence's voice came on next: "I can't believe you were ever friends with that monster. I mean, his face is so *gross*. He's a total Frankenstein, no, make that Zitzenstein." Then her voiced dropped to a dramatic Slavic accent, "I am Franken von Zitzenstein. I break into girls' lockers and leave creepy notes, and I vant to eat your brainz!"

And then Lauren laughed like it was the funniest thing.

The secretary came on then, telling the girls that one of them had accidentally set her bag on the button for the PA speaker. They apologized and went on to announce something about a talent show the school was putting on that night. I barely heard the snickers of those sitting around me in class. All that really registered was the sound of Lauren's laughter as my heart shattered into a hundred thousand pieces.

Life got bad after that. I'd only been invisible before. But after Kadence coined the nickname Zitzenstein, I found it in permanent marker on my locker. Jocks would ram my shoulder in the hallway and say it under their breath to me, either that or "stalker." I was beaten up a few times. The more popular Kadence and Lauren became, the worse the bullying got. But none of it hurt as much as Lauren laughing so hard the first time Kadence called me the name.

I've played through these memories so many times that I fast-forward through them in seconds as I glare at the men behind bars.

But I see something different on their faces than on the old bullies' faces in high school. They aren't just disgusted and amused at their own power to pick on someone weaker than themselves. They're afraid. Oh, they're taunting me. They think I'm a sick freak who likes to hurt girls for kicks. But there's fear underneath it too. Because I'm an unknown. What did I do to her? Nobody knows. People are always afraid of what they don't know. And part of me is glad for their fear. Because at least fear is better than disgust, isn't it? Fear at least has a degree of power to it. Disgust means you are the victim. Fear means you are their master.

If nothing else, I think, *at least there's that.* At least there is that. So I smile at them. I grin an evil fucking grin and make eye contact with each one that I can see from my vantage point. I hope it's a face that will haunt their dreams. I hope they think they're looking into the face of the devil himself.

There was never any real hope of rebirth for me. I get it now. I was always gonna be a monster one way or another. A phoenix is a bird that burns up and then is reborn again from the ashes, but I'm like one that stayed ash and never became a bird again. Then I smirk darkly. More like the origami one I made that was crumpled and tossed away with the half-empty neon-green slushies and candy wrappers in the dark trash can where I'm sure Lauren threw it.

I keep the grin plastered on my face the whole way to my cell. Until the barred door clanks shut behind me and the noise echoes off the gray-painted cement walls. The other inmates are silent now.

I sit down on the cot attached to the wall and fist the worn, dark-gray blanket in my hand. The same stupid hand that only hours ago was caressing Lauren's cheek. Because along with the rest of the accusing eyes of the world, Lauren now thinks the worst of me. And is she entirely wrong?

No. No, she's not. Christ. I thud the back of my head into the wall. You can't hurt people and then pretend it never happened. Consequences were always gonna catch up with me in one form or another. My eyes start stinging. I slam my palms against them. For real? I'm gonna start crying? Now? After all these years? I haven't cried since I got home from school that day she laughed over that goddamned loudspeaker.

I drop and yank the scratchy sheet and blanket over my body. Squeezing my eyes shut hard, I pretend I can go back to a time before monsters, before prison bars. Before the name Kadence Mulligan was even a whisper on the wind. Back to just a boy and a girl laughing and running through the woods, the taste of peanut butter on their tongues.

TWENTY-TWO

KADENCE

Found Video Footage
Kadence Mulligan's Laptop
Date Unknown

Image opens.

Kadence sits on a stool on what appears to be a stage set of some kind. A heavy, red velvet curtain hangs behind her. There is a red oriental rug on the floor. Her hair is piled on her head in curls, with a Rosie-the-Riveter bandana tied around it to keep it in place. She has on heavy cat-eye makeup, red lipstick, and a tidy, narrow-fitted button shirt tucked into a vintage, gray pencil skirt. She appears agitated as she taps her foot.

"Lauren said she wanted me to go solo," she begins. "I never would've done it if she hadn't given the okay. But then, when her voice didn't get better as quickly as we hoped, she started getting really weird." Kadence throws her hands up in the air, as if in exasperation. "It was these weird passive-aggressive moves, like she'd say, 'Great show the other day. But what happened with that last line of the song? That wasn't how we used to practice it.' As if the way we used to practice things was the only way they could go.

"I know it was hard for her, but I had to change things as I saw fit. The music was evolving. I know it hurt that it was evolving without her. I got that. So I understood when she said it. But some of the stuff that came later just made me go, what the heck is going on, Lauren?"

Kadence gets up from the stool and begins to pace back and forth, even though the top part of her head is no longer in view of the camera, only her mouth and body. She continues, "Some of her comments started getting nasty, which was never the way that Lauren and I were with each other. She'd say, 'Kady, I'm not trying to be mean, but I don't think you're a strong enough guitarist to hold that song on your own.' Lauren was always saying that. Like it made her comments less hurtful if she stuck that on at the beginning." Kadence makes air quotes. "'I'm not trying to be mean, but...'"

Kadence shakes her head. "It shocked me at first, but I got used to it and knew that whenever she said that, whatever came next was going to rip my heart out. *I'm not trying to be mean, but* you were really messing up the melody during the bridge of that song. *I'm not trying to be mean, but* without the harmonies, this other song totally falls flat. *I'm not trying to be mean, but* you're not getting the views on your new video like we got on our old stuff and I'm not sure you can make it as a solo artist. *I'm not trying to be mean, but* you know I'm the lyricist and I'm not sure you should be trying to write songs on your own."

Kadence sits back down on the stool hard, her shoulders crumpling. In the next second, they are shaking. It's clear that she's crying. When she looks back up at the camera, her expression is broken. "It's getting worse and worse. I know that I'm this confident person on the outside. And I guess"—she hiccups—"I guess that Lauren and I have had this symbiotic relationship over the past six years. I really relied on her, and I didn't think that it was unhealthy or anything. She's never turned on me like this before.

"I don't know, maybe it's because she's so upset about her voice. That's probably what it is." Kady wipes her eyes. "I should try to be more understanding. She's probably hurting so bad that she has to take it out on someone, and unfortunately right now that someone is me. But you know, I'm hurting too, and it's not fair. I don't deserve to be put down all the time. Lauren was never in it one hundred percent. Not like me. She wasn't the one putting in all of those hours trying to make us a success online. She wasn't the one making the videos happen and advertising and getting the word-of-mouth going.

"Ugh!" Kadence throws her hands up again. "I don't even know what I'm saying! Or why I'm recording it! It's not like I'll ever post this. I just have to get this off my chest. I have to be able to talk to someone, even if it's not a real, live person, even if in reality I'm only talking to myself." Her shoulders slump again and she bows her head. Then slowly she gets to her feet and walks toward the camera.

A few moments later, the image goes dark.

TWENTY-THREE

JUDE

Sheriff's Office
Friday, April 6
10:00 a.m.

The next morning a guard leads me out of my cell in cuffs. I'm led into a small room. It's cinder block. A dingy light blue. Cheery.

Two detectives sit in chairs opposite the one that the guard leads me to. I sit down, careful to keep my face a blank mask. The guard attaches shackles to my ankles and links a chain up to my handcuffs. I smirk. They must think I'm a very dangerous criminal. Oh look, I'm reverting to I-don't-give-a-shit Jude. Guess it's easier being him, at least in here. Glad some defensive mechanism is kicking in, because, truth is, most of last night I was scared shitless.

"Don't I get a lawyer?" I ask.

The first guy across the table is blond and on the shorter side but solid, like he was a wrestler in high school even though now he's gotta be in his late forties. He leans forward with his elbows on the table. "Only guilty people need lawyers. I'm Detective Kopitzke and this is Detective Miller. If you've got nothing to hide"—he spreads his hand wide—"then why don't we have a little chat?"

Yeah. I'm not an idiot. I wince overdramatically. "Really? You're starting off with the oldest line in the book?" I shake my head as if disappointed. "For shame, detective."

The detectives smile easily. The one who hasn't talked yet leans forward. He's older than the other guy, mid-fifties with high color in his cheeks and a mustache that looks like it belongs in the eighties. A sheen of sweat covers his balding head. "Are you asking for a lawyer?"

I hesitate while maintaining my mask of being a smirking, overconfident punk. Dad can't afford a lawyer, and I don't want the public defender. The public *pretender*. I think I'm smart enough not to say the wrong thing and incriminate myself. And I'm curious to know what evidence they based this arrest on. How bad is this?

"Nah, guess not." For now anyway. I shrug, then wink at the first detective, the one whose name started with K something. "Why would I need a lawyer when I can have a relaxed chat with you two gentlemen?"

Detective K continues. "So you acknowledge that we have explained your rights and you are willing to continue?"

I roll my eyes. "Yeah. So let's hear it." I lean back in my chair.

"A warrant to search your house proved very fruitful," the second detective, Mustache Man, finally pipes up.

My jaw tenses. Crap. If they searched my house, my room, then this isn't good. "And how did you get a warrant for that?" Who says TV never taught me anything?

"The local news station was filming the concert," Detective Mustache goes on. "And when they took a shot of the crowd, they caught you on camera with your own recording device. You seemed very intense on the video. Unusually so, and not merely in the manner of an avid fan. You appeared angry. And so we did some checking up on you.

"Turns out that Jude Williams used to go by the name *Nathan*

Williams. School records indicate that you were accused of stalking Kadence Mulligan and Lauren DeSanto, and later that your mother reported incidents of you being bullied because of it. She lodged an official complaint when she removed you from the school district and had you go live with her."

My hands ball into fists, a reaction that does not go unnoticed by either detective.

"That was enough to get us a search warrant," Detective Mustache finishes. I'm really starting to hate this guy, his blotchy cheeks, and the rodent that died over his lip.

"And then what we found," says Detective K, "well, what we found has us troubled, Jude." He opens a folder and spreads out several pictures. The first is a picture of my video camera. The next few are screenshots from videos I've taken.

They aren't just videos from the night that Kadence disappeared. They're videos of Lauren and Kadence over the past eight months, ever since I moved back to Pine Grove. In my defense, most are from the first few months. The first picture shows them in the lunch room, laughing together. It was right when school started, before Lauren lost her voice. There's another picture from a video of Kadence sneaking off into a bathroom with a boy who is definitely not Mason.

And then finally there's one of Lauren sitting bundled up in the courtyard all by herself. The snow was falling that day. During the spring and fall, the courtyard is filled during lunch with everyone eating out there, but in the dead of winter it's totally empty. But this was a couple months ago, in February. Things were bad between Lauren and Kadence because of Lauren's voice.

I swallow, ashamed. For the most part, I'd stopped following them around. The pictures and the videotaping—I'd cut out all that creepy shit I'd been doing when my head was so messed up by the meds.

But that day, Lauren...she looked so sad. So I followed her into the courtyard. I wanted to go up to her and ask what was wrong. To try to make her feel better and get her to laugh like in the old days. But of course I couldn't. There were too many years, too much history between us. She sat under a tree and watched the snow fall. And she was so beautiful that the old compulsion got hold of me. I pulled out my video camera and recorded her for the entire twenty minutes she managed to brave the freezing weather. I switched back and forth between watching the zoomed-in camera screenshot of her face and looking up to see the real thing. To be in the moment with her even though she didn't know I was there.

I'm not proud of it. I recognized it for the invasion of her privacy it was. It was the last time I ever recorded Lauren. Kadence, well, she was a different story.

"You see how bad this looks." Detective Mustache's voice breaks into my thoughts, bringing my ugly reality crashing back in.

I shrug. *Say nothing*, I remind myself.

"And then there's the notebook," Detective Mustache says. "Or should I call it more of a poetry *diary*?" He smirks and holds my beat-up, leather-bound notebook in his hands. In spite of the cuffs, I want to lunge for it. The skin on my neck feels hot and itchy, and my teeth grind together. My book, those pages...I can't stand the thought of his blunt, fat fingers touching them for another second but there's nothing I can do about it.

Detective K takes the notebook from Detective Mustache and I feel a small measure of gratitude. I get that this is good cop/bad cop and that I'm being played as far as feeling any sympathetic connection with Detective K, but whatever. It still makes me feel better to get my journal out of Detective Mustache's grubby hands.

"So, Jude, tell us what you know about Kadence Mulligan's disappearance."

I remain stonily silent.

"Where did you go after Kadence Mulligan's concert at Cuppa Cuppa on Friday, March 30?"

More silence from me.

"Okay," Detective K goes on, "next question. Can you tell us your whereabouts from March 30 at midnight to one p.m. on March 31?"

I stare coldly at both detectives. I don't have the energy for the jackass act anymore.

"See the thing is," Detective K says, "if you can't tell us where you were, things look bad for you. Let me make clear just how bad." He opens the journal, and I can see that they have marked certain passages with little yellow tabs. He begins to read: *Hatred, like pus, gathers and bursts from the blisters you burned in my skin.*

"You know, I get that." Detective K says. "We all get angry sometimes. But this next one, Jude, well, this is where it gets a little problematic." He starts reading, and I cringe from the first few words, knowing exactly which entry he's reading. It's from a long time ago. Right in the middle of the bad times.

I dream of my hands,

Long-fingered dreams,

Knuckles against the blush skin of your throat.

Will you cry out? Will you beg?

Will you scream like the day you were born?

Or will you die silent,

Silent like the cold, cold night.

"And then, well, Jude," Detective K flips to the end of the journal, to the last few pages, "there's the most recent entry. You were nice enough to give this poem a title." He reads the poem I wrote most recently: "Buried in the Wood."

TWENTY-FOUR

LAUREN

Riverview Trailer Park
Friday, April 6
10:00 a.m.

The woods are lovely, dark, and deep. Lovely, dark, and deep. I can't get this line out of my head as I stare into the woods behind the Riverview Trailer Park. It's not just the woods. I *feel* dark and deep. I haven't slept more than a few hours each of the last seven nights. I mean, I'm dead on my feet. *Dead* on my feet. Ha. It's almost laughable, but I don't let myself go there. Enough with the inappropriate emotions. The less sleep I get, the harder they are to manage. When exactly will the horror of this moment set in? Four hours from now? Six? Next week?

The constant pressure behind my eyes and the pounding in my head isn't helping either. I don't need a mirror to know that I look like hell. I feel like hell, but I suppose that—at least—is appropriate.

I should have stayed home. I know that. But I had to be here. I'm not alone either. At least a hundred people have shown up to help with the search. School was even canceled because so many students wanted to come.

Three large German shepherds are waiting in crates in the back of a Washington County Sheriff's Department pickup truck. I suppose they're going to lead the search.

It's all so freakin' surreal. How is it that just yesterday I was in the woods with Jude? The instant replay of the cops cuffing him in my front yard flashes in my mind again. The shouts, the lights, my mom's pale hand covering her mouth. It was all I could see as I lay in bed last night, unable to sleep.

Then this morning, the detectives sat me down and showed me videos Jude had taken of Kadence and me. "Stalker," we'd called him once upon a time. An old song by the Police drifts through my mind. *Every breath you take. Every move you make...*

And now I'm, I'm...

I'm second-guessing my decision to be here, that's what I'm doing. A few girls from school walk by, and when they notice me looking, they glance away. Despite Jude's arrest, people are still acting like me being here is an attempt to deflect attention from my own guilt. Hardly. Being here only makes me feel my guilt more keenly, but it's not because of what they think. I can't really blame them for what they're thinking. I'd probably be thinking the same thing.

A man in a shirt and tie is instructing ten younger-looking deputies. They're all wearing brown field jackets with "Washington County" printed on the back. They're all wearing radio headsets. The man in the tie is pointing and marking off a grid on a map.

The Mulligans are standing nearby. Mrs. Mulligan is clutching her husband like she might fall down. They were already old, but they look ancient now, far older than the last time I saw them a week ago. Has it only been a week? It seems like a year.

I'm hanging out at the back of the crowd. We're all wearing protective gloves and the recommended long pants tucked into our socks to protect us from wood ticks and stinging nettle. It's kind of a jungle back here.

Back when Jude was Nathan, he and I had a fort in these woods. We'd take his dog, Coco, back here on rabbit-hunting expeditions, though we never actually caught one. It was more the idea of it that we liked. A hunting adventure! I don't think either one of us could have handled hurting a rabbit back then.

Funny how things change.

Part of me would give anything to go back to that more innocent time. My stomach lurches at the memory of Nathan the boy and Jude the man. *Stalker.* What happened to him? *You,* a voice in my head whispers. *You* happened to him. I look around me, my breath coming in quick puffs in the cool air. What happened to all of us? How could it have come to *this?*

I shouldn't be here, I think again. But just as I'm about to go, the dogs are released from their crates. One of the deputies gives them some articles of clothing to smell: Kadence's paisley blouse and Jude's leather jacket. I feel sick. The dogs bark and wag their tails excitedly. I wonder if the dogs will pick up on my scent in the lining of Jude's jacket. I wrap my arms around my body, imagining the dogs lifting their noses in the air and then charging straight for me.

I sense the presence of someone right behind my shoulder. I tense instinctively but don't turn. No one has spoken to me since I arrived. No one has come within twenty feet of me. But I can feel the heat of another person. It feels male. Very male. I don't know how I know this, but I do. I can hear him breathing.

I'm about to walk away when a voice says, "I'm so sorry, Lauren."

I flinch and turn. It's Mason. Again I have the ridiculous urge to laugh because he's holding a hockey stick and I wonder if it's like a security blanket for him. I don't laugh though. Mainly because he does look really, really sorry.

"What are you sorry for?" I croak out.

His face looks pained. "For having doubted you. You don't look like you've been sleeping too good."

I give a little shrug, then bow my head and study my feet.

"Me neither," he says, which doesn't seem fair because he's as good-looking as ever. "How have you been feeling?"

"I have no idea," I say on an exhale. I don't plan on saying anything more, but Mason is looking at me expectantly so I add, "My parents are constantly asking me that too, and I have no idea. I know I'm supposed to feel a certain way. People expect me to be sad or mad or...scared. But most of the time I don't know what to feel, or if I even know *how* to feel." I throw my hands up in the air, exasperated. "And then when I do feel something, it seems like it's the wrong thing to be feeling. I don't know. I-I just...And being out here—" I break off again, unable to finish the sentence as I look around us. So much for being the word girl. I've got nothing.

He nods and steps a little closer. "Don't worry, Lauren. We'll find Kady." His words are perfect. And they stab at my heart. "This whole thing has been doubly hard on you. It's not fair how you've been treated. I've missed seeing you at school."

I raise one eyebrow. It's taken me a while, but I'm finally getting better at detecting a lie when I hear one. Mason and I have never really talked about what happened between us. I bet my absence from school has made his days a lot more comfortable. "You've missed me?" I ask, and my doubt is clear.

He smiles a little, knowing he's been caught. "I mean, I've noticed that you weren't there."

"Right." I shake my head slightly and turn my attention back to the deputies.

"I heard you were hanging out with that Williams kid," he says quickly. "I mean...before..."

"A little," I say with a shrug of one shoulder. Word gets around fast.

"Lauren." He puts his hand on my shoulder like he's trying to keep me from walking away. I wasn't going anywhere though. I can't even feel my feet. "What I'm trying to say, Lauren...is that I'm so glad he didn't hurt you too."

My hands start to tremble. "Thanks." What else do I say to that?

"And I feel bad about the cops...you know...getting the wrong idea about the fight in the cafeteria. I should have been supporting you. That was wrong of me. You know, not to be there for you."

"It's okay. It's been a weird time. For all of us." At least I can give Mason absolution.

He breathes out in a long, slow breath, then turns to stare into the woods. "I can't stand the thought of Kady being out there somewhere."

"I know," I say. I squeeze my gloved hands into fists. I wish I had a guitar or my uke. Or better yet, a drum. Something to smash out all the emotions I can't name.

"I had to be here today," Mason says, "but if we find her, I really hope I'm not the one to do it. I don't think I could handle that. My imagination is already driving me crazy. The real thing...it would be too much."

"Odds are against us," I say. "There's got to be a hundred people here."

"One twenty-seven," he says. "I saw the check-in sheet. It's nice to know how many people care about her. She was such a good person. She didn't deserve for some freak to take out his rage on her." He sniffles and wipes at his eye.

Mason was always such a sweet guy. Too good for Kady. It's a mean thought to have in this moment, but that doesn't make it less true. "Hey," I say, reaching out awkwardly to pat his arm. "We don't know what happened to her yet."

"I have a pretty good idea."

I glance at him to check his expression. Is he just being pessimistic, or does he actually know? Before I can figure him out, I'm distracted by his sudden decision to swing his hockey stick through a patch of tall grass, like a farmer with a scythe.

"What's the stick for?" I ask because by now I really have to know.

He looks down like he forgot he was holding it. "Kadence gave it to me for Christmas. I used it to score the winning goal against Roosevelt. I thought it would help me clear brush today, look under things."

"Sounds like you do want to find her then."

"Like I said, I'm hoping someone else does, but I thought the stick might bring us some luck."

The man in charge picks up a hand-held loudspeaker and addresses the crowd. "We'll be breaking into twelve groups of about ten people," he says. "You'll each be given a team leader and assigned a portion of the grid. The plan is to spread out in a line and walk from the boundary of the trailer park straight back to the highway. If anyone finds anything of interest, notify your team leader.

"Team leaders, if it's something that we need to check out, you are to alert me via radio."

At that point they start calling names and assigning us to teams. Everyone stares when my name is called, but Mason squeezes my hand as if his approval should satisfy the group.

A few minutes later we are standing in a line, evenly spaced, staring into the woods. Someone blows a whistle and we start walking. Mason is nowhere near me now. Though Mrs. Fitzpatrick from the convenience store by my house walks on my left, and the high school volleyball coach walks on my right, I am in my own little bubble, staring at the ground. I don't share Mason's hope that we'll find anything.

There are no search dogs in my group, but I can hear them bellowing as they pull their handlers ahead of our line.

The ground is soft from the recent melt, and the ground cover is thick with nettles and broken twigs and branches. It's slow going. I climb over a fallen branch, happy for the gloves that protect my hands when I stumble and fall. No one helps me up. That's okay. I understand. It takes longer to clear a name than it takes to smear one.

We are forty-five minutes into our gruesome task when the dogs start howling and someone blows a whistle in three sharp bursts. I freeze, feeling the icy rush of fear run down my arms. No. No way.

Everyone starts running to the sound. I am several seconds behind, not feeling the earth under my feet. It's like running on a trampoline, unable to find the right purchase on the ground. The pine branches slap against my face, and tears are streaming from my eyes.

When I catch up to the rest of the group, I push through the circle of people standing around a dark rectangle of newly disturbed earth.

TWENTY-FIVE

JUDE

Sheriff's Office
Friday, April 6
10:30 a.m.

"We've got your videos that prove you were obsessed with Kadence Mulligan"—Detective Mustache slams his hand down on the table over the scattered photographs—"your poetry, which all but details how you planned to strangle Kadence, and then there's this."

He pulls out my laptop. I guess somehow they were able to get past my password. I shrink farther into my seat. I feel another rush of wordless anger and fury.

Detective Mustache clicks several times and then spins the laptop around on the table to face me. He's opened the calendar application on my personal Outlook. Where obviously I already know what he's trying to show me. In it I've detailed dates, times, and locations. Showing that I followed Kadence and Lauren. I had their schedules down pat. I knew when Kady got her weekly mani-pedis. Not that pointing out, *Hey, look, most of those notations are from August through December when I was a little nuts on meds* is much of a defense.

Especially since I *did* continue to follow Lauren. But only to her doctors' appointments. I noted exactly how long each one lasted. I was worried about her, and I guess I thought knowing how long the appointments were could give me some indication of whether or not her voice was getting better. And Kady, well, I kept track of her concerts and other things because I knew it was hurting Lauren not to be singing with her anymore. And you just had to watch that witch.

But looking into each of the detective's faces, I know that my stupid, paltry explanations will sound like just that. Stupid excuses. Excuses offered by a jackass trying to get out of what looks like damning evidence. Like it fucking matters. They'd already convicted me before I'd stepped a foot in this stupid-ass room. I feel the heat rising up my neck and reach up to scrub my hands over my face. But of course, my wrists catch in the cuffs and only make it halfway there. Which makes my agitation all the more obvious. I want to laugh. I look guilty even when I'm trying specifically not to.

"So you see, Jude," Detective K says, "this doesn't look too good. But if you confess now and tell us where Kadence's body is, then it will go easier for you in the long run. Judges take this kind of thing into consideration. How helpful you've been along the way."

I feel my eyes widen.

He leans in, blocking my view of Detective Mustache. "Look, I get it. We've all been obsessed about a girl at some point. So this went a little further than you meant. It got out of hand.

"You followed her home after the show at Cuppa Cuppa and tried to talk to her, and she wouldn't listen. You got angry. Lost your temper. A guy can get frustrated after paying a girl attention for all that time and then when you finally talk to her, she blows you off. It was late at night, no one around. So maybe you got mad, and maybe it was an accident. That's understandable. Accidents happen.

"And then your truck was right there and you just tossed her in. Is that how it happened, Jude?"

I bang my hands on the table hard, so hard the chains on my cuffs rattle. "Shut up! That's not what happened. I didn't kill Kadence Mulligan!"

Detective Mustache comes in now, palms planted on the table. "Oh no? You've got motive, opportunity. Hell, you've even got a truck to move the body."

"No, that's not what—"

"And all those big, dark woods behind the trailer park to bury her." He cuts me off. "You were obsessed with Kadence Mulligan. Everything we've looked at"—he gestures at the table—"makes that perfectly clear. Why else would you be following her and her friend around like this? Why else would you be stalking their every move?"

They're twisting it. This was never about Kadence. Well, it was, but it wasn't.

"I wasn't stalking them."

"Taking pictures? Video?" Detective Mustache looks back at the laptop. "K. hair appt. Four seventeen to five thirty-nine p.m.," he reads from the calendar. "Mighty specific for someone who's not a stalker. And these increasing numbers all along the bottom of every day. Mind enlightening us about what those are? Counting up to something? Something happen once it hits a certain number? Did Kadence's time run out?"

Dickhead isn't even making any sense now. "They're YouTube views, dipshit. Of their videos." Then I drop my head to my hands so I can finally scrub my face hard with the heels of my palms. I should shut up at this point. I haven't slept enough and everything's all screwed up in my head, but Dickhead Detective Mustache isn't having it.

"Why were you following them?" he shouts in my face.

"*Because I love her!*" I shout back.

I'm so wound up that I've jumped to my feet too, but I'm half bent over because my hands are cuffed to my ankles and the chain isn't long enough. My chest heaves up and down, and my blood whistles in my ears. *Damn it!* I wasn't supposed to lose my temper. But all this crap they're saying. The look on their faces right now, as if they've won some great prize. It's probably a good thing they have me handcuffed or else I'd punch their smug faces.

"So," says good cop Detective K, "you loved Kadence Mulligan?"

I cringe at the thought and then I start laughing. I hear the manic edge to it, but what the hell else am I gonna do? These goddamn idiots. With all their *detectiving*. "Christ, no," I say, finally getting myself back under control. I look away from them toward the cinder-block wall. "Not her," I murmur under my breath. I don't know if they heard and I don't particularly care.

I look back and forth pointedly at each of the detectives. "I'd like my lawyer now." I have no illusions about a lawyer actually doing anything useful, but asking for one should get me out of this room for the moment, and that's good enough for me.

TWENTY-SIX

LAUREN

Behind the Riverview Trailer Park
Friday, April 6
11:00 a.m.

I know what this dark patch of earth is. I'm not an idiot. But I cannot wrap my brain around what this means. How could Kadence have ended up here? Here? The tears dry on my cheeks as bone-deep confusion paralyzes me. It's Billy with the frog all over again, except of course this is no frog. This is a grave. For a body. Kadence's body. Deep in the ground behind the trailer park. How? I don't understand.

Of all the places that Kadence thought she was going, this was not one of them. I thought—I never thought—I can't seem to keep an idea straight in my head as I grip the bottom of my jacket.

Two young deputies are already digging. Murmurs pass through the crowd as the other officers push us back. I look up and see that many people have turned their backs on the scene. They cover their mouths. A few look on in morbid fascination. Some girls are crying on the shoulders of the guys who came with them. Not me. I don't cry. The panicky thoughts have passed. Now I feel nothing.

It doesn't take long for the deputies' shovels to find the bottom of the grave. They are careful. They are respectful. They don't want to harm the body. It feels almost religious—how they move, how solemn the crowd is. Mrs. Fitzpatrick even pulls out her rosary beads.

I've never been good with religion. To me, it looks more like the deputies are harvesting a potato.

After the deputies brush away the remaining thin layer of dirt, they gently flip back a sheet and the entire crowd gasps. My own chest heaves. There is no relief, no easy end to this, and again I'm left wanting to laugh, cry, and scream all at once.

Because it's not Kadence. It's the body of a dog. Buried with her favorite item, one of the neon-orange chew toys Jude always bought for her after she destroyed the last.

It's Coco.

TWENTY-SEVEN

KADENCE

Found Video Footage
Kadence Mulligan's Laptop
Date Unknown

Image opens.

Kadence sits on a stool in front of the red velvet curtain again. She's in full makeup, but one of her false eyelashes looks improperly applied and hangs halfway off, giving her the appearance of a drooping eye. Her usually full magenta hair is flat on one side, like she's been sleeping on it and hasn't looked in the mirror. Though her makeup is thick, there are still visible shadows underneath her eyes.

"Hello, my beautiful Kady-Dids!" she says cheerfully, giving a wide, toothy smile, but within seconds, it falters, then collapses completely. She gets off the stool and comes forward as if she's about to switch the camera off, but then she says, "You know what? You are my fans, and I know you'll love me no matter what. Right, guys?"

She sits back down on the stool. She takes a deep breath and looks away from the camera. She blinks hard, the false eyelash that's barely attached flapping wildly. She notices and angrily pulls at it until it detaches. She winces slightly, but then a moment later yanks at the other one until it comes free too. She drops them to the floor, still breathing heavily and not saying a word. Finally, after another half minute of full silence, she looks back up at the camera.

"I try to make this a positive show, you know, guys? I try to look on the bright side of life. But sometimes..." Tears track down her cheeks.

"I've talked a lot about Lauren and me on the show. Well, today I want to tell you a story about a boy. Not *my* boy." Kadence smiles sadly and swipes at her cheeks. "This is a story about Lauren's boy. You see, when I told you the story of how I met Lauren that day in seventh grade, I didn't tell you the whole story.

"Before I became Lauren's best friend, she had another best friend. A boy named Nathan. I never knew that. She never said anything about him being her friend. Not a single thing. All she ever said was that this Nathan kid was sort of creepy and that he would follow her around. She told me he said mean things to her. Naturally, I tried to protect her from him. Whenever he came close, I steered us in the other direction." Kadence looks up at the camera and her eyes are full of emotion as if she's pleading with her audience.

"He backed off the rest of that year. It didn't get really ugly until eighth grade when Lauren complained to her counselor that Nathan was stalking her." Kadence's face scrunches up and she shudders. "Word got around. Lauren made sure of it. I assumed it was the truth—I never imagined she could be vindictive and lie about something like that."

Kadence squares her shoulders and sits up straighter on the stool. "But it turns out that sometimes you never really know someone. Even the person who's so close to you that you call her sister..." Another tear runs down her cheek, but she doesn't stop talking. "Anyway, I didn't think anything about this. Yes, it was sad that this boy was bullied because of what Lauren told everyone. Bullied so bad that he had to change schools. But like I said, I didn't think anything of it." Kadence shakes her head.

"I know that was selfish of me not to think more about it, but I was young. I guess that's no excuse." She shakes her head again and looks off to the side. She swallows hard and then continues, looking back up at the camera. "I didn't know the full story until the boy came back this year and confronted me.

"He changed his name, changed his look. He'd really gotten himself together, moved past all the hurtful things that Lauren had done to him. And that's when he told me that he hadn't been just *some guy* to Lauren. He had been her best friend before I came to town and she completely dropped him. Started ignoring him like he was nothing, like he'd never existed. Just like that, poof!

"They'd spent practically every day together for like four years, and then one day she cut him loose like he was nothing. He told me that hurt worse than any of the things people said to him, more than any of the times he got beat up." Kadence swipes at her eyes again. "I'd never seen someone look so raw like that, this guy who was a stranger to me really, coming up and telling me all of these things that I knew were so dark and deep to him. But he was baring his soul to me and all because he wanted to warn me.

"He was telling me who Lauren really was. He said I needed to know. He said this because"—Kadence's voice breaks—"because there were rumors about the way she was looking at my boyfriend."

Kadence's whole body shakes on the stool now in open sobs, and her words can barely be heard. "I don't know if he told me as a way"—sob—"to get back at her...or, or"—sob—"because he was genuinely"—sob—"worried about"—sob, hiccup—"me. But I followed them to this fort in the woods, and I saw"—she gulps for air—"I saw...them making out. Heavily. All over each other."

She is silent several long minutes while she gets herself under control. The video keeps recording through it all. She goes offscreen for a minute and then comes back with a box of Kleenex. She wipes her eyes and blows her nose and then goes offscreen again, coming back without the Kleenex. She sits back down on the stool again. Her breathing is calmer in spite of her puffy eyes and slightly reddened nose.

She looks straight into the camera. "I thought I knew Lauren DeSanto. But I was wrong, and what Nathan told me only confirms it. Lauren was never the girl that I thought. I'm not the first person that she's done this to. Stabbed in the back. Betrayed by messing around with their boyfriends. There have been others. Another girl back when we were in eleventh grade, the same girl who beat us in the eighth-grade talent show, who I guessed Lauren still felt threatened by.

"Turns out Lauren slept with her boyfriend and totally destroyed her confidence until she moved away from our school. I mean, I can barely believe it, but after what happened with her and"—she gulps, tears shimmering in her eyes again—"and my..." She swipes angrily at her eyes. "After what happened to me, I went and talked to that other girl's boyfriend. At the time, I'd never believed the rumors, but he confirmed it. And now with Nathan's story and what's happened to me, it's a pattern. I guess she gets off on this stuff."

Kadence's jaw tightens and she looks furious. "Lauren seems like a shy, unassuming girl. Like you'd never think she could pull off a lie if she wanted to. But that's the way she wants to come off. It's the ultimate mask. She's a wolf in sheep's clothing, and I'm going to confront her about it all. She had the audacity to ask me to play at the coffee shop where she works. As if she hadn't all but slept with my boyfriend! As if she hadn't betrayed me deeper than any friend can betray another."

Kadence shakes her head in disbelief and swipes angrily at another tear. "But that's fine with me. I'm going to go sing at her coffee shop.

And afterward I'm going to talk to her. I'm going to say everything that's ever needed to be said. And she is going to answer for what she's done."

The image goes dark.

TWENTY-EIGHT

JUDE

Sheriff's Office
Saturday, April 7
12:01 p.m.

They can't hold me. Without a body or any physical evidence tying me to a crime, they can't keep me. And my thirty-six-hour hold is up. Screw you, county bastards.

The property clerk eyes me warily from behind the counter as she hands me two extra-large Ziploc bags with all of my personal items: clothes, belt, wallet, cell phone in one, boots in the other. I grab them a little more roughly than is necessary. I stop myself from baring my teeth at her. *Want to gawk at the scary murder suspect some more? Let me at least give you a show.* 'Cause yeah, pretty sure this is a sneak peek of the rest of my life if Kadence is never found.

Suspected murderer. There's a label you can't outrun by switching school districts. I heard from the latest arrival in the cell next to me that I'm already headline news. And that they dug up Coco. My jaw flexes. Poor ol' girl. My good, good dog. I still can't get used to the idea she's gone, but at least she went peacefully in her sleep. And now those shit-heads have disturbed her grave.

I step behind a curtain and yank my pants on, then pull my thermal on over my head. I jerk my belt through the loops on my pants furiously and pull on my boots without bothering with the laces. I want to get the hell out of here.

I jam my wallet in my pocket and then I'm out the door. The freezing wind whips through my thin, long-sleeved shirt. The clerk kindly informed me that they're keeping my jacket for an indefinite period of time in case they need to use the search dogs again. No, of course they couldn't use my cheap two-dollar socks. It's gotta be my damned prized bomber jacket.

No one's here to pick me up, even though they called my dad. They even got hold of him. Parking lot's empty. I'm surprised that I'm surprised.

My jaw flexes as I use my thumb to flip through the contacts on my phone. It's a short list.

I call Rocky. He picks up on the second ring. "What's up, man?"

I stare at the ground. Is he serious? "Um. You been around? Heard what's going on?"

"What's going on?" He sounds genuincly confused. "Me and the fam are visiting my dad a few hours up north. What's up?"

Well, damn. Guess he's not gonna be able to swing by to pick up my sorry ass then. "Nothing. Just a misunderstanding." I kick at a rock on the ground and jam the hand not holding the phone into my pocket. "Forget about it."

"Jude." The sounds of laughing, screeching kids in the background fade, as if Rocky has moved into a different room. "You don't sound so good. What's up, dude? Problems with your old man?"

I laugh bitterly. For there to be problems, that'd mean Dad would have to actually acknowledge my existence. "It's nothing. Everything's fine. You have a good time with your family. See you when you get back." I hang up before he can say anything else.

I squeeze my eyes shut for a long moment, then open them and scroll through the rest of my contacts. My thumb hovers over Lauren's name. Before I can stop myself, I push Connect. It rings four times, then goes to voice mail. It rang just long enough for me to wonder if she clicked "send to voice mail" herself or if she genuinely wasn't around to hear the call. I click "end call" before it gets to the beep. Then I ignore my quickly numbing fingers and type out a quick text:

Me: Lauren, you know I had nothing to do with Kady's disappearance, right? You believe me, yeah? Please.

I hit Send before I can chicken out. The wind starts blowing so loud it's whistling in my ears. I stare at my phone until the little phone light turns off. There's no return text.

She's just not by her phone. It's probably in the other room. Maybe buried in her purse where she can't hear it. I mean, she's gotta understand there's no real evidence against me, right? She knows me. After everything we shared, those kisses in the woods...she has to know...

But then my jaw hardens. *What does she know, Jude? Huh? What exactly does she know?* The police probably told her you were stalking her and Kadence. Showed her what they found in your room—the pictures, the videos, the calendar. They'd have made it clear that you're a sick freak.

She's afraid of you now. She'll never talk to you again, much less ever let you touch her. She'll never climb behind you on your bike and wrap those sweet arms of hers around your waist, never again whisper your name in that needy way after you've kissed her...

I don't realize I'm stomp-pacing back and forth with my hands balled into fists until I'm interrupted when the door opens behind me. I pause and turn to see the property clerk standing with her body half shielded by the door. "I called a cab for you," she says, pointing at a yellow taxi that's pulling into the parking lot.

"Here." She offers me a twenty-dollar bill. The gesture is personal—not a gift from the county—but I can't tell if it's because she feels bad my dad didn't come or because she'd rather not have a potential murderer hanging around outside her window. I want to laugh. I want to scream. Instead, I turn my back on her offer and slip into the back of the cab. Owe nothing to anyone. New words to live by.

When I get home, Dad's truck is in the driveway. I pay the cab driver with my last twenty bucks and step out onto my gravel driveway. The trailer, *home, sweet home*—if that's what you can call this beat-up box of rusting steel and aluminum siding—looks as crappy and stupid and useless as my whole goddamn life. The fury that lit outside the sheriff's office starts all over again, and this time it's not a slow burn. I blow my lid.

I run up the weather-worn steps, throw open the door, then slam it behind me so hard the whole trailer shakes. Dad's sitting in the same place he always is on that same pumpkin-colored velvet couch from the seventies. It's worn through the fabric down to the cushion in an ass-shaped impression where he sits. So washed up he can't even be bothered to come get his own goddamn kid out of jail.

He glances up for one second. One glance. That's all he gives me, then his gaze goes back to the TV. One glance. Yep. That's apparently all I'm worth. I'm so furious that my breath is coming out audibly. My chest moves up and down, up and down like one of those old-time bellows. Still, my father doesn't notice.

Or maybe he does hear me, but having a son booked on suspicion of murder doesn't fit into his narrow goddamn little life of working at the garage, coming home, drinking his goddamn beer, and watching his goddamn sports.

I feel the veins standing out in my forehead as I stomp through the living room. I go straight to the bathroom and strip off every single thing I'm wearing and get into the shower. I don't wait for the water to warm up. I know I'm rank. I haven't showered or brushed my teeth in two days. I have to get clean.

The blast of cold water is good. It makes me feel something other than the blinding rage. It distracts me from the thoughts of my fingers around my father's throat. After a few minutes, the water warms, then turns to blistering heat. I put a hand on the wall and lean my head into the spray, holding my position until the water turns cold again. I crank the handle hard to the right and stand under the dripping showerhead, still breathing so hard I'm dizzy with the rush of blood.

I'm not quite under control yet. There's too much crap in my head. I had so many plans, but everything got shot to hell. I don't know what I'm doing anymore. I don't know what any of this is for. I don't know if I ever did.

I slam an open palm against the tile wall. All I know is my world got turned upside down when I showed up for school one day in seventh grade and my best friend suddenly stopped talking to me. Everything since then has been all screwed up, right until this goddamn second. My body shakes as I reach for a towel and dry myself off. My hand fumbles through my pants on the ground. I find my cell phone and check to see if there are any texts. But the screen is blank.

No texts.

No Ren.

I shove open the door to the bathroom and stalk toward my room in only a towel. *I just need a little space,* I think as I throw open the door and step into my room. *I need to calm down.* But then I see what's become of the one place I always felt safe with my darkest thoughts.

They never had to come out into the light of day if I could keep them contained here in my room or buried in the pages of my journal.

But now my room's screwed. My journal's gone. All the drawers in my dresser have been emptied, crap all over the floor. My mattress and box spring are overturned and cut, gutted down to the springs. Fingerprint powder dusts every flat surface. My books, vintage poetry I collected from the half-price bookstore, are flung on the ground like someone swept the bookshelf with their arm. Some of the them lie open, spines split. One of my favorites, a collection of Robert Frost poems, has a large boot print across its front cover.

My neck is hot. All of me feels hot. The blood is back screaming in my ears. *Two roads diverged in a yellow wood. Two roads diverged in a yellow wood.*

I jerk on some clean clothes from the pile that has been tossed on the floor. From my closet, I yank out my heaviest coat. It has a fleece lining though it smells like oil from being worn at the garage a lot. I pull it on.

I walk back out to the living room. Dad doesn't acknowledge me. I grab his keys from the ugly ceramic bowl on the counter, then reach for a bottle of Jack and a pack of smokes from the cupboard. Dad keeps all his vices in one place. Handy.

"What do you think you're doing?" he asks.

I just flip him off and walk for the door, holding the bottle underneath one arm and tucking the cigarettes into the pocket of my coat. Suddenly Dad gets some life in him. He stands up and blocks the door. This makes me laugh.

He glowers at me. "Don't you think you've gotten into enough trouble? You are not leaving this house with that bottle."

I swear there's a flash of burning light behind my pupils and then I'm drawing back my arm. My fist connects with the stubbled flesh of his jaw in a hard, decisive punch. With a weird sort of detachment, I note that it doesn't sound like punches do in the movies. More of a quick thwack than a satisfying, reverbed Hulk smash noise. I feel the hit all the way up my arm to my shoulder, and it hurts like a mother. Dad crumples to the floor. I don't know if he's knocked out, but he doesn't get up again. I don't say a word as I step over his body and close the door behind me.

TWENTY-NINE

MASON

Sheriff's Office—The Interview Continues
Monday, April 2
11:52 a.m.

Kopitzke: What more can you tell me about Lauren and Kadence's relationship?

I know what he's getting at. Ever since I gave him my account of the fight between Kadence and Lauren, I wished I could take it back. Girls fought. My little sisters loved each other, but they could go at it like curly-horned mountain goats. Why should Kady and Lauren be any different?

Mason: Kadence and Lauren loved each other. That fight last week didn't mean anything.

Besides, there wouldn't even have been a fight if not for me. In fact, sometimes I wonder if I am to blame for all of their rocky patches.

The first time there was a little bit of trouble, maybe even the seeds of what finally blew up into this big recent fight, was sophomore year. Kadence and I had been dating for three months, and it had been seriously the best three months of my life. We were sitting on my back deck and eating the leftover chow mein I'd made the family for Friday dinner the night before. Kadence put her chopsticks in her mouth like walrus tusks. It was really cute, and she could laugh like nobody else. It was the kind of laugh that made you laugh too, even when you knew it wasn't *that* funny.

Of all the time we spent together, I loved our weekend time the best. That's when she was most herself. Easy. Casual. No makeup. I was kind of proud of the fact that I was the only one who saw her real face.

It was always a shock on Monday mornings when I'd see her again in full getup, because that girl loves her makeup. Or maybe she was just so insecure she needed to wear a mask around everyone else. No one else saw that. The insecurity. But she didn't need the mask with me. I knew Kadence. I knew her better than anybody else knew her. Even better than Lauren.

Anyway, we were on my back deck waiting for Lauren to pick Kadence up. They had an appointment with a real recording studio to record their new song. They said they were making a "rough cut," which I guess is like a demo or something. When Lauren finally texted that she'd "be there in five," Kady jumped up and pulled a bag out of her backpack. She ran into the bathroom, saying she had to "fix her face." I didn't think anything needed fixing. To me she was perfect.

That's what made me a total dick. Here I had this perfect girlfriend, and while she was in the bathroom I was out on the front step with her friend, checking her out. I didn't mean to, I swear. It was just that sometimes you can't help looking.

Lauren never wore anything too revealing, not like Kady. But I don't know, that kind of modesty has its own, you know, appeal. And B.K.

(Before Kadence), Lauren was the kind of girl who was really more my type. She was short but curvy. Tan and dark-haired. Smart too. Book smart, and there was nothing more intriguing than a girl with a book.

Hey, Mason, she said that afternoon.

Hey.

Kady's here, right?

Yeah, she'll be out in a second.

I forcibly averted my eyes from her chest. And that's where my brilliant conversation skills came to an end because God knows how hard it is to talk to a girl when you're wondering what her skin feels like.

See, this is what I mean when I say everything was my fault. I thought I appreciated Kadence, but it wasn't until she was gone that I realized how good I had it. I never deserved her, but Kadence thought I *did*. That's why I had no business thinking about Lauren. Ever.

"What's going on out here?" Kadence asked, coming up behind me and stepping out of the house. Her eyes were outlined in thick black eyeliner, pulled into cat-eyes at the corners.

"Nothing," Lauren said because of course to her, it was nothing. "You ready?"

"I was born ready," Kadence said with a wink to me, then she took my face in her hands and kissed me in a way that was nearly indecent for public display. It did the trick though. Like a wet paper towel on a blackboard, Lauren was wiped clean away.

"I can't wait to see you tomorrow," she whispered in my ear. That's how great Kadence was. She made me believe in the future, and I could stand as much confidence as I could get in that department.

Dad traveled a lot with his new job, and Mom worked all the time too. That left me in charge of my little sisters. Between them and hockey practice, it didn't leave much time for anything else. It was tough sometimes.

Kopitzke: You think Kadence and Lauren are that close? That they love each other?

Mason: I didn't mean it like that.

Kopitzke: No, I understand what you meant. What about next year, then? Are they planning to go to college together?

Mason: No. Kady isn't going to school next year. She wanted to focus on her music. *Wants.* She wants to focus on her music.

Kopitzke: What about you? College next year?

I shrug. I've been accepted to State, but I don't have much for college savings. I was counting on a hockey scholarship coming through for me, but it's not looking good. Mom and Dad said we'd figure something out, but I don't see how.

When I start to get down, I think about what Kady always says: *Life is short, my darlings. Reach for the stars before they burn out!* It's a little cheesy—okay, maybe a lot cheesy—but when you're with her, she makes you believe that nothing's out of reach. The stars. A good life. A life with *her*. Because even without a hockey scholarship, I have Kadence.

Kopitzke: What about your family? Did they love Kadence like everyone else seems to?

Mason: My little sisters think she's a princess or something because she's so pretty and she sings to them. It's like Snow White or something. Or Ariel. Man, Meredith's crazy about Ariel, and Kadence could look just like her with her hair, plus Kadence knows how to play all the games they like.

Watching Kady play with my sisters always made me imagine what it might be like to be married. To be Mr. and Mrs. Sisken and have a family of our own. Kind of freaky to be in high school and thinking about things like that, but Kadence could make me think all kinds of crazy things—like maybe even running away with her to Mexico. We could run a seaside bar where she could sing every night, and I'd mix drinks and make all this fancy Mexican food. Not like, for real. Just one of those stupid fantasies. But I don't know. A little house here in Pine Grove wouldn't be too bad. Some day.

Mason: Can I go back to your first question?
Kopitzke: You can do anything you'd like, Mason.
Mason: You asked me what Kadence and Lauren were like together. It just came to me. The best way to describe them...Do you know what mole sauce is?

Kopitzke shakes his head.

Mason: We did a food unit in Spanish class. It's this sauce made out of chili peppers and chocolate. That's the way it was with Kadence and Lauren—two very good but very different things that are exceptional together.

Spicy and sweet, I think. Although sometimes I don't know which girl is which. You take one look at Kady with all her beauty and style and think, *spice*. Yet for all of Lauren's sweetness, that girl has a wicked side too.

I almost say something more, then think better of it and close my mouth. Lauren would never hurt Kady. Not for real. She loved her too much.

I close my eyes. The fluorescent lighting is starting to make them burn. I hear a soft shuffle of something sliding across the table, and when I open my eyes, there's a clear plastic bag on the table. The bag is sealed with tape marked: EVIDENCE and DO NOT BREAK SEAL.

Kopitzke: Do you recognize what's in this bag?

I don't answer out loud, but I nod my head. It's a uniform shirt from Cuppa Cuppa. There's an obvious bloodstain in the center, just under the logo. I understand what the detective's showing me, and I understand his unspoken questions. Do I want to rethink my answers? Is Lauren DeSanto really the girl I think she is?

THIRTY

JUDE

Williams Residence
Saturday, April 7
2:09 p.m.

My boots crunch on the gravel driveway as I walk to the truck. I yank open the door and shove the bottle of Jack under the passenger seat. Soon I'm headed down the open road.

I end up driving aimlessly for a couple hours, listening to a rock station at full volume, screaming along until my throat and ears ache and some of the rage burns off. I only turn around when there's just enough gas to get me back to Pine Grove. Rebel without a freakin' cause, no joke. I flip the old radio dial roulette style, and it lands on Willie Nelson singing about all the girls he's loved before.

"Yeah. You and me both, old man."

Then as I pull back into town, Johnny Cash comes on, singing "Hurt." Damn this is a good song. Like the exact song I was meant to hear right now. I pull off to the side of the road so I can listen to it without any distractions. I run a hand down over my face when it's over, feeling...*affected*.

It's only then that I look around and see that I'm stopped across the street from the junior high. It's deserted since it's the weekend. I didn't mean to come here. Least I don't think I did. Then again...isn't this where everything always comes back to? Back to Lauren. Back to this place. The place where Lauren ditched me, where Kadence christened me "Zitzenstein" and "stalker," where even God himself abandoned me.

I park and get out of the car, but not before I remember to grab the bottle of Jack. It's freezing, the kind of cold that cuts through your coat and down to your bones, then through those too. *The winter wind is like the Holy Ghost*, my grandma used to say when she was knee-deep in her "special" tea she drank all day long—years later I learned the special ingredient was Southern Comfort. *Accept Jesus in your heart*, she'd say, *and the Holy Ghost comes in so deep inside you, he's down in your bones*.

Always scared the crap out of me. Doomed from the start with DNA like that, I'm telling you.

I stride past the junior high, across the road toward the high school, then into the woods behind it. At least I know where my feet are carrying me now. Let's go be a normal high school kid for once. Let's go get drunk in the F.U. Fort.

I come up to the ramshackle wooden structure and pull open the flimsy door. It's Saturday, so no one else is here. Yep. This is my way of doing high school. Without any of the actual students. I already have the top off the bottle and send a healthy swig down my throat before collapsing onto the nasty gold-plaid couch.

Christ, that *burns*. I manage not to cough like a pansy. I take another swig and lay my head back on the couch until I'm looking at the slanted tin roof of the shack.

I relax into the couch. Or try to. Damn, this couch is uncomfortable. I shift my butt trying to get in a comfortable position. It's impossible.

Something's digging into my thigh. That's the problem. I frown. Whatever it is doesn't feel like a spring or slipped frame board. Closing my eyes, I try to ignore it for another couple minutes until finally I'm annoyed enough to check it out. I get off the couch and crouch in front of it.

I lift up the cushion and frown. What the hell? There's an old army tack box hidden under the cushion. A space has even been hollowed out to fit the box. I can't decide if it was genius to try to hide something out in public like this or a totally dumb-ass move.

I stare at the box for a moment wondering if I should open it. Who the hell am I kidding? I flip open the latches and lift the lid. Inside is a laptop wrapped in three coats of plastic and sealed in one of those big vacuum Ziploc bags. It takes me no time to unwrap the laptop and flip open the cover. The battery is still thirty-seven percent charged and there's no password. Curiouser and curiouser. After all, if you're gonna leave your laptop out in public, at least put a password on it. I click around trying to find out who this fool is.

Opening the My Documents folder gets me subfolders labeled by class. I click on some of those files and find drafts of assignments. A few more clicks and I get a paper with none other than Kadence Mulligan's name at the top.

What the hell? I jerk back from the laptop like it's gonna bite. Is this some kind of trick? A way for the cops to get more physical evidence against me? My fingerprints on her laptop or something?

I take a few steps around the small room, looking back and forth. *Crap, crap, crap.* I drag my hands down my face. I need to think for a second. Who the hell would be trying to frame me? And how did they know I'd be here? I didn't even know I would come here until I stopped the truck.

No. I try to calm my racing heart. No one's trying to frame me. I push open the door to the fort and look outside. No cops. No reporters jumping out and shouting, "Gotcha!" either.

I shut the door again and stare down at the laptop. The screen stares back. Damn thing's taunting me. Kadence's laptop. How the hell did it get here? Lauren said the cops didn't find it with Kadence's stuff, so everyone assumed it went missing when Kadence did. So how's it here?

I sit down and pull it into my lap again. My fingerprints are already on it, so why not? I close all the document files and look through the other folders. In the My Pictures folder there's only a bunch of images of Kadence performing at shows. Self-obsessed much? With that a bust, I'm not expecting much when I click on the My Videos folder.

But I don't find videos of her performances. No, this is something else. Diary-type videos for YouTube that she must never have posted. If she had, they would've been playing them on all the news shows. There aren't any dates, but in the first video she talks about it being winter and wearing a scarf to protect her voice. In another she's talking about Lauren and even me in a roundabout way.

It's crazy, watching these. I hated this girl. She's being her normal, super-artificial self in these videos. All *I'm-so-friendly* and *Gosh-darn, aren't-I-likable*? It's why I slipped up even after the meds were out of my system and would videotape her sometimes. I wanted evidence. Like if I could catch her in the moments where she was showing her true witch face, then I could...I don't know, prove to the world that she wasn't what they all thought. Or at least prove it to Lauren.

I can't help clicking and watching the next video and the next and the next. I frown as the tone of the videos starts to change. Then I get to the last one.

Wait, what?

I thought I knew Lauren DeSanto. But I was wrong. The Jack Daniel's is forgotten, the cold is forgotten. I stare at the blank screen after the video finishes. Kadence's words ring in my head. *Lauren was never the girl that I thought. I'm not the first person that she's done this to. Stabbed in the back.*

I stare at the laptop, mind racing. The other girl Kady talks about, the one who had to leave school, has to be Mary Blake. I watch the video again, paying attention to every word this time. *Lauren slept with her boyfriend and totally destroyed her confidence until she moved away from our school.* And then at the end of the video, Kadence shakes her head and swipes at her tear-stained cheeks: *I'm going to go sing at her coffee shop. And afterward...she is going to answer for what she's done.*

My mind floods with everything the people we've talked to over the past week have said. How, when Lauren explained to Caleb how Kady had outed him to his father, he responded, "You know what? She told me the same thing about you."

Why'd I assume that Kady had been the one who was lying, not Lauren? Yeah, there were a few moments here and there when I wondered. When Lauren's reactions to things seemed a little off. Or sometimes I'd wonder why she wasn't talking about Kady more...But that was Lauren, I thought. She was funny that way. It didn't mean she didn't *feel* it just because she wasn't showing it like other people did.

But what if she...No way. Or could she...?

Christ. I squeeze my eyes shut and push my palms into my forehead. Because then again, all I could ever see was Lauren. I was always blind to anything else.

I flip through the week's events like movie clips. Mary shouting, "You ruined my life!"

I let the new thought in. What if it really *was* Lauren who had hooked up with Nick and set Mary up with Donny? I slide my palms down against my eyes. This is too much. Christ, if it's true, if it was Lauren who was the master liar in this game, then maybe she was actually capable of hurting Kadence. Of covering it all up. The possibility hits me like a punch to the guts.

But maybe not. I scrub my hands the rest of the way down my face.

I could be jumping to the wrong conclusions, couldn't I? Could Lauren still be innocent in all this? My conversation with Kadence didn't exactly go down like she made it sound. It was back in early January, but she made it seem like it was recent. And I certainly never "bared my soul to her." I didn't tell her about Mason's interest in Lauren because I was "genuinely worried" about anything—least of all Kadence. It was just a last card to play in my already fizzling plans for revenge. I'd stopped the meds in December, and I felt lost.

Kadence hardly seemed that impressed that I'd "gotten myself together and moved past all the hurtful things" that they'd done to me either. In fact, she laughed in my face when I told her that I was Nathan. I didn't feel pissed or vindicated or anything much at all after the conversation. Just...empty. There wasn't satisfaction in revenge, it hit me then. It just made for this vague, ugly feeling in my stomach. I let most of it go at that point, except for the occasional impulse to catch Kady out and unmask her for the fake she was.

But it strikes me now that maybe both girls were twisted, not just Kadence. Lauren certainly spent enough time around Kady to have picked up her tricks.

So what the hell's really going on? And why is Kadence's laptop here, still with battery life no less? Kadence's parents could be strict, with her dad being army and all. I guess I can maybe understand why she couldn't keep a laptop full of personal thoughts in her house. She *could* have put it here before she ever went missing. If no one's used it since then, it'd still have battery life after a week and a half. But why hide it here in such a public place and with no password on it? Kadence was smarter than that. Above all, she was smart.

But then again, so is Lauren. She's the one who made their lyrics so powerful. The lyrics kept their music from being too sugar sweet. Christ, if Kadence had been writing the lyrics, I don't even want to think about how shallow those songs would be. Lauren was the one slipping in the literary stuff and writing lyrics that had people on the Internet making .gifs like crazy and reposting them everywhere. Not that anyone remembers that now that they've all turned on her. Damn it, how can I still feel so much for her, even while I'm thinking she might have done something to Kady?

The darkness in you calls to the darkness in me.

I wish I had my notebook to write that down. I say it again in my head, and then over again once more. *The darkness in you calls to the darkness in me.*

I close up the laptop. Then, on inspiration, I slip the bottle of Jack into the Ziploc bag, place it in the tack box, and secure the latches. The next visitors to the F.U. Fort will find a nice surprise.

I walk back to my dad's truck, the laptop tucked under my arm. I breathe in the cold, biting air. There's something about winter. It's so crisp, clean. Another cutting wind blows in and I think about Grandma and her Holy Ghost again. It wasn't until I got older that I realized she wasn't talking about an actual ghost, that it was supposedly the part of God that was like the wind. I breathe in deeply, letting the wind into my lungs.

I like the idea of breathing in a little bit of God on this insane day. It brings a calmness that I haven't felt in a very long time. I'm going to confront Lauren. But the rage that drove me out of the house is gone. I'm not afraid either, no matter what I find out. Either Lauren DeSanto is a twisted liar, maybe even a murderer, or she's innocent. That I'll finally have some answers to the riddle gives me a sense of peace. Soon I will know who Lauren really is and why she left me all those years ago.

I've been mixed up for a long time now. Maybe it was never about becoming a new man, and maybe I was never really a monster. Maybe I'm just *me*, and it's time to figure out who that is.

Either way, it's time to learn the truth.

THIRTY-ONE

LAUREN

DeSanto Residence
Saturday, April 7
7:00 p.m.

I lie in bed, staring at the fake stars on my ceiling and thinking about how much more time I spend staring at them than at the real deal. Kadence helped me glue them up there when we were in eighth grade. Even after my birthday bedroom remodel, the stars remained. Kadence always told me to reach for the stars. "Reach for the stars before they burn out," she'd say. I press the heels of my hands into my eyes.

It seems so symbolic. I thought what I had was real. With Kadence. With Jude. Now everything is more confusing than ever—it's been a fake, glow-in-the-dark kind of life, and right when I finally get what I've been reaching for, it's nothing but plastic.

After finding Coco earlier, I left the search party and came home. I actually managed to fall asleep for a few hours, but now I am all but swallowed up with my own self-pity. Which sucks. It's not anything I'm proud of. I'm thinking that I'm basically a pathetic mess, probably destined for a mental breakdown, when my window rattles so loudly I nearly have a heart attack too.

BUM...*Ba*-BUM. BUM...*Ba*-BUM.

Jude.

I didn't answer his earlier call or his text because I wasn't ready to talk to him and I didn't understand how or why he was out of jail.

I'm still not sure my head is clear enough to talk to him, but there's nothing I want to do more. I want answers. I *deserve* answers. After everything the detectives showed me this morning, I deserve to know the truth. I need to know why Jude was spying on us. Filming us. Was it some form of irony? A joke? Finally doing what we'd falsely accused him of all those years ago?

And helping me investigate Kadence's disappearance, was that a joke too? Was any of it real? Those moments I thought we'd connected...that kiss...

The knock comes a second time. Still I hesitate. When a long, drawn-out silence follows, I panic that I've waited too long. I launch myself from the sheets and yank open the curtains. My heart stutters, then pounds against my sternum when I find Jude standing there, facing my window. I might have even given a little shriek.

I open my window, but he doesn't come in like before. Instead, he shakes his head and curls his fingers, beckoning me to follow.

For several seconds, I stand there and stare at him, backing away. Is he serious? I shake my head. No way.

He tilts his head slightly to the side, studying me in that way he sometimes does. I squirm uncomfortably, like a worm that's been washed onto the sidewalk after a rain. Completely exposed.

Jude steps toward me, bracing his hands against the window frame. "I take it the detectives showed you some stuff?" His blue eyes are piercing as he searches mine. "Do you really think I'd hurt you, Ren?"

But then a shadow crosses his face, and I don't know. I really don't know.

My heart is beating as fast as a hummingbird's wings. I stare back at him. Breathless. And then my answer comes to me: "No," I whisper, my raspy voice almost giving out on that single word.

And the thing is, I mean it. I spent years side by side with Kadence Mulligan, the master liar, the queen of feigned sincerity. Enough to recognize a lie when I hear it now. With Jude, I only hear the truth. "No, I don't think you'd hurt me."

Without letting myself think any more about it, I grab my jean jacket, some wool socks, and slippers. They aren't the best choice in footwear but my sneakers are in the front hall, and I don't want Mom and Dad to know I'm leaving.

I run across the grass to meet him. "Did you escape or something?"

Jude makes a noise that tells me I'm way too naive for my own good. "Yeah, I went totally *Shawshank* on them." Then, when I don't laugh, he adds, "They didn't have enough to hold me, but I bet you aren't surprised to hear that."

"I never thought you did it," I say, my breath burning in my lungs.

"And why is that?" he asks. There's a strange bite to his question that I don't understand.

"Because I know you." I smile encouragingly. "You're angry. You have every right to be. But I don't think you'd ever really hurt anyone. Not even Kadence."

Jude stares at me with a look that again is impossible to decipher.

"What's wrong?" I ask.

"Nothing." His eyes are narrowed like he's trying to read me too. "Are you sure that's it?"

"Is what it?" I ask. I shift my weight. The grass is wet and it's soaking into the soles of my bedroom slippers.

"Is that the only reason you knew it wasn't me?"

I tilt my head like he did earlier, trying to hear the real question behind his words. "Isn't that enough?"

Jude rolls his eyes and takes me by the elbow. "Come on," he says. "My truck is parked around the corner."

"Why?" I ask. It's the first time I feel the tickle of unease. "Can't we talk here?"

"There's something you need to see."

He guides me through the darkening backyards, around the Johnsons' swing set and the Webbers' hot tub. We cut the corner of the Obodzinskis' yard, then Jude pulls open the driver's side door of his truck and pushes me inside. I don't say anything. Neither does he.

I move all the way to the passenger window and turn my body to fully face him. I need to go on offense. I want answers to my own questions before I need to see anything he wants to show me. But he doesn't do or say anything. He stares at the steering wheel. There's a line of muscle in his jaw, pulsing against his clenched teeth.

Finally I can't stand it anymore. "What? What am I doing out here?"

Jude bends down and pulls something out of his backpack on the floor between us. I know what it is immediately. It's Kadence's missing laptop. My stomach sinks.

The cops might have released Jude, but it looks like they were right about him after all. Apparently my genius internal radar is on the fritz, and I just got into a truck in a deserted cul-de-sac with a criminal.

"Where did you get that?" I ask, even though the better question is, why am I not getting out of his truck?

Just as I'm reaching for the handle, Jude opens the cover and double-clicks on a desktop thumbnail. Kadence's face appears on the screen. It's a jolt to the system to hear her voice again. Jude pushes the computer onto my lap and my hands go to steady it.

"Now, we're going rockabilly, baby!" Kadence says with a sweep of her hand. "This vibe fits a lot better with the new world of indie musicians. I think I'm categorized as indie folk or indie pop or maybe both on the download sites. They can't make up their minds where to put me. But you know that's fine with me. I like being indefinable. Music should be in a world without labels."

I push the laptop away from me onto the seat between us. Jude's sitting at the furthest edge of the driver seat, not crowding me. "What is this?" I stare at the image of Kadence on the screen. Another rushing mix of emotions chokes me. For a second I forget about how Jude got his hands on the laptop because I can't believe the words that just came out of Kadence's mouth.

"This is a bunch of crap," I finally manage to sputter. "Kadence subscribed us to TuneCore so we could put a couple of our songs on iTunes. She spent like two whole days trying to decide what to write down for our genre. She's all about the label."

"I didn't mean to click on that video," Jude says as if he doesn't care about Kadence's rockabilly bullshit. He scrolls to the midway point in the next video and says, "Explain this one to me."

Once again, Kadence's voice fills the truck cab. I watch the video as she pretends to be completely wrecked about me and Mason. Maybe she was, but I doubt it. I heard how she talked about him when he wasn't around. The "pretty but stupid hockey-star arm candy." He's such a good guy, and she was just in it because she liked how they looked together.

And Mason and I didn't "all but have sex!" What does that even *mean*?

That stupid day. I don't even know how it happened. I just remember that Mason left a note in my locker: *Would you please, please meet me after school (by flagpole)? I really need to talk to you, and it can't wait. Mason*

How could I say no to that? It felt weird to be with him alone, without Kady. I'm pretty sure I wouldn't have gone if his note hadn't sounded so sad or been so sweet.

After the final bell rang, we took a walk on the path that led to the football field, which brought us to the woods. We went inside the F.U. fort. We talked about Kadence, which is why Mason's kiss took me completely by surprise. I mean, not like I had a ton of experience at the time. As in, none. But still, I never saw it coming.

One moment we were sitting on that ratty old couch in the fort, commiserating about how Kadence was always canceling plans lately, always too busy for us. The next minute Mason was leaning in, and I was frozen in place. I mean, what was I supposed to do? Kiss him back? Push him away? Hope for a case of spontaneous combustion?

When it was over, we both knew it was a terrible mistake. I don't even know how Kadence found out about it. Not from me, and most definitely not from Mason. That guy loved her so much he wouldn't do anything to jeopardize it. Maybe she knew that I sometimes fantasized about being with him, or at least having someone like him. Maybe she made her accusation without knowing the truth, and my apology that day in the cafeteria just confirmed her suspicion.

The video continues and Kadence talks about a conversation she had with Jude. My eyes flicker up to him, but his face stays neutral. I get the idea that the conversation didn't go down exactly like Kady said it did in the video. A part of me hurts to learn that Jude had been talking about me to Kadence.

But all other thoughts are obliterated when the video ends. Kadence is crying so convincingly. It's her poor, tragic girl act. I'd believe it myself if I hadn't seen her turn it on and off whenever she needed it, say if she did badly on an exam or had too many tardies. The only time tears were acceptable. But never did I think she'd use that particular talent of hers against me.

Kadence starts talking through her tears. "Lauren seems like a shy, unassuming girl. Like you'd never think she could pull off a lie if she wanted to. But that's the way she wants to come off. It's the ultimate mask. She's a wolf in sheep's clothing, and I'm going to confront her about it all. She had the audacity to ask me to play at the coffee shop where she works. As if she hadn't all but slept with my boyfriend! As if she hadn't betrayed me deeper than any friend can betray another."

I can feel the blood draining from my face. How can she say that? How can she do this to me? It's all lies, but...Oh my God, if this video ever got in the wrong hands...Are Jude's the wrong hands? I look up at his face. He can't ever show this to anyone. He can't.

"Well?" he says.

"I didn't sleep with Mason. I didn't 'all but sleep' with him either," I add, quoting Kadence. "I mean"—I take a deep breath—"if you care."

"So you say."

"So I say because it's the truth." When he doesn't respond, I groan in frustration. "None of this would be happening if Mason hadn't put such a sweet note in my locker."

A strange look clouds Jude's face, like a mixture of grief and rage. "I guess you're just a magnet for sweet locker notes." His tone is sarcastic, and it pisses me off.

"And what the hell is that supposed to mean?" I ask, and my voice cracks.

"Are you going to go around telling the whole world that Mason's a stalker too?"

"What are you talking about?" Jude's not making any sense, and I'm exhausted with this whole thing.

"Oh, I get it," he says, his voice full of bitterness. "When I leave you a letter saying I wanted our friendship back, I'm a creeper." He throws up his arms. "But if *perfect Mason Sisken* leaves you something sweet, you're all forgiving?"

"Y-You never left me a letter like that," I sputter. "You sent me a threat. You wrote all kinds of vile things. You were just a kid, but your note scared the *shit* out of me, Jude." I lean toward him, my index finger pointed in accusation as I recite the words that are burned on my memory. "'You bitch! Why are you being such a little cun—'"

"Stop!" Jude cuts me off, looking horrified. "Don't say that word." I watch as he goes pale, then paler. And then—too many years too late—I know why. I sit back against the truck seat and stare out the windshield as I try to make sense of it all.

Jude didn't leave me that horrible note, just like Mason never left me that sweet one and...oh, God, was there a third note too? Mason must have thought I'd asked *him* to meet me after school. No wonder it was all so awkward at the beginning.

I glance over at Jude. He looks like he's going to be sick. His hand goes to his hair and his breath falters. "I didn't write that. Did you even get the phoenix?"

I don't understand what he's talking about, but I'm barely listening anymore. Kadence got me with the same trick twice. The realization that I'd been played fills me with dread. "Where did you find her laptop?"

"In the fort," he says quietly, his eyebrows drawing together.

"In the fort," I repeat slowly as if it's a foreign language. How is that possible? "What she's saying in these videos, Jude. It's all lies. She tricked me and Mason into going to the fort that day."

I can practically see the battle raging in his mind. He has to know that I would never lie to him. Not about this. Not about anything.

"Believe me," I say. "Believe me for the same reason that I believe in you."

"Do you?" he asks. "I mean, the last time I lived here, you took Kadence's word over mine."

"And look where that got me," I rasp. "I'm sorry for how I treated you in the past. So sorry."

Jude shifts in his seat, seemingly uncomfortable with my apology, but I continue. "I've had to learn a lot of lessons the hard way, but Jude..." I reach out and touch his arm. "I've never had to learn the same lesson twice."

I can tell he wants to trust me, but Kady's performance in her videos is just *that* persuasive. Even when she's caught in a lie, she demands to be believed.

When he doesn't respond, I ask him what he's going to do with her laptop. "Are you going to give it to the cops?"

"No. I..." He gulps at the air, then says, "I trust you, Ren."

"Good," I say. "Because it's not just the lies. There's something else that's off about these videos."

"What part?"

I don't know how to answer him. It's just...*something*. "Let me see that again," I say, taking the laptop from him and setting it back on my knees. I open a third thumbnail and let the video play.

This time Kadence doesn't look sad. She looks exhausted. But then, like I said, she was always a good actress.

"Lauren was always saying that," Kadence says to the camera. "Like that made her comments less hurtful if she stuck that on at the beginning." She makes air quotes. "'I'm not trying to be mean, but...' It shocked me at first, but I got used to it and knew that whenever she said that, whatever came next was going to rip my heart out. I'm not trying to be mean, but you were really messing up the melody during the bridge of that song."

I groan in outrage at the laptop. Who is she kidding? What is this? Am I allowed to be furious with someone who—yes, screwed me and Jude over but nonetheless—is missing? Who might be hurt, or worse...

murdered? I haven't let myself really believe it. Kady is...well...*Kady*.

Finally it hits. All the confusing emotions I haven't been able to name—the frustration, the guilt, the unexplainable upset that doesn't seem to fit with everyone else's sadness—it's because I simply didn't believe that Kadence was hurt at all. At least not in the beginning.

I thought she simply disappeared on one of her camping trips. She was pissed about Mason and me, probably for her pride's sake more than anything else, so she took off. Yeah, she was gone for longer than normal. But just like she said in one of these stupid videos, she liked being *inexplicable*.

But then there was all the news coverage, and still no Kady. That's what was most inexplicable because she would've eaten that stuff up. I mean, her dad was on-screen begging for her return. Nothing got to Kady like her dad. And all my confidence about this just being another attention-getting prank started draining away. Even now, I'd rather be furious at her. It's so much easier to feel rage than—than—

I swallow hard and open the last video. I click Play. I'm not sure if I do it to hear her voice again or to reignite my anger by listening to her accusations. As if that can put off the grief for longer.

Then I suck in my breath. Because that thing I couldn't put my finger on...it's there right in front of me. I freeze the frame and stare at the screen, trying desperately to come up with a rational explanation for what I see.

But it's useless. I keep coming back to only one conclusion. This is not old footage from before Kadence disappeared. It's new. It's right there on her face.

Holy crap! *Crap, crap, crap.* Kadence has made these videos since the last time I saw her. I know because of the small cut by her eye. She's tried to cover it with makeup, but I can still see it. She got the cut when she turned to say good-bye to me at Cuppa Cuppa that Friday night.

"Abyssinia!" she said as she passed through the doorway, looking back over her shoulder at me, but she misjudged her exit and banged the corner of her eye against the door frame. I had to cover my mouth so not to laugh out loud because, truth be told, I thought it was pretty funny. First she slices up her hand and then she tries to make a really cool exit (Exit, stage left!) and she ends up banging her face, her head snapping back, yelling "Ow!"

Not as smooth as she'd hoped. I'd almost forgotten about it. And now...and now...what is that girl doing? I blink furiously, all my mixed-up emotions from only moments ago disappearing.

She's out there somewhere, but not held captive in some madman's basement or dead in the ground. She's, like, out there...out there and making freakin' videos and staging this whole thing to ruin my life?

"Lauren?" Jude asks. "Your mind is going a thousand miles per hour. I can practically smell the smoke."

"It's nothing," I croak out, irritated by his interruption. Where could she be? Not in the tree house. I'm sure the police have already checked the places I mentioned to them. Besides, there's no power out there to connect her laptop. She couldn't be at anyone's house because of the risk of getting caught by parents. The empty maintenance shed behind the school football bleachers wouldn't be good this time of year. She'd camped out there a few times in the past when her parents were driving her crazy, but only during the summer months. There's too much traffic out by the fields while school is still in session.

But there is the warehouse down by the river.

As far as I know, she never broke in there before, but she's talked about it. She thought it would be a great set for a music video. It's been empty for years but maybe she could have found somewhere to plug in. There was a library nearby with free Wi-Fi. Could she have gone there and not been recognized? Doubtful because by now it's not only her parents' fliers that have her face plastered all over town. There's the local news too. Someone would have had to recognize her. She couldn't just stroll into a library.

"Lauren," Jude says again, this time more insistent. "What's going on?"

When I think about Kadence's attention to detail, the sheer amount of thought that went into her ruse disappearance, I am blown away. The amount of planning it took to hide out for this long would be impressive if it wasn't so sick. Like diagnosable, get-her-a-straitjacket sick.

And I can't help but think: When Kadence is found, because she will be found, how will she react? Will she be like a cornered animal? Will she lash out? I can't imagine Kadence curling up in a fetal position and accepting the backlash. She'll fight. She'll claw and bite and spit her way out of the corner.

"I'm going home," I say. "I need time to think." I don't dare tell Jude what I know. I don't want him to go looking for Kadence. I don't want him to be involved anymore than he already is. I've messed up his life enough already.

Still, it occurs to me that—if I did check out the warehouse—it would be safer to take Jude with me. But then I drop that idea as quickly as it comes. Kadence won't give up the act if I don't diffuse the situation first. Bringing Jude would be like throwing gasoline onto a fire.

Jude doesn't stop me when I get out of his truck.

■   ■   ■

Ten minutes after leaving Jude's truck, I am leaving my house again. This time I'm going out the front door—my parents are already in their bedroom watching TV—and this time with a serrated knife stashed in my bag. I don't mean any violence. It's against my new constitution. But I'm not an idiot.

Kadence has always been high-strung and unpredictable, especially when she senses a threat. No one can deny me a means of self-defense.

I just hope it doesn't come to that.

Outside, the evening air is cool and full of energy. I don't work so hard to hide the knife now. I let it slip out of my sleeve, catching the handle in my palm before it drops to the driveway. The streetlight glints off the blade. I shiver, and not because it's cold as all hell.

I won't need it, I tell myself. It's only a precaution.

For a second I think I hear something. Not a car, not a jogger, but... something. But I'm being paranoid. It's Saturday night and already dark; people in my neighborhood are settled in for the night. I am alone.

I pull the car out of the driveway and head out of the cul-de-sac, taking a left at the road that will take me nearly all the way to the warehouse, which is along the river. I was there once before when Kadence took me along to scout music video locations last summer. We couldn't get inside, and when I brought up permissions and the permits we'd need to get, Kady just rolled her eyes at me.

It's only a mile by the way the crow flies, but at least a fifteen-minute drive with the number of stop signs and curvy meanderings this road will take. That's fine. It gives me a little time to think. It gives me time to come up with a Plan B in case Plan A is, like, capital C catastrophic. Either way, if I'm right and Kadence is at the warehouse, her little hideaway attention-seeking stunt is coming to an end. Tonight.

I'm less than two blocks from home when a car behind me flashes its high beams. It shines in my rearview mirror. *Jerk*, I think, and adjust the mirror so I'm not totally blinded. A few more turns, a few more stops, and I pull into the convenience-store parking lot that's across the street from the empty warehouse—a two-story brick building with boarded-up windows.

Tall clumps of grass grow through the cracks in its darkened parking lot, which is dimly lit with a light mounted at each rooftop corner of the building. So I guess the owner has maintained some electrical power.

I should feel some kind of validation. Power means Kady could have made her videos here. But now that I've arrived, my confidence begins to wane. What am I supposed to do now that I'm here? Do I go in? It's hard to picture Kady being in there. I'm even a little embarrassed by how overly dramatic I've made this whole thing. What was I thinking, bringing a knife? This seemed like a much better idea an hour ago. In fact, the warehouse gives me a serious case of the creeps. Like horror movie, *only-an-idiot-with-a-bad-script-would-go-in-there* kind of creeps.

A half hour passes. Maybe more. I check my phone. Okay, it's been more, and the only thing I've seen is a raccoon climbing into a dumpster. Then another fifteen minutes and I still haven't worked up the courage to go inside.

A homeless person shuffles around the far corner of the building, arms loaded with bags. At first I think it's a woman because the body moves gracefully, but then I notice the short dark hair and realize it's just a really skinny man.

I'm about to check my phone again, when the vagrant puts his hand on the warehouse door handle. He turns to look over his shoulder, as if he's afraid of being followed. It's the level of wariness that catches my attention.

The second thing I notice is his backpack, and my heart stutters in my chest.

I would know it anywhere because I was the one who picked it out for Kadence before school started this year. It's turquoise and lime green, the colors she would have painted her room if her parents would have let her. It's completely recognizable.

That skinny homeless man has Kadence's backpack! What the hell? Suddenly my thoughts are going a mile a minute. Things that didn't make sense. Yes, Kadence did like to go strange places to camp. And yeah, she did like publicity. But this would have been excessive, even for her. And there's another explanation. She could have made those videos the same night she hurt her eye. What if she recorded them after the concert at Cuppa Cuppa, then put them in the F.U. Fort?

Maybe that's even when she was grabbed. A hundred new scenarios are playing out in my head—all with Kadence as victim instead of as the wicked witch.

I wouldn't be surprised if I wasn't the only one she talked to about making a music video here. Or what if she *did* come out here alone, thinking herself as invincible as always? Something could have easily gone wrong. If someone grabbed her, stole her stuff, hurt her...

Like this man with her backpack. Is she still in the warehouse? Is she still...alive?

I grab the knife that I'd laid down on the seat beside me. My breathing picks up. How quickly my thoughts turn from protecting myself from Kadence to protecting her from this strange man.

Without thinking, I slip the knife up my sleeve and step out of the car. That's when Jude appears.

Quickly, so quickly I don't know what's happening, he grabs the car keys from my hand and pushes me back inside my car. Just like earlier, he joins me, forcing me to slide over. He slams the door behind himself.

I sit—paralyzed with shock. A glance in my rearview mirror shows his dad's truck parked at the end of the lot directly behind me. "You followed me."

"You brought a knife?" he asks without glancing down. He must have felt it when he was shoving me so unceremoniously into the car.

I turn toward the windshield, eyes flicking back to the warehouse. I've got to get inside. Kady could be in there. "It's not what you think," I say, my voice trembling.

THIRTY-TWO

JUDE

The Warehouse Parking Lot
Saturday, April 7
8:45 p.m.

"Lauren." I scrub my hands through my hair. "Christ, Lauren, you can't do this." I look through the windshield at the warehouse. Before I let Lauren see who or what's behind that door, I've gotta tell her everything. She has to know before it's too late. Revenge won't get her anywhere. "There's something I haven't told you."

"Jude, there's no time—" She reaches for the door handle, but I put a hand on her forearm to stop her. I feel the knife, hard under her sleeve. *Mother of Christ.*

"Lauren"—my voice is heated—"this is hard enough for me to say, and you've gotta listen." I take a deep breath. She still seems impatient, but she waits for me to finish.

"There's something I haven't told you," I repeat. "After you made fun of the gift I worked so hard on, that dumb phoenix thing, which God, I know now you never even got"—I plow on before she can try to leave the car again—"but when you said those things over the loudspeaker…"

"Jude." Her eyes are pained. "I never meant—" She breaks off and reaches over to squeeze my hand. I force myself to meet her gaze. She's so beautiful. So open. The way she's looking at me...like she sees me, like she sees something in me, something worthy.

I squeeze her hand back, probably too hard. Then I pull away, 'cause I can't handle her pulling away first. And that's exactly what she'll do in about ten point two seconds once she hears all I have to say. I swallow and continue.

"And then everyone started bullying me. It was a bad time." We both know that's an understatement. She doesn't know just how much, and I don't ever want her to know how bad it was.

I look out the window. "When I moved to my mom's, I was so angry." Crap, I don't even know how to explain it. "Really, really angry. And then when I went on this intense medicine that cleared up my skin, people were treating me better all of a sudden, like at school and stuff. But it was still there. All that anger. More than I'd ever felt before. I thought I hated you."

She winces again and now I try to go on as quickly as I can. She has to know that I get her impulse to grab that knife. That the darkness in me calls to the darkness in her. Maybe she'll be able to forgive me and we can both just drive away from here.

"I know it wasn't you I hated. I get that now." I laugh humorlessly. "I learned a lot of crap the hard way this year. I—" My words are fumbling again, but I know there's a big idea here. God, I need her to understand. Please let her understand. "That's what hate does. It makes you think it's all about someone else. But really, it's only in you, like, feeding on itself. But it's a fucking parasite. Eating you alive. That's what it did to me anyway."

Her brows knit in confusion. Crap, I'm rambling, probably not making any sense. It's time to just say it.

217

"I saw those music videos on YouTube of you and Kadence doing so great, saw how many hits you were getting, millions of them. You were like some kind of sensation or something. And it pissed me off even more. I was so angry that you were both doing so well when I was still miserable. The medicine I was taking can have these bad side effects. Like mental, emotional side effects. It was making me a little off. Even more angry." I take a quick breath. "So I wanted to come back here because I wanted revenge. And Ren, I don't want you to make the same mistake. You've gotta understand that before you walk into that building."

When I look back at Lauren, her eyes aren't sorrowful and empathetic anymore. No. They're wide. Jesus Christ. She's afraid of me.

"What did you do, Jude?"

"I never meant for things to go as far as they did," I say quickly. "I swear to you."

"What. Did. You. Do?" Her grip is tight on the knife again, and she's moving her body closer to the door. And I can't say I blame her.

I sag against my own door. "It was the night before one of your concerts last fall. I see how stupid it was now. So freaking dangerous. I wasn't thinking. Didn't realize..." I squeeze my eyes shut in pain.

"What did you do?" she rasps.

"I poisoned you," I blurt out. Damn it, that wasn't how I meant to say it. Not so blunt.

"You..." Her voice is trembling. "You what?"

I reach for her, but she pulls back. So I try words instead. "I got detention for smoking on school property. As part of my detention I had to work in the cafeteria for a week. It was spaghetti-and-meatball day, and I knew you didn't like that and would go for the sandwich option."

"Jude..."

"It was this stupid split-second decision. The lunch lady had told me earlier to toss out a packet of chicken that had accidentally been left out overnight, but I hadn't done it yet. When I saw you coming, I pulled out one of those slices and put it on your sandwich real quick."

I rush on when she doesn't say anything, just stares at me open mouthed. "I swear I only meant to make your lunch taste like shit. Maybe make you throw up, at the most. I was so mad and messed up back then. I don't know if that's an excuse, the meds I was on—but I swear I was only trying to ruin your *day*, not your *life*."

The words are tumbling over themselves as I try to get them all out at once. "I never meant for you to have to go to the hospital or to get your stomach pumped, or God, for your throat to get infected." I cringe at the words coming out of my mouth. "I swear, if I had known, I never would've done it. It was stupid, just a horrible decision I made in the spur of the moment." My voice breaks. I can see the horror overtaking her face. Her eyes flick back to the warehouse and then widen again as she brings them back to me.

I have no idea what she's thinking, but before I can say anything more, she's reaching for the door.

"Please, wait, no! I never meant for—" But she's already out and sprinting into the night. Away from me.

I follow her out of the car and shout, "Wait, stop! I swear, Lauren! I would never hurt you again. Come back, it's too cold out here. Please come back!"

I run in the direction I think she went, but it's so dark it's hard to tell. I pause, trying to listen for her footsteps. Damn it. I still have her keys. This is a horrible part of town. She can't be out here by herself. I have to find her.

THIRTY-THREE

LAUREN

The Warehouse Parking Lot
Saturday, April 7
9:17 p.m.

My feet pound against the pavement and the whole time I'm thinking, *Why do I keep doing this?* Why am I such an idiot? First falling for Kadence's bullshit and now Jude's. A moment ago, he was looking at me with so much sorrow and regret that it nearly broke my heart. I totally bought it!

But it was just another lie. Or...was it? Despite the flicker of doubt, I don't slow my steps.

Jude said he didn't mean for everything to happen, but he still meant for me to get food poisoning! My voice is still ruined!

Even if it was just a...What did he call it? A "stupid split-second decision," he's still a liar. His voice echoes in my head: *I wanted revenge.*

A tremor of fear ripples through me, and I keep running.

I thought I'd finally figured out who to trust, but I've had it all backwards. I'm no better at reading people or situations than I ever was. I don't know where I'm going, only that I need to get away from

Jude. I can't trust him. He seemed so sincere back in the truck, but there's no more room for mistakes. I've spent the last four years side by side with the best actress around. What if Jude's just more of the same?

My feet pound against the pavement, sounding like *slap, slap, slap*. Oh my God, what if Jude *did* have something to do with Kady's disappearance and he's working with the man inside the warehouse who had Kady's backpack? I feel like I'm losing my mind.

My breaths come in even quicker pants as I duck behind a brick building, then glance around frantically to make sure I haven't trapped myself in some dead-end alleyway. I'm at least two blocks away now, and I stop to catch my breath.

There aren't any footsteps behind me. Did I really lose Jude, or is he still out there looking for me? If he is, how am I supposed to get back to the warehouse?

I shiver, even though I'm sweating under my jacket. I squeeze my eyes tight and let the tears run down my cheeks. My palms press against the damp brick. My fingernails dig into the rough facade. I need to go back. I still need to go into that warehouse, but I know now that I can't do it alone.

I should call the cops. I should call my parents! I dial Mom's number but it goes to voice mail. JJ! He always has his phone on him. I'm about to dial again when my fingers freeze over the keypad.

But what if I'm wrong about all of this? I've been wrong before. Maybe that skinny guy found Kady's backpack somewhere. *Crap*. I can't keep a coherent thought in my head. If I call the cops, or even JJ or my parents (who will call the cops), I'd be putting myself and *Jude* back in the middle of the storm again. Jude was just let out of jail. Despite everything he confessed, do I do that to him again?

All this time, I've been swearing that I'm not the girl I used to be. I can think independently. I don't judge people. Or...at least I don't jump to conclusions without giving people a chance. I'm all about healthy living, for God's sake! I'm scared. Maybe even scared of him. But that moment of self-doubt has me changing my plans. I don't call the cops. I don't call my parents again, or JJ. I call Mason.

"Lauren?"

"Mason," I say, still short of breath.

"Lauren, are you all right?"

"I-I might have f-found Kadence."

"What?" he asks, his tone as confused as I feel. "Where are you? Is she all right?"

"I don't know." I'm crying now. "Mason? Mason, can you come get me?"

"Lauren, you're freaking me out. Did you say you found Kadence?"

"Can you please come?" My hand shoots inside my jacket pocket, and I'm relieved to find that the knife is still there.

"Shit, Lauren, where are you? Should I call 911?"

"Three blocks north of the Kwik Trip. On Cherry Street. Over by the river. Just you though, Mason. No cops."

"We have to call the cops."

"Please. If I'm right, I promise we'll call them right away, but if I'm wrong it'll make things worse. They'll start questioning me again. I can't handle that. Please, Mason."

He swears under his breath because he knows I'm right. "Fine, Lauren. If you're sure. No cops. Not yet anyway. How do I find you?"

"Text me when you're close to the Kwik Trip."

"I'm already in my car," Mason says, his voice soothing, but I can hear the tension behind his words. "Ten minutes. I'll be there in ten minutes."

But it's fifteen minutes by the time Mason's text comes through, saying that he's close. It's so dark that I'm at the passenger door before Mason even sees me. He gives a little jump, then he unlocks the door and I slip inside.

There are food bags and candy wrappers on the floor. I know him well enough that in any other circumstance he'd be apologizing for the mess—he hates it when his friends leave their garbage in his truck—but now is not the time for apologies. Both of us are freaking out. The thought of someone having Kady, hurting her...I hope Jude got frustrated and took off.

"Where is she?" Mason asks immediately.

"I don't know for sure, but I think the old warehouse," I rasp, my voice even rougher than usual from crying.

Mason doesn't react. He just drives to the empty lot and throws his truck in park. We don't bother to be inconspicuous. Jude's truck is gone.

"I think we can get in over there," I say, indicating the door. Mason grabs me by the hand and drags me at a run toward the door. There is a small crack where it didn't latch properly and we step inside. It's dark and we both pull out our phones to use as makeshift flashlights.

With my other hand, I wrap my fingers around the handle of the knife.

What I can see of the floors are nasty, so I try not to look too closely. It stinks in here, like pee and sour garbage and I don't know what else. Broken crates and other trash are stacked high against some of the walls and in the corners. Mason puts his finger to his lips as we listen for any sound of movement. After a few moments there is a soft shuffle. A foot in the dust, a turn of a page, a bird's wings.

Mason beckons me to follow him. He doesn't make any comment on the fact that I have a kitchen knife clenched in my hand. Maybe he thinks I'm more capable of using it against someone than he is. He's probably right. Mason has never been anything but sweet. Even as hockey players go, he always plays a clean game.

The warehouse is divided into several large rooms with wide doorways. We peek around each door frame before stepping into the next room. I expect to hear a man's voice. I hope to hear Kadence. But besides the soft scrape of movement, it's quiet. It could be raccoons. Or pigeons in the rafters.

But as we step from the third room and into the fourth, we both freeze in our tracks. There is a small light in this room, illuminating the man I saw before. He's in the corner, lounging in a nylon camping chair and flipping through a magazine. Two full garbage bags sit beside the chair, though they seem too soft and round to be filled with garbage.

"Kadence?" Mason asks, testing out the name. I glance at him, not understanding.

The man shrieks, hands going to his head. He swings around with his back to us and a second later pulls off what I then realize is a wig. Revealing pinned-up magenta hair.

It's Kadence.

She hastily pulls out the pins, then combs her hands through her long hair, trying to fluff it out. It's oily from being underneath the wig and the apparent lack of shower facilities, but otherwise she looks fine. Perfectly healthy. Safe.

This I find to be annoying. But I can only watch with stunned fascination as she grabs lipstick and a compact from her pocket and tries to make herself look presentable. *Presentation is everything.* Another one of her quotable quotes. She had one for every occasion. And what exactly will she say on this occasion? How will she try to explain this one away? I wait for it.

Lips coated cherry red, she puts the lipstick back in her pocket and clears her throat.

"Miss me?" she asks with a Cheshire smile.

THIRTY-FOUR

JUDE

The Warehouse
Saturday, April 7
9:50 p.m.

I've circled the block a couple of times in my truck looking for Lauren. No trace. She can't have gone far on foot. I'm idling at the stop sign across the street with my lights off when I finally catch sight of her again. She's walking up to the warehouse and she's not alone. Mason's with her. That asshat who Kadence caught in the fort with Lauren. I get that she probably hates me now and will most likely never speak to me again. Seeing her with Mason still makes me want to punch something, preferably his pretty All-American boy face. I choke the urge back down and focus on what they're doing.

Lauren and Mason approach the door of the warehouse and slip inside. I jump out of the truck and immediately follow. Lauren's heading in there with a freaking knife. No way I'm letting her out of my sight. I don't care if Mason Best-Guy-in-the-World Sisken is beside her. I don't trust anyone to protect her but me. Now isn't that the irony of ironies.

I don't pay much attention to the piss-smelling warehouse as I enter a minute or so behind them. I'm silent and they don't notice me. I hear them up ahead and soon I can follow the light of their phones, tentatively checking each step is clear with my foot before putting my weight down. I'm careful to keep quiet.

They enter one of the side rooms. I pause outside, give one quick peek around, then hide behind a stack of crates inside the doorway. Once again, I am watching them from the shadows, but I can see everything from here: Mason and Lauren. And Kadence. The witch herself, looking nice and hag-like, though she was trying to make herself presentable again when I glanced in. Gotta say, I preferred her with the man's wig on.

Earlier when Lauren and I first got here, I recognized Kadence's little rat-like figure as soon as I saw her scurrying in the warehouse door. There was a certain genius to it. Without her hair, makeup, and all her freaking diva clothes, no one would recognize Kadence Mulligan. Not decked out as a homeless dude, certainly. She could have been going to the convenience store across the street for food all this time and no one would've been the wiser. In fact, I think I may have even seen her around the garage where I work—the homeless person with that bright-colored backpack—but I wasn't paying as much attention then as I was today.

Because today I recognized her. Probably only because I used to watch her from afar so often. Ugh, freakin' disgusts me now, even if I did have my own messed-up logic to it back then. At least it gave me the opportunity to memorize her stupid jaunty walk and the way she sways her hips. I recognized it half an hour ago, even when she was trying to disguise it with a pretend off-kilter thug shuffle.

Then I hear the words that come out of her mouth. "Miss me?" As if she doesn't have a care in the world.

"M—? Miss you?" Lauren asks, and on those words, her voice breaks through. Loud and clear and completely...normal!

The sudden return of her voice takes everyone by surprise. Lauren's hand goes to her throat. I whisper, "*Oh, thank you, God.*" But my relief is overshadowed by Lauren's rage and by what I know she must still carry up her sleeve.

"We thought you were *dead!*" Lauren yells. Her voice is still coming out strong and full-throated, but I can barely spare a thought for it. "What is going on, Kady? What sick game is this?"

"So are you and Mason a thing now?" Kadence asks, stretching her hands leisurely over her head. "Don't answer that. Here's a better question: How did you find me?"

"How did we find you?" Lauren stares at her incredulously. "*How did we find you?*" Her voice is almost a shout. "Do you know what everyone's been saying? Do you know what you've done to me? To Jude?" My heart does a funny little skip when she says my name. She still cares. At least a little.

Lauren advances a stride toward Kadence but then stops. "They've accused us of murder! What have you been doing out here, Kadence?"

Kadence drops her arms and glares. "What have I been doing? Well, Lauren..." She looks down, and when she looks back up again, her face is tormented and her eyes are full of tears. "My best friend and my boyfriend betrayed me. I loved them more than I loved anybody else in the world, and then I walked in on them..." She buries her face in her hands and starts to sob. Her entire body is racked with it. My eyes narrow.

She gulps in breath after breath, only barely managing to get herself under control long enough to say through hiccups, "I had to get away. I had to get away from it all! So I went to where I knew there would be no distractions, no Internet, no reminders, no friends, and no gossip, where I could be alone with my thoughts and write music and pour out my pain. I'd been planning to do a music video here and no one knew about this place. But I had no idea that the whole country was looking for me. I had no idea I'd made everyone so upset."

She gives another great heave of breath. "If I'd known"—she presses her hands to her chest—"you have to believe me...if I'd known, I would have come back immediately. As soon as I learned about all the terrible misunderstandings, I called my parents right away and set up a press conference to let everyone know I was okay. You don't know how much it meant to me to know that all my fans and loved ones have been so worried about me. And please believe me when I say that I'm so sorry. I'd been so crushed. I hope that those of you who have also been ripped to shreds by love can understand and forgive."

Kadence looks at the floor, and when her face comes back up, the furrowed brow and the sorrow-filled expression are gone. Instead, she's grinning.

"And end scene." She bows dramatically.

The three of us stare at her, shocked into silence. My mom told me never, ever, under any circumstance, to call a girl a bitch. But I can't think of any other word for what I just witnessed.

"But why?" Mason manages to ask.

Dude sounds on the edge of tears. I take it he was buying into that little performance of Kadence's and then was confused as hell by the ending when she turned back into the Kadence that Lauren and I know so well. From everything I've gathered over the past eight months, this guy has been blind to all that she truly is. I feel a little bad for him. I don't think he's dumb. He just wants to see the good in people. Too bad there's no good in Kadence Mulligan.

"Why?" Mason asks again. "Because I kissed her? Kady, I'm sorry. It wasn't anything more than that. I don't know where you heard that it was, but I swear that kiss meant nothing. There's nothing between us."

Kadence laughs at this and then sighs at him fondly like he's a puppy. "Oh, you gorgeous idiot. You were the perfect high school boyfriend, someone nice and wholesome to bring home to the Major, but never quite quick enough, were you?" She snaps her fingers in front of his face as her gaze sharpens. "And when I set up one simple loyalty test, you couldn't pass that any easier than the rest of your exams. Didn't you ever ask each other about the Post-it notes that you found in your lockers that day?"

Mason and Lauren exchange a glance. He's blinking like he can't comprehend what's going on, like the girl saying all these things is an evil twin and his real girlfriend will appear at any moment. Kadence continues in a singsong voice. "'Would you please, please meet me after school (by flagpole)? I really need to talk to you, and it can't wait. Signed Mason'; 'Please. Need to talk. Meet me by the flagpole? Signed L.' Wasn't too hard to get the handwriting right, but then I've always been good with that."

Kadence smiles charmingly at me through the crates I'm standing behind, and I suck in my breath. She must have seen me come in, but she doesn't let on to Lauren and Mason.

"I learned that little trick early with that stalker Nathan." She's toying with me, knowing that I am now doing exactly what she accused me of all those years ago. Stalking in the shadows.

I want to rush out to Lauren and let her know I'm here and that if she would let me close to her again, I'd never leave. Instead, I hold my ground.

"You set us all up," Lauren says.

Kadence's easy manner shifts, her face hardening. "No. I'd seen the way you and Mason looked at each other. You thought I didn't notice. That I was too busy. You thought I was stupid. As if! So I set up a little test. To see if you would be loyal." Her gaze cuts back and forth between Lauren and Mason, her blue eyes cold as razors. "And guess what? You failed."

"Babe, I—" Mason starts, hands up in entreaty, but Lauren cuts him off.

"So that's what all this is about?" she asks, her voice still strong. "You setting us up with some twisted loyalty test that you had already manipulated?"

The cold smile is back on Kadence's face. "Well, I'm not an idiot, am I? I knew you would fail. I was counting on it."

Mason takes a step back as if he's been dealt a physical blow.

"My YouTube views had flatlined. How was the Major supposed to brag to all his friends if I wasn't anything special anymore?" Her eyes go slightly unfocused as she looks past Lauren and Mason. She's not looking at me either, but at some point past the wall. "Do you know it was him who came up with my name? Not Mom. He always liked music even though he could never play or sing too well. He was so proud when we started being successful with the YouTube channel and making news. *Kadence*. A special musical name for a special musical girl, he tells his friends. Everyone else calls me Kady, but never the Major."

My mouth flattens. Hello, daddy issues. I almost feel a moment of compassion, except that then she flips a hand at Lauren dismissively. "Then you had all your drama this year. And it was harder than I thought going on as a solo act."

I see Lauren's shoulders flinch when Kadence summarizes her throat troubles as *drama*.

"So I got to thinking, how can I make my videos go viral again? I'd toyed around with vlogging, but I couldn't get the videos as perfect as I wanted, so I never posted them. Besides. Everyone's blogging-vlogging blah, blah, blah these days. And then I had an epiphany. I needed to make news. Big news." She grins.

"You wanted them to suspect me." Lauren states it with sudden realization. "You wanted all of this to happen. That's why you left your car door open. You planned to put your blood on that shirt. And then plant the laptop."

Kadence smiles. "Aha, she finally catches up! But I had no idea about that creeper Nathan's bizarre vendetta." Her grin widens. "Bonus for getting the whole town out to search for my body in the woods. That was some great TV!"

"But if you've been here," Mason asks, still with that bewildered shock on his face, "then how did you even know what was going on outside?"

Kadence tilts her head, giving him another look as if he's an adorable but especially stupid puppy. "The library is only seven blocks away. They're very nice to the poor, young homeless men trying to search for jobs on the Internet and get their lives back together."

She juts her lower jaw out and drops her voice, adopting a more masculine stance. "Had to run away from my last foster home. Stood up to that son'a bitch when he went after my li'l sister. He almost kilt me, but I got Beth Ann outta there. I take care of her now. Trying to make a better life for us. But life's rough on the streets, y'know?"

Kadence stands up straight again, popping one hip out and laughing. "They pushed me to the front of the waiting list for the computers every time. I think this one junior library chick even had a crush on me."

"And the laptop?" Lauren asks between clenched teeth. "Those videos?"

"Oh, that was a genius idea I had a couple days ago." Kadence tosses her hair. "I had some of those old videos on the laptop like I said, but then the news coverage was dying down and I thought I'd bump it back up. And why just local news? Why couldn't I make national? Everyone loves video footage of a missing girl. I had to improvise a little to make them look like they came from before, but I already had some props for my next music video—" She gestures at the opposite corner from where she was rooting around when Lauren and Mason came in, to where a velvet curtain and stool I recognize as the backdrop for some of the later videos are still set up.

Then she frowns. "But since I haven't seen anything online and *you* seem to know about it, I'm guessing you found my computer? Well"—she rolls her eyes—"that's not the way it was meant to go at all. I hid it in the fort a couple of days ago and someone was supposed to find it, get all excited, and run straight to the media." She sighs. "The best-laid plans. Oh well. I guess since you've all found me now, the jig is up and it's time to come out of hiding."

She runs her fingers through her hair, fluffing it some more. "I've already got my speech prepared after all."

Then she smiles dazzlingly into her small compact mirror. "The views on my videos are already through the roof, and after all, that's what matters."

THIRTY-FIVE

LAUREN

The Warehouse
Saturday, April 7
10:12 p.m.

With a feral yell I launch myself at Kadence. I'm not even sure my feet touch the ground. One second I am standing with Mason at the far side of the room. The next moment I have my arm wrapped around Kadence's throat, arching her backwards. The compact in her hands smashes to the ground, the mirror shattering. She may be seven inches taller than me, but I have the advantage with her back bent, my knife at her side.

Mason has gone pale. His eyes are blank. He doesn't do anything to stop me. He better not.

"Since it's apparently confession time, tell us everything," I hiss in her ear. I don't think about the consequences. I don't think about anything except how time seems to have slowed, and how I want to draw out her agony. I want her to feel. I want her to hurt. "Tell us about Caleb. Tell us about Mary. I want to hear it from your mouth."

She looks sideways at me, half amused and half confused. I am not the Lauren she knows. I'm not even the Lauren I know. Before, she always had me under her thumb. She always played me so well. All of a sudden I'm going off script. I'm surprising her.

Kadence narrows her eyes as if I'm no threat, but she's careful not to twist her torso. She feels the tip of the knife, and that realization gives me a rush of power. For once, I'm in control.

"Caleb," Kadence says with an air of dismissal. "He was just a little boy who was too afraid to talk to his daddy about the fact that he rubbed off to boys instead of girls." She shrugs. "So I helped him out of the closet."

"You told him it was me who told his dad to go downstairs that night."

She shrugs again. "Well, no one ever really liked you, Lauren, so it made more sense that way."

She's forgotten I'm the one holding the knife. Or she doesn't believe I'll use it. Or maybe she just can't help being Kadence. I give the knife a little jab—just enough to focus her attention—and keep pressing for answers. I want my conscience to be clear when I finally act.

"And Mary?"

Kadence tips her head to the side with a groan of boredom. "She was a drama queen about the whole thing."

My rage and fury are suddenly such real things that I can taste them in my mouth. "She was raped," I finally manage to say through gritted teeth, "because of you."

Mason sucks in his breath as Kadence swings her head to look at me out of the corner of her eye. "I never touched her. That was all Donny. Some of us had to make the hard choices to get us to the top. Mary Blake the Rake was being recruited by freaking Nickelodeon." She shakes her head. "There was only going to be one breakout singing group from our school, and I did what I did to make sure it was us. You could thank me, you know."

"So you screwed her boyfriend, told Mary it was me, then convinced her to get revenge on Nick by going out with Donny? You knew his reputation. Tell me you didn't know what would happen. *Tell me*," I demand. And I realize that even now, I don't want it to be true. Kadence was my best friend once. I don't *want* her to be a monster.

But she doesn't deny it. She only clicks her tongue at me. "There are statistics to these things. Only one act was going to make it. Maybe not even that! I was simply ensuring that if one of us was going to hit it big, it was going to be you and me, not her. And God, it wasn't like *you* were going to take one for the team and do what needed to be done to get her out of the way." She's so calm that it pisses me off.

"No, Kadence. I wouldn't have." My voice is cold, absolutely unrecognizable. "I would have never done that. That would take a sociopath."

Kadence's pulse beats fast against the inside of my elbow—like a staccato drum, like a metronome.

My body trembles, but the hand holding the knife is firm. A million thoughts zing through my head at once. Kadence reacting so casually to the fact that a girl was raped. *Raped!* What she's put us all through the past week. The town turning against me...hell, the whole Internet. Jude going to jail. I feel hot and cold at the same time. I feel almost giddy with the surges of electricity tingling underneath my skin. I recognize—in almost an abstract way—that this is what people mean when they talk about an adrenaline rush.

But then my thoughts all take aim and focus.

"Remember how I told you that my dad took me hunting?" I jab her in the ribs with the point of my knife. I want her to pay for all the lives she's ruined. "Just one hard push, up and under the ribs. Right here"—I put a little more pressure on the tip of the knife—"to get straight through to the heart."

I can sense Kadence's mind working, twisting out a plot to talk her way out of this. She's finally taking me seriously.

"But Lauren, hon, come on. I did all this for us. Have you looked at how many views we've been getting lately? And your voice seems to be getting better." She sounds so genuine. How does she do that? Lie like that even after everything she's said? If I didn't know her so well, I'd be tempted to believe the feigned sincerity in her voice. "It'll just be us again. We have the numbers now, and with the press coverage, I bet we'll totally get signed by a label. Come on, let's get out of here. You and me against the world. Let's do this for real."

But I've heard enough words at this point, too many words. She can't rewrite this song because it's already been sung. I tried to tell her that once before. You can't rewrite a song.

I push the knife against Kadence's side, and she cries out when she realizes that time has expired.

"Lauren," a voice says from the shadows, calm and controlled. "Lauren, you don't want to do that." It's Jude.

I blink hard, glancing away from Kadence only long enough to see him approaching. How long has he been here? I almost laugh. Of course he's here. Despite all the hell he's put me through, I'm glad he is. While neither one of us is innocent, at least...I look down and tighten my grip on Kady's neck...at least we aren't as guilty as her. Jude and I would have never hurt each other if not for Kady's twisted interference.

My heart softens as Jude holds his hands up, palms forward. It's only right that it ends with all of us here together, and Jude deserves this moment as much as I do.

Jude continues walking slowly to me, hands still up. Mason glances over at him but shows no surprise, still motionless, his mouth slightly open.

"Stay back," I say as gently as I can. I don't like the look on Jude's face. It's like he wants me to put down the knife. Doesn't he see I'm not doing this only for me? I'm doing it for him too. And for Mary and Caleb and all the others. Not that long ago, I thought it was too late to fix all the things that were broken between me and Jude. I thought there was too much regret to ever wipe away. But I can fix this. I can fix both of us. It would be so easy.

"No," Jude says softly, still walking toward me. "This isn't you, Ren. And this isn't just about you and Kadence either."

"Exactly!" I say, gratified that he understands. "You're right. You're a part of this too. She has to answer for what she's done to us." A part of me still thinks I should feel threatened by his advance, but that part of me is growing smaller and smaller, like the sun pulling away to a pinprick of light as I sink deeper and deeper into the blackest water. The Nathan I know, the Jude I know, would never hurt me. The Jude who hurt me was simply pushed too far. Because it wasn't just Kadence who did that to him. It was me too. I saw him being bullied after we called him a stalker. The names they called him, teasing him about his acne. For years. God, has all this been some kind of penance to pay?

"Ren," he says, "put the knife down. You don't want to hurt her. She's not worth it. She's not worth it because of what it would do to you. You're worth ten of her. Ten thousand of her."

How can he say that to me, of all people? I failed him when he needed me most, that lonely boy back in seventh grade who I completely abandoned. My best friend.

"I'm sorry," I say to Jude, my voice quaking. Even though I still have Kadence by the neck, my knife in her side, Jude is all I can see. "I'm so very, very sorry. How can you ever forgive me for what I did to you?"

"Lauren," he says again, "I already forgave you. The second I saw you at your bedroom window last week, and probably a long time before that even. That was just the first time I realized it. But can you forgive *me*? Will you look at me, Ren? Please," he begs.

237

The room is silent until I obey. Finally, I lift my eyes and our gazes lock. "Can you forgive me?" he asks again. "Saying I didn't mean for you to lose your voice doesn't excuse what I did. All I can say is I'm sorry and beg you to believe me when I say I will never hurt you. It kills me that I ever did and you have cause to doubt that."

He squeezes his eyes shut, and it's as if I can see the weight of guilt slamming into him like a thousand-pound lead ball. "But I'm so, so sorry. I hate those words"—he runs his hands down his face hard before looking up at me—"because they aren't enough. If you were willing to give me the chance, I'd spend every opportunity showing you I'm the kind of guy you can trust." Then his face falls a little. "But I understand if you can't ever get past what I did."

He moves to take a step back from me, but I speak up to stop him. "I forgive you." These words at least are so easy to say. I can't ever forgive Kadence, but Jude was never malicious like her. And his anger at the way we ruined his life is different from Kadence's complete disregard for the feelings or lives of others. Jude must be a much bigger person than me. Actually there is no question about it. He's always been the better person.

"I love you," he says simply, baring everything to me. "I have since we were kids."

I squeeze my eyes shut and shake my head. His words are too painful to hear. How can it be so easy for him? I doubted him, thought the worst of him, not even thirty minutes ago. But he never lost faith in me. Even when he thought I might have done something to Kadence, he brought the videos to me and asked me about them. He never condemned. I don't deserve him.

And then, it's like Jude has read my mind. "You're a good person, Ren. This isn't the way your song is gonna end. You deserve more. So much more."

My heart shatters into a million little pieces. Kadence must sense it.

"Lauren," she says. She has the audacity to speak, to taint this holy moment.

"Shut up!" I say, shoving her away from me, suddenly repulsed by the idea of even touching her. She turns and smirks like she always knew she'd come out of this okay. "I'm done," I say. "I'm so done. I'm disgusted with this whole thing. I don't want anything more to do with you."

Jude closes the gap between us and takes me in his arms. My knees buckle with exhaustion, and I'm glad he's strong enough to keep me from falling as I quietly go to pieces.

"Jude. Lauren," Mason says finally. Quietly. Almost apologetically. I'd forgotten he was here. "You can go home now," he says.

I turn my head from Jude's chest to look at Mason. He looks tired and sad. Still, it's better for him to learn what Kadence is now rather than wasting any more of his life on her.

"It's okay," Mason says. "I can take Kadence home."

Jude lifts his chin from the top of my head. "Seriously?"

Mason shrugs, looking uncomfortable. "Figure she needs a ride." Then he turns to Kadence and adds, "Is that okay, Kady? Can I take you home now?" Even now, after everything, I can see the wistful longing on his face as he stares at her. I swear, he can still see his whole perfect fantasy future laid out with her. As if it could still be possible. I feel so sorry for him.

She rolls her eyes. "Sure. You can help me with my stuff." She kicks one of the overstuffed garbage bags by her chair.

"Come on," Jude says, tugging at my elbow. And we leave before I change my mind and decide to scratch her eyes out after all.

THIRTY-SIX

WXLN News
Sunday, April 8
6:00 p.m.

"And now," says the news anchor, face solemn, "breaking news out of Pine Grove. Kadence Mulligan, the YouTube sensation beloved here in Minnesota and all over the world through her fans online, was discovered dead early this morning."

Several pictures of Kadence Mulligan flash across the screen—one of her that looks like a high school photo, and then two more of her from *America's Talented Kids*. The last is a short video of her singing, though without the audio.

The female co-anchor speaks as the photo montage continues. "Mulligan has been missing for nine days, since her performance on March 30 at Cuppa Cuppa coffeehouse, where she was last seen. Police discovered Mulligan's body at a warehouse not even seven miles from her parents' residence after a distress call was received through 911."

"For more on the story," the anchor says, "we turn to local

correspondent Kristi Clemens with Washington County Sheriff Vu Nguyen."

The screen changes to Kristi Clemens and the sheriff standing in front of a warehouse surrounded by police tape and police cars. The sheriff is in a shirt and tie. His sleeves are down but they're wrinkled as if they've been rolled up all day.

A small crowd has also gathered. A few people wave at the camera. Kristi Clemens stares off into the distance with a slight frown as if in concentration or waiting for something, pressing an earpiece to her ear.

A few seconds later, Clemens stands taller and arranges her face into a serious expression.

"Sheriff Nguyen"—she turns to the man beside her—"we're standing outside the warehouse where Kadence Mulligan's lifeless body was found early this morning. Walk us through what happened here last night."

The sheriff nods. "Well, 911 received a call shortly after midnight last night, stating that a young female was not breathing."

"Young female. Kadence Mulligan."

He nods. "Yes. Kadence Mulligan, though that was not determined until later."

"And you say she wasn't breathing? What was the cause of death?" Clemens's eyes are bright as she pushes the microphone toward the sheriff, then brings it back to her own mouth quickly. "And who made that 911 call?" She shoves the mic quickly back in the sheriff's face.

He blinks as if startled by so many rapid-fire questions but recovers quickly. "She was found by an acquaintance of hers from school. Her death is being reported as a catastrophic medical event."

Clemens's eyebrows drop low as she nods along. "And what *exactly* does that mean? Catastrophic medical event?"

241

"That is yet to be determined. An autopsy will be performed shortly. We expect the preliminary report tomorrow morning."

"What about your previous prime suspects from when this was still categorized as a disappearance or worse? Lauren DeSanto and Jude Williams? Are they being held in custody?"

The sheriff clears his throat. "There are no suspects in the case at this time."

"But isn't it true that the deceased's missing laptop was found in one of the suspects' possession—in Jude Williams's vehicle?"

The sheriff looks startled, but then he stands up straighter. "There are no confirmed suspects at this time. Thank you, and again, we will have more information in the morning. Right now all we know is that it is a horrible, horrible tragedy."

He turns away and the camera swings fully to Kristi Clemens. "Indeed, a horrible tragedy here in Pine Grove, Minnesota. Less than two weeks ago, this reporter was present for what would turn out to be Kadence Mulligan's last concert."

The screen plays a long shot of Kadence singing the chorus of "Sweet Regret."

Hazardous deeds
Should only be done
by those who can't look back.
What's won is won;
what's lost is gone;
But oh sweet regret, sweet regret.

The screen cuts back to Clemens standing in front of the warehouse.

"We will keep you up to date with more breaking news on this *tragic* case as this community demands answers about what took bright teen star Kadence Mulligan far too soon." Bright white teeth flash. "Kristi Clemens reporting."

THIRTY-SEVEN

LAUREN

DeSanto Residence
Sunday, April 8
6:00 p.m.

Jude and I didn't learn about Kady's death until this morning. Mason texted me around 4:00 a.m. to let me know what happened. *Nuts in the gas-station junk food she was eating. No EpiPen. I called 911, but it was too late.*

The sheriff found Kady's laptop in Jude's truck shortly after dawn. I don't know what that will mean. No matter what Mason tells Kopitzke, I'm afraid for Jude. I still can't understand it, how we got to this point. Kady is dead. I can't find my bearings. Nothing seems real.

I don't leave my bed all day. My parents remain close, but they've left me alone to grieve. There's nothing they can do to make things better. I feel sorry for them. For Jude. For Mason. For me. Mostly for Kady. Despite everything, this wasn't how it was supposed to end.

I struggle to know how to react. I don't know what to feel. I've never lost anyone close to me. All my grandparents are still alive. It scares me to think that Kady isn't here. She must be somewhere. Where is she?

It's impossible that she simply doesn't exist. She was always larger than life and now...

Last night, after Jude and I left the warehouse, I felt amazing. I'd conquered my demons, conquered Kady, or at least her hold on me. I'd become the person I wanted to be—strong and if not completely forgiving, then at least willing to be the bigger person and walk away.

But now she's *dead*. And I'm thrown right back into not knowing anything anymore. Should I have stayed? Would she be alive if I'd stayed and forced her to ride home with me? Should I have called the cops when I first thought about the warehouse? Yes. That's what I should have done. *Shoulda, woulda, coulda.*

I don't even know how to cry. It should be simple, but my body is a foreign thing. I can't formulate a thought. I can't muster up a tear—not one lousy tear—for my best friend. It's not because I don't want to. I just can't find myself in all of this. I still remember her ugly words at the warehouse. But I also remember the girl who befriended me in seventh grade. The girl whose eyes would light up when we made music together back in the early days.

Every muscle in my body constricts. I feel like I could turn inside out. I open my mouth to scream but no sound comes out. I didn't want this. I never wanted this. Kady made me angry and confused and all kinds of things I'd never felt before, but I never wanted her to die.

The whole time she was missing, I never really thought she was dead. Kadence Mulligan couldn't be dead. The world is a strange and unfathomable place if something like that could be true. But it is. Kady is gone.

Jude comes over. My parents don't protest. They let him into my bedroom and close the door behind us. He curls up beside me and doesn't say a word. There's nothing to say.

In the background, my small TV starts to play the familiar bars of the local news show. The local news anchors' voices—barely louder than a whisper—trickle across the room.

Jude gets up to turn off the TV, but I stop him. I want to see Kady.

I sit up, and the screen fills with photos and video of her singing. There's such life in her eyes.

My chest seizes and finally a sob rips up and out of me, racking my body into ugly convulsions that I cannot stop. I'm drowning, and I think I may die too.

"Shhh, shhh," Jude says. He cradles my body in his lap, wraps me in his arms, and rocks me sweetly, rhythmically.

Though my eyes are now clouded with welcomed tears—tears that tell me I am human and not a monster—I watch the screen, desperate for another look at Kady, but it's that blond reporter now talking to some official onscreen.

What about your previous prime suspects from when this was still categorized as a disappearance or worse?

"That's enough," Jude says. He sets me gently on the bed and gets up.

Lauren DeSanto and Jude Williams? Are they being held in custody?

The sheriff clears his throat. "There are no suspects in the case at this time."

"But isn't it true that the deceased's missing laptop was found in one of the suspects' possession—in Jude Williams's vehicle—"

Jude clicks off the TV.

The silence beats at the walls, and I am afraid. For me. For Jude. And for Mason. What must he be going through right now? I hope he's not alone.

"Is this my fault?" I ask.

Jude stops halfway between the TV and my bed. His face is somber. "How could any of this be your fault?"

I don't know how to answer that rationally, but I can't shake the feeling that somehow I'm to blame.

"Ren," he says, and his voice is like a balm to my ragged heart. "Ren."

"She was my friend, Jude. Forget about everything else. I didn't want it to end like that. On a fight." *Another fight.*

"Shhh," he says again, sitting on the bed beside me.

He pulls me against his body, and it's warm. It's solid. It's so real. It's in that moment that I realize how much I need this. How much I need *him.*

"It isn't your fault," he says, "and I'm not going anywhere until you believe that."

"Then you're going to be stuck here for a very long time," I say, my voice breaking on a cry that turns into a laugh. How can I laugh? How is it possible that Jude could bring that out of me? It's sacrilege.

Before I can apologize, he says, "I can think of worse things than being stuck with you."

His tone is somber, and I know it's true. There are far, far worse things. Without saying a word, I know both of our thoughts are on the twisted but beautiful girl whose body has already long grown cold.

THIRTY-EIGHT

MASON

Sheriff's Office
Tuesday, April 10
3:30 p.m.

I take a deep breath and let it out slowly, wishing I could forget the worst night of my life. Kopitzke is sitting across the table from me again in the same light-blue cinder-block room as before. I hope it's my last time in a room like this.

Kopitzke turns on his tape recorder and runs through his standard script about date and time, then he gets to the heart of it. "What happened after you and Lauren found Kadence in the warehouse three nights ago, on Saturday the seventh?" Kopitzke asks.

I take another deep, shaky breath and begin. "Kady was upset when we found her," I say. Lauren and Jude were questioned right before me. I wish I knew what they said, but I'm not too worried about any contradictions between our stories. It is what it is.

"She was scrambling to, like, look presentable. I don't think she was ready to be found. She was mad, like she was blaming us for finding her."

"What did you make of that?" Kopitzke asks.

I shake my head and stare down at the table. My throat feels thick and I try to swallow. Someone has scratched *Zeppelin* into the wood, and I trace it with my finger. "She was acting weird, but I wasn't really conscious of any of that at the time. I was just so happy to see her again."

I look up at him through tears and pray I can hold it together. "I'd convinced myself she was dead. Seeing her again was like seeing a ghost. Seriously. I think I might have been in shock."

"Let's back up," Kopitzke says. "What did you mean, she was scrambling to look presentable?"

Had I said that? This whole thing is so surreal. I shrug one shoulder. "I guess she'd been in disguise. Wearing this wig thing so she could look like a guy when she went out and not be recognized. To buy food or go to the library. Without her makeup." I swallow again. "And looking like a homeless person, no one knew her." I gouge at the Z in *Zeppelin* with my thumbnail.

"Anyway, Jude and Lauren...Obviously, they wanted to call you guys right away and let you know that Kadence was alive, that she'd concocted this whole hoax. But Kadence didn't want any cops. I think she needed some time to process the fact that we found her. She was really shaken up and wasn't ready to go home yet. So I told Jude and Lauren that they could go home and that I'd take her when she was ready." I look up at Kopitzke quickly. "I was going to call you guys as soon as I got her home. I swear."

"And did Williams and DeSanto go?"

I exhale. "Yeah. They left. I heard both of them drive away."

"And they didn't come back?"

"No, they didn't come back. In the end, I was the only one there for Kady." I loved her so much. I would have done anything for her. She had to know that. I swallow hard yet again, letting the weight of that statement sink in. Dang it, what's wrong with my throat? It's like there's a boulder sitting in there that I can't get down.

"I told her I'd stay with her until she was ready to go home. So that's what we did. Waited. We didn't talk much. She did say how sorry she was for upsetting people and for getting Lauren and Jude brought into this. She said she didn't mean for any of that to happen."

"At some point did she decide she was ready?"

"Yeah. About an hour later, maybe? I helped pack up her things."

"What things?"

"She had this big garbage bag full of stuff. She had some of her show clothes stuffed in there, the flashy stuff. I don't know why. There were blankets to stay warm at night and then the clothes she must've gotten at thrift stores to pretend to be the homeless guy. Lots of magazines too. I guess that's how she'd been keeping busy during the days. She had her backpack and her purse too. Not a lot."

Kopitzke leans forward, and I lean back in my chair. He says, "We found plastic bags from the Kwik Trip at the scene."

I nod, feeling sick to my stomach. "She'd been buying food there. Nothing good. Snacks mainly. She had some hard candy and some granola bars. I could tell she'd already eaten a couple bananas because the peels were at the top of another bag she was using for actual trash. She offered me some of the granola bars. We ate a couple."

I stop talking at that point. I don't want to go any further, but Kopitzke stares at me. Waiting. After a while the silence gets too uncomfortable. I inhale and exhale slowly. "Then all of a sudden her eyes got real big and her face looked weird. It got all red and her eyes started watering. She put her hands around her throat. I was like, 'What is it? What's wrong?'

"I thought she was choking at first and tried to do the Heimlich maneuver but nothing came out. I remembered her allergy and

searched for the EpiPen but couldn't find it. That's when I called 911."
My voice cracks. "By the time anyone found us though, it was too late."

I shudder at the memory of Kady's face. She'd been clutching her throat and gasping for air that wouldn't come. Then the rash broke out and her face began to swell. "I never want to see anything like that again." My voice is a choked whisper.

"Allergies are nothing to mess with," Kopitzke says. "We couldn't find an EpiPen in her things either."

I shake my head. "I thought it was because I was so scared. My hands were shaking. She usually had it in her purse but it wasn't there. She was always so careful."

"There were no peanut ingredients listed on the granola bars she bought, but after the preliminary autopsy came back, we had them tested. The food came back clean, but there were peanut oils on the outside of the wrappers themselves. We think it was an accidental transfer. Most likely someone stocking the shelves at the convenience store."

"Good," I say.

"Good?"

"I'm just saying, with the way she was acting and talking, not like herself at all—I don't think I could stand it if I thought she did it to herself on purpose."

Kopitzke nods and stands up. I take that as my signal that we are done. Before I go, I have a thought. I scrub my hands roughly through my hair and bow my head. "Do you...do you think if I'd listened to Lauren and called you guys right away when we found her, do you think that Kady would still be alive?" All I can see is Kady's swollen face at the end. Our last kiss, and then holding her in my arms, sobbing as her body went limp.

Kopitzke puts his hand on my shoulder. "Don't beat yourself up too much, son. It's a damn shame, but you couldn't predict this. If you want,

I can talk to your parents about getting you a counselor. We work with grief counselors often enough, and there are a few who are really good with young people."

"Thanks," I say. I swipe roughly at my eyes. "I want to go home now. Is that all right?"

"That sounds like a good idea, Mason. I'll give your parents a call tomorrow."

When I walk out of the sheriff's office, I can feel a dozen pairs of sympathetic eyes follow me. I wonder how long people will look at me like this.

Outside, the midafternoon sun bounces off the white concrete sidewalk and into my eyes, temporarily blinding me. I make a visor with both my hands and search the parking lot.

THIRTY-NINE

JUDE

Sheriff's Office—Parking Lot
Tuesday, April 10
4:32 p.m.

Lauren and I stand outside the sheriff's office, waiting for Mason. When they found Kady's laptop in my dad's truck at the ass crack of dawn on Sunday, I thought it was going to start all over again. The accusations, the trumped-up charges, Kady upending our lives even from the grave. But then the autopsy results came back late last night and confirmed that it was all an accident. There's no one to blame, not even Kadence herself. Funny how things work out. And sad. Despite everything. So fucking sad.

Even in my darkest times, I never wished anyone dead. I'm still not sure how Lauren's handling it all. She hated Kadence in the end. There's no doubt about that. The girl was a sociopath. But Lauren's not. They were best friends for years, and that meant that Lauren loved her. Kadence's funeral is in a couple of days. Lauren said she wants to go. I'll do whatever she asks. I just want to protect her from all hurt and sadness at the same time.

Kopitzke had the three of us who were with Kady that night come in today for some kind of final interview. He talked to Lauren first, then me, then had Mason go in. Mason's still inside and his interview is taking longer than either Lauren's or mine did. Maybe because he was there in that last hour with Kadence before she died.

"Do you think it's going okay for him in there?" Lauren asks. Her voice is anxious from beside me. Her hand has a death grip on mine where our fingers are interlaced. She's been nervous all day—for Mason, for me, about everything. But even that is all mixed up with grief. The grief is everywhere for her but wound together with so many other things. As complicated as Kadence herself ever was.

I picked Lauren up on my bike to bring her here. Her dad hates the thing. Doesn't like me much better, but he can see that Lauren is less anxious when she's with me.

When Mason finally steps outside, she runs to him. I walk up behind her, meeting them in the middle of the parking lot. I want to know what happened as much as Lauren does.

"I'm fine, guys. Really." Mason looks rough. He runs a hand through his shaggy hair. He's usually clean-shaven, but I can see a couple days' growth. There are bags underneath his eyes. I wonder if he's slept since it happened.

"No charges, right?" I ask Mason. I'm still having trouble wrapping my head around the fact that—for once—those idiots in the sheriff's department got it right and believe the truth.

"No." He breathes out heavily. "No charges."

Lauren puts the hand not holding mine on his shoulder. "Mason, I'm so glad Kady wasn't alone. That she had someone who loved her there with her in the end." She lets go of my hand to give Mason a long hug, then releases him. The guy looks so haggard when she pulls away, just destroyed. Lauren notices too and puts her hand on his arm again. "When was the last time you slept? Go home, get some rest."

"Yeah, I guess so." He gives Lauren a wan smile, swiping at his eye with his shoulder, then throws a chin nod my way before heading in the direction of his mom's car.

I feel a burst of anger at Kadence Mulligan all over again. I know the allergies weren't her fault, but she dragged Mason through the mud and she did that on purpose. Then he had to watch her die. I bet it's an image he'll never get out of his head, and for that, I feel sorry for him.

I feel sorry for Lauren too as she mourns Kadence's death. As for me...well...I'm no monster, and I do feel sorry and sad. But it's more in the general way that the loss of life, especially someone so young, hits you.

Could Kadence Mulligan have ever been anything other than a sociopath? Could she have changed? I don't know. We'll never know. And that's what's really sad—the loss of life's opportunities.

I search for Lauren's hand again and lace my fingers through hers. She squeezes back just as tightly.

FORTY

MASON

Sheriff's Office—Parking Lot
Tuesday, April 10
4:45 p.m.

Mom's car is parked not too far from Jude's bike, at the edge of the parking lot. She and Dad are sitting in a grassy patch under a shade tree with Annabel and Meredith, waiting for me to be done. As I get closer, Mom smiles that same sad smile she's been giving me for a week. "All done, honey?"

"All done," I say, shoving my hands deep in my pockets. I can't look at them.

"Are you hungry?" Dad asks.

I shake my head.

"That's fine," Mom says. "That's fine."

I nod and walk to the car, slipping in the backseat. Annabel gets in from the other side and slides to the middle of the seat. Meredith sits on her other side. The girls both reach for me and wrap their arms around my chest. Then they let go and dutifully buckle up their seat belts. I lean my head against the window.

"Let's get you guys home," Mom says from the front seat. She glances over her shoulder at me, and just like that, the ghostly memory of Kadence's voice is whispering in my ear and I'm back in the warehouse three days ago. The night that will forever be on loop in my head.

■　■　■

"That's it?" Kadence asked after the heavy warehouse door clanked shut behind Jude and Lauren. Then she laughed incredulously. "After all I just said, I'm forgiven, and you want to give me a ride home?"

"Of course," I said. "You have no idea what it's been like thinking you were gone forever. It's been a nightmare."

"You really are something else," she said with a shake of her head. It didn't sound like a compliment. I tried to ignore it.

"So, you'll let me take you home?" I raised my hand toward her face. It was such a habit of mine to touch her hair. My hand hung in the air.

"Sure, what the hell," she said with a shrug. It was like I'd suggested watching a movie we'd both already seen. "But I need to pack my stuff." She glanced around the room. It was strewn with a mix of her bright concert clothes and the old flannel and denim that were just another kind of costume, weren't they? The two bags beside her camping chair were stuffed with more of each, along with blankets and a fluffy sleeping bag.

How long had she been planning to stay here? I couldn't believe she'd already lived like this for over a week. How could she have left me to worry for so long? If she needed to get away, why hadn't she told me? I was the one she could always be honest with. I was the one person who knew her.

But I guess I had that all wrong. I'd never really known her at all.

"Fine," I said. I picked up one of the garbage bags and it split down the middle, spilling out the sleeping bag and blankets. "Wait here. I've got my hockey bag in the back of my truck. We can load it up and get out of here." And I meant right away because I wanted nothing more than to get out of that dusty rodent motel.

She made a noise that could have been taken as either agreement or disagreement, busy holding up one of the show outfits to her frame, a dress that looked like it came from the twenties, and looking down at herself with a furrow between her eyebrows as she modeled it.

I turned away, again only focused on getting out of there. If I could erase all of the things that Kadence had said, all that she had confessed to Lauren and to Jude and to me, I would have. I would have washed away all those horrible, disgusting words that poisoned that sweet mouth of hers.

She'd never loved me. It had all been an act. I was just another player on her stage. Naive boyfriend, star hockey player. All our moments together were only scenes to her. With me she got to play the fresh-faced innocent. And I'd let her. She'd given me hope for something better, something that never ever existed.

I'm not really sure when the idea came to me.

It was somewhere between stepping out of the warehouse and arriving at my truck. I wanted to make things right. I wanted life to go back to the way it was before, when life was simple. Life B.K.

I wondered what my little sisters were doing. We didn't get our tea party in this morning. Actually we hadn't had one in a while. Maybe I could make it up to them tomorrow. Go back to the way things were.

I flipped down the tailgate and retrieved my hockey bag, emptying out my skates, pads, and jersey. I slung the empty bag over my shoulder, slammed the tailgate shut, then went to the passenger side. My buddy Chad had left a brown paper sack on the floor.

When I opened the door, I was gratified to see that it was still there. I unrolled the top and peered inside inhaling the distinct aroma. I took a deep breath and drove my hand into the bag, bringing out a fistful of peanuts.

I cracked open the first shell and tossed the nut into my mouth, opening the next and the next and the next. They were fat and salty. Substantial between my teeth.

I chewed them slowly and with purpose. I ate a few more. Then I went back to the warehouse.

"You took your time," Kadence said. She'd fixed her makeup. She almost looked like herself again. "I was starting to miss you."

"You have no idea," I said. "The last eight days have been hell."

She pouted her lips. "Aw, sweetie. I promise. I'll never put you through that again."

"I know you won't," I said with a smile, dropping my hockey bag on the floor and hiding her purse. "Congratulations on all the views on your videos, baby. Your numbers are huge. Your music is going to get someone's attention now for sure. Come here. Life is short, my darling."

She grinned, appreciating my use of her catchphrase. She took three long strides toward me and wrapped her arms around my waist. She tipped her head back, and her lips parted as I slipped my hand behind her neck.

And that's when I kissed her like I would never kiss her again.

FORTY-ONE

JUDE

Sheriff's Office—Parking Lot
Tuesday, April 10
4:45 p.m.

As Mason's parents' car disappears into traffic, Lauren turns to me and buries her face in my chest, wrapping her arms around my waist. I hug her back just as fiercely. The thing I still can't believe is that I'm holding her in my arms. That after all these years and everything that went down, she still wants me back.

Last night, I sneaked into her room. We spent a couple of hours holding each other in the dark. I was afraid of today, that they were going to, like, decide it was all my fault somehow and throw me back in jail. But there's no more fear now. Sadness, yes. But also the future and all the many, many possibilities. It's like I can finally breathe out when I didn't even realize I was holding my breath.

I pull back from Lauren and look down at her seriously. I search her eyes, those deep, dark pools. "I love you."

"Love you too." Her voice is a whisper, but it's not because she's rasping anymore. It's more like a caress, like a song. I take a moment to memorize the velvet shades of it. Possibilities. Lauren without Kadence. All that Internet positioning that Kady worked so hard to build can be Lauren's now. Kady made herself news. In a horrible irony, her death sent views on their music videos skyrocketing, just like Kady always wanted. If Lauren was inclined, she could take that momentum and make it hers. Somehow, though...I see my girl taking a different path. But still with music, always with music. It's too much a part of her.

The day is finally warming up, the cold front of the last few days passing. There will be the funeral in a couple days, and dealing with Kadence's death will probably have Lauren hurting for a long time. But if she lets me, I'll be here for every step of it. And eventually she's gonna be okay. We're both gonna be okay.

And maybe along the way, on days like today, we can take little breathers. Remember that while there's all the sad crap, there's the good stuff too. After everything, maybe remembering that is more important than ever.

"Come on, Ren. Want to go back to the waterfall? Just get out of here for a while?" I nudge her with my shoulder. "I hear it's a really great place for...talking."

I can tell she appreciates my attempt at levity because the edges of her mouth tilt up. It's the smallest smile but I swear it's brighter than the spring sun.

"Nah," she says after a moment. "I think I want to discover someplace new with you." She grabs the helmet off my handlebars, then straddles the bike. Goddamn it, I've never seen anything as hot in my life.

I try to play it cool, but I can tell she knows how much she's affecting me. She loves it too. Her tired eyes warm and widen under my gaze. I step on the bike in front of her and grab her thighs, yanking her forward so she's pulled tight against me on both sides. This elicits a startled little yelp out of her, which makes me grin.

"The open road it is." I roar the throttle high.

SING TO ME, CALLIOPE

Words and Music by Lauren DeSanto

Sing to me, Calliope.
Your words take me away.
Sing to me, Calliope.
I don't want to stay.
Write it down in stone, my love,
of all that we have lost.
Let it never be forgotten
that we paid a bitter cost.

It's the last chance for Calliope,
One last song for you and me.
Dance on the island,
Dance on the sea.
It's good-bye, baby,
Good-bye to you and me.

Sing to me, Calliope.
They mock what you've become.
Sing to me, Calliope,
for what is done is done.
Make your music all they hear
and make them cry for me.

Let it never be forgotten
that my tears have filled the sea.

It's the last chance for Calliope,
One last song for you and me.
Dance on the island,
Dance on the sea.
It's good-bye, baby,
Good-bye to you and me.

As we dance upon the sea,
we were never meant to be.
Never meant to be.

ACKNOWLEDGMENTS

First, a thank-you to Sammy Brown, Anne's daughter, and Sammy's dear friend and musical partner, the late Zach Sobiech, for giving us the idea to write a story about two teen YouTube musicians. (Though it behooves us to say that Sammy and Zach were *nothing* like Lauren and Kadence and used their music to do so much good in the world.) Feel free to check out Sammy and Zach's videos and music, all of which support osteosarcoma cancer research.

As always, a big thank-you to our agent Jacqueline Flynn and editor Wendy McClure for their insight and enthusiasm. Also much gratitude to Ellen Kokontis, Kristin Zelazko, Diane Dannenfeldt, and Andrea Hall.

In our opinion, every writer needs a no-holds-barred critique group. Ours was Li Boyd, Kerstin March, Lauren Peck, and Jacqueline West.

Thank you to spouses and family, without whose support none of this would be possible.

Finally, to the readers, librarians, bloggers, and kidlit community: Rock on!